THE ALEXANDER SHAKESPEARE

General Editor
R.B. Kennedy

Additional notes and editing
Mike Gould

ROMEO AND JULIET

William Shakespeare

COLLINS
CLASSICS

Harper Press
An imprint of HarperCollins*Publishers*
77–85 Fulham Palace Road
Hammersmith
London W6 8JB

This Harper Press paperback edition published 2011

A catalogue record for this book is available from the British Library

ISBN-13: 978-0-00-790236-1

Printed and bound in Great Britain by Clays Ltd, St Ives plc

MIX
Paper from
responsible sources

FSC™ C007454

FSC™ is a non-profit international organisation established to promote
the responsible management of the world's forests. Products carrying the
FSC label are independently certified to assure consumers that they come
from forests that are managed to meet the social, economic and
ecological needs of present and future generations,
and other controlled sources.

Find out more about HarperCollins and the environment at
www.harpercollins.co.uk/green

Life & Times section © HarperCollins*Publishers* Ltd
Gerard Cheshire asserts his moral rights as author of the Life & Times section
Shakespeare: Words and Phrases adapted from
Collins English Dictionary
Typesetting in Kalix by Palimpsest Book Production Limited,
Falkirk, Stirlingshire

3

Prefatory Note

This Shakespeare play uses the full Alexander text. By keeping in mind the fact that the language has changed considerably in four hundred years, as have customs, jokes, and stage conventions, the editors have aimed at helping the modern reader – whether English is their mother tongue or not – to grasp the full significance of the play. The Notes, intended primarily for examination candidates, are presented in a simple, direct style. The needs of those unfamiliar with British culture have been specially considered.

Since quiet study of the printed word is unlikely to bring fully to life plays that were written directly for the public theatre, attention has been drawn to dramatic effects which are important in performance. The editors see Shakespeare's plays as living works of art which can be enjoyed today on stage, film and television in many parts of the world.

CONTENTS

An Elizabethan playhouse. Note the apron stage protruding into the auditorium, the space below it, the inner room at the rear of the stage, the gallery above the inner stage, the canopy over the main stage, and the absence of a roof over the audience.

The Theatre in Shakespeare's Day

On the face of it, the conditions in the Elizabethan theatre were not such as to encourage great writers. The public playhouse itself was not very different from an ordinary inn-yard; it was open to the weather; among the spectators were often louts, pickpockets and prostitutes; some of the actors played up to the rowdy elements in the audience by inserting their own jokes into the authors' lines, while others spoke their words loudly but unfeelingly; the presentation was often rough and noisy, with fireworks to represent storms and battles, and a table and a few chairs to represent a tavern; there were no actresses, so boys took the parts of women, even such subtle and mature ones as Cleopatra and Lady Macbeth; there was rarely any scenery at all in the modern sense. In fact, a quick inspection of the English theatre in the reign of Elizabeth I by a time-traveller from the twentieth century might well produce only one positive reaction: the costumes were often elaborate and beautiful.

Shakespeare himself makes frequent comments in his plays about the limitations of the playhouse and the actors of his time, often apologizing for them. At the beginning of *Henry V* the Prologue refers to the stage as 'this unworthy scaffold' and to the theatre building (the Globe, probably) as 'this wooden O', and emphasizes the urgent need for imagination in making up for all the deficiencies of presentation. In introducing Act IV the Chorus goes so far as to say:

> . . . we shall much disgrace
> With four or five most vile and ragged foils,
> Right ill-dispos'd in brawl ridiculous,
> The name of Agincourt, (lines 49–52)

In *A Midsummer Night's Dream* (Act V, Scene i) he seems to dismiss actors with the words:

The best in this kind are but shadows.

Yet Elizabeth's theatre, with all its faults, stimulated dramatists to a variety of achievement that has never been equalled and, in Shakespeare, produced one of the greatest writers in history. In spite of all his grumbles he seems to have been fascinated by the challenge that it presented him with. It is necessary to re-examine his theatre carefully in order to understand how he was able to achieve so much with the materials he chose to use. What sort of place was the Elizabethan playhouse in reality? What sort of people were these criticized actors? And what sort of audiences gave them their living?

The Development of the Theatre up to Shakespeare's Time

For centuries in England noblemen had employed groups of skilled people to entertain them when required. Under Tudor rule, as England became more secure and united, actors such as these were given more freedom, and they often performed in public, while still acknowledging their 'overlords' (in the 1570s, for example, when Shakespeare was still a schoolboy at Stratford, one famous company was called 'Lord Leicester's Men'). London was rapidly becoming larger and more important in the second half of the sixteenth century, and many of the companies of actors took the opportunities offered to establish themselves at inns on the main roads leading to the City (for example, the Boar's Head in Whitechapel and the Tabard in South-wark) or in the City itself. These groups of actors would come to an agreement with the inn-keeper which would give them the use of the yard for their performances after people had eaten and drunk well in the middle of the day. Before long, some inns were taken over completely by companies of players and thus became the first public theatres. In 1574 the officials of the City of London issued an order which shows clearly that these theatres were both popular and also offensive to some respectable people, because the order complains about 'the inordinate haunting of great multitudes of people, specially youth, to plays interludes and shows; namely occasion of frays and quarrels, evil practices of incontinency in great inns . . .' There is evidence that, on public holidays, the theatres on the banks of the Thames were crowded with noisy apprentices and tradesmen, but it would be wrong to think that audiences were always undiscriminating and loudmouthed. In spite of the disapproval of Puritans and the more staid members of society, by the 1590s, when Shakespeare's plays were beginning to be performed, audiences consisted of a good cross-section of English society, nobility as well as workers, intellectuals as well as simple people out for a laugh; also (and in this respect English theatres were unique in Europe), it was quite normal for respectable women to attend plays. So Shakespeare had to write plays which would appeal to people of widely different kinds. He had to provide 'something for everyone' but at the same time to take care to unify the material so that it would not seem to fall into separate pieces as they watched it. A speech like that of the drunken porter in *Macbeth* could provide the 'groundlings' with a belly-laugh, but also held a deeper significance for those who could appreciate it. The audience he wrote for was one of a number of apparent drawbacks which Shakespeare was able to turn to his and our advantage.

Shakespeare's Actors

Nor were all the actors of the time mere 'rogues, vagabonds and sturdy beggars' as some were described in a Statute of 1572. It is true that many of them had a hard life and earned very little money, but leading actors could become partners in the ownership of the theatres in which they acted: Shakespeare was a shareholder in the Globe and the Blackfriars theatres when he was an actor as well as a playwright. In any case, the attacks made on Elizabethan actors were usually directed at their morals and not at their acting ability; it is clear that many of them must have been good at their trade if they were able to interpret complex works like the great tragedies in such a way as to attract enthusiastic audiences. Undoubtedly some of the boys took the women's parts with skill and confidence, since a man called Coryate, visiting Venice in 1611, expressed surprise that women could act as well as they: 'I saw women act, a thing that I never saw before . . . and they performed it with as good a grace, action, gesture . . . as ever I saw any masculine actor.' The quality of most of the actors who first presented Shakespeare's plays is probably accurately summed up by Fynes Moryson, who wrote, '. . . as there be, in my opinion, more plays in London than in all the parts of the world I have seen, so do these players or comedians excel all other in the world.'

The Structure of the Public Theatre

Although the 'purpose-built' theatres were based on the inn-yards which had been used for play-acting, most of them were circular. The walls contained galleries on three storeys from which the wealthier patrons watched, they must have been something like the 'boxes' in a modern theatre, except that they held much larger numbers – as many as 1500. The 'groundlings' stood on the floor of the building, facing a raised stage which projected from the 'stage-wall', the main features of which were:

1 a small room opening on to the back of the main stage and on the same level as it (rear stage),
2 a gallery above this inner stage (upper stage),
3 canopy projecting from above the gallery over the main stage, to protect the actors from the weather (the 700 or 800 members of the audience who occupied the yard, or 'pit' as we call it today, had the sky above them).

In addition to these features there were dressing-rooms behind the stage and a space underneath it from which entrances could be made through trap-doors. All the acting areas – main stage, rear stage, upper stage and under stage – could be entered by actors directly from their dressing rooms, and all of them were used in productions of Shakespeare's plays. For example, the inner stage, an almost cavelike structure, would have been where Ferdinand and Miranda are 'discovered' playing chess in the last act of *The Tempest*, while the upper stage was certainly the balcony from which Romeo climbs down in Act III of *Romeo and Juliet*.

It can be seen that such a building, simple but adaptable, was not really unsuited to the presentation of plays like Shakespeare's. On the contrary, its simplicity guaranteed the minimum of distraction, while its shape and construction must have produced a sense of involvement on the part of the audience that modern producers would envy.

Other Resources of the Elizabethan Theatre

Although there were few attempts at scenery in the public theatre (painted backcloths were occasionally used in court performances), Shakespeare and his fellow playwrights were able to make use of a fair variety of 'properties', lists of such articles have survived: they include beds, tables, thrones, and also trees, walls, a gallows, a Trojan horse and a 'Mouth of Hell'; in a list of properties belonging to the manager, Philip Henslowe, the curious item 'two mossy banks' appears. Possibly one of them was used for the

> bank whereon the wild thyme blows,
> Where oxlips and the nodding violet grows

in *A Midsummer Night's Dream* (Act II, Scene i). Once again, imagination must have been required of the audience.

Costumes were the one aspect of stage production in which

trouble and expense were hardly ever spared to obtain a magnificent effect. Only occasionally did they attempt any historical accuracy (almost all Elizabethan productions were what we should call 'modern-dress' ones), but they were appropriate to the characters who wore them: kings were seen to be kings and beggars were similarly unmistakable. It is an odd fact that there was usually no attempt at illusion in the costuming: if a costume looked fine and rich it probably was. Indeed, some of the costumes were almost unbelievably expensive. Henslowe lent his company £19 to buy a cloak, and the Alleyn brothers, well-known actors, gave £20 for a 'black velvet cloak, with sleeves embroidered all with silver and gold, lined with black satin striped with gold'.

With the one exception of the costumes, the 'machinery' of the playhouse was economical and uncomplicated rather than crude and rough, as we can see from this second and more leisurely look at it. This meant that playwrights were stimulated to produce the imaginative effects that they wanted from the language that they used. In the case of a really great writer like Shakespeare, when he had learned his trade in the theatre as an actor, it seems that he received quite enough assistance of a mechanical and structural kind without having irksome restrictions and conventions imposed on him; it is interesting to try to guess what he would have done with the highly complex apparatus of a modern television studio. We can see when we look back to his time that he used his instrument, the Elizabethan theatre, to the full, but placed his ultimate reliance on the communication between his imagination and that of his audience through the medium of words. It is, above all, his rich and wonderful use of language that must have made play-going at that time a memorable experience for people of widely different kinds. Fortunately, the deep satisfaction of appreciating and enjoying Shakespeare's work can be ours also, if we are willing to overcome the language difficulty produced by the passing of time.

Shakespeare: A Timeline

Very little indeed is known about Shakespeare's private life; the facts included here are almost the only indisputable ones. The dates of Shakespeare's plays are those on which they were first produced.

1558	Queen Elizabeth crowned.	
1561	Francis Bacon born.	
1564	Christopher Marlowe born.	William Shakespeare born, April 23rd, baptized April 26th.
1566		Shakespeare's brother, Gilbert, born.
1567	Mary, Queen of Scots, deposed. James VI (later James I of England) crowned King of Scotland.	
1572	Ben Jonson born. Lord Leicester's Company (of players) licensed; later called Lord Strange's, then the Lord Chamberlain's and finally (under James) the King's Men.	
1573	John Donne born.	
1574	The Common Council of London directs that all plays and playhouses in London must be licensed.	
1576	James Burbage builds the first public playhouse, The Theatre, at Shoreditch, outside the walls of the City.	
1577	Francis Drake begins his voyage round the world (completed 1580). *Holinshed's Chronicles of England, Scotland and Ireland* published (which	

Shakespeare later used extensively).

1582		Shakespeare married to Anne Hathaway.
1583	The Queen's Company founded by royal warrant.	Shakespeare's daughter, Susanna, born.
1585		Shakespeare's twins, Hamnet and Judith, born.
1586	Sir Philip Sidney, the Elizabethan ideal 'Christian knight', poet, patron, soldier, killed at Zutphen in the Low Countries.	
1587	Mary, Queen of Scots, beheaded. Marlowe's *Tamburlaine (Part I)* first staged.	
1588	Defeat of the Spanish Armada. Marlowe's *Tamburlaine (Part II)* first staged.	
1589	Marlowe's *Jew of Malta* and Kyd's *Spanish Tragedy* (a 'revenge tragedy' and one of the most popular plays of Elizabethan times).	
1590	Spenser's *Faerie Queene* (Books I–III) published.	
1592	Marlowe's *Doctor Faustus* and *Edward II* first staged. Witchcraft trials in Scotland. Robert Greene, a rival playwright, refers to Shakespeare as 'an upstart crow' and 'the only Shake-scene in a country'.	*Titus Andronicus* *Henry VI, Parts I, II and III* *Richard III*
1593	London theatres closed by the plague. Christopher Marlowe killed in a Deptford tavern.	*Two Gentlemen of Verona* *Comedy of Errors* *The Taming of the Shrew* *Love's Labour's Lost*
1594	Shakespeare's company becomes The Lord Chamberlain's Men.	*Romeo and Juliet*

1595	Raleigh's first expedition to Guiana. Last expedition of Drake and Hawkins (both died).	*Richard II* *A Midsummer Night's Dream*
1596	Spenser's *Faerie Queene* (Books IV–VI) published. James Burbage buys rooms at Blackfriars and begins to convert them into a theatre.	*King John* *The Merchant of Venice* Shakespeare's son Hamnet dies. Shakespeare's father is granted a coat of arms.
1597	James Burbage dies, his son Richard, a famous actor, turns the Blackfriars Theatre into a private playhouse.	*Henry IV (Part I)* Shakespeare buys and redecorates New Place at Stratford.
1598	Death of Philip II of Spain	*Henry IV (Part II)* *Much Ado About Nothing*
1599	Death of Edmund Spenser. The Globe Theatre completed at Bankside by Richard and Cuthbert Burbage.	*Henry V* *Julius Caesar* *As You Like It*
1600	Fortune Theatre built at Cripplegate. East India Company founded for the extension of English trade and influence in the East. The Children of the Chapel begin to use the hall at Blackfriars.	*Merry Wives of Windsor* *Troilus and Cressida*
1601		*Hamlet*
1602	Sir Thomas Bodley's library opened at Oxford.	*Twelfth Night*
1603	Death of Queen Elizabeth. James I comes to the throne. Shakespeare's company becomes The King's Men. Raleigh tried, condemned and sent to the Tower	
1604	Treaty of peace with Spain	*Measure for Measure* *Othello* *All's Well that Ends Well*
1605	The Gunpowder Plot: an attempt by a group of Catholics to blow up the Houses of Parliament.	

1606	Guy Fawkes and other plotters executed.	*Macbeth* *King Lear*
1607	Virginia, in America, colonized. A great frost in England.	*Antony and Cleopatra* *Timon of Athens* *Coriolanus* Shakespeare's daughter, Susanna, married to Dr. John Hall.
1608	The company of the Children of the Chapel Royal (who had performed at Blackfriars for ten years) is disbanded. John Milton born. Notorious pirates executed in London.	Richard Burbage leases the Blackfriars Theatre to six of his fellow actors, including Shakespeare. *Pericles, Prince of Tyre*
1609		Shakespeare's Sonnets published.
1610	A great drought in England	*Cymbeline*
1611	Chapman completes his great translation of the *Iliad*, the story of Troy. Authorized Version of the Bible published.	*A Winter's Tale* *The Tempest*
1612	Webster's *The White Devil* first staged.	Shakespeare's brother, Gilbert, dies.
1613	Globe theatre burnt down during a performance of *Henry VIII* (the firing of small cannon set fire to the thatched roof). Webster's *Duchess of Malfi* first staged.	*Henry VIII* *Two Noble Kinsmen* Shakespeare buys a house at Blackfriars.
1614	Globe Theatre rebuilt in 'far finer manner than before'.	
1616	Ben Jonson publishes his plays in one volume. Raleigh released from the Tower in order to prepare an expedition to the gold mines of Guiana.	Shakespeare's daughter, Judith, marries Thomas Quiney. Death of Shakespeare on his birthday, April 23rd.
1618	Raleigh returns to England and is executed on the charge for which he was imprisoned in 1603.	
1623	Publication of the Folio edition of Shakespeare's plays	Death of Anne Shakespeare (née Hathaway).

Life & Times

William Shakespeare the Playwright

There exists a curious paradox when it comes to the life of William Shakespeare. He easily has more words written about him than any other famous English writer, yet we know the least about him. This inevitably means that most of what is written about him is either fabrication or speculation. The reason why so little is known about Shakespeare is that he wasn't a novelist or a historian or a man of letters. He was a playwright, and playwrights were considered fairly low on the social pecking order in Elizabethan society. Writing plays was about providing entertainment for the masses – the great unwashed. It was the equivalent to being a journalist for a tabloid newspaper.

In fact, we only know of Shakespeare's work because two of his friends had the foresight to collect his plays together following his death and have them printed. The only reason they did so was apparently because they rated his talent and thought it would be a shame if his words were lost.

Consequently his body of work has ever since been assessed and reassessed as the greatest contribution to English literature. That is despite the fact that we know that different printers took it upon themselves to heavily edit the material they worked from. We also know that Elizabethan plays were worked and reworked frequently, so that they evolved over time until they were honed to perfection, which means that many different hands played their part in the active writing process. It would therefore be fair to say that any play attributed to Shakespeare is unlikely to contain a great deal of original input. Even the plots were based on well known historical events, so it would be hard to know what fragments of any Shakespeare play came from that single mind.

One might draw a comparison with the Christian bible, which remains such a compelling read because it came from the collaboration of many contributors and translators over centuries, who each adjusted the stories until they could no longer be improved. As virtually nothing is known of Shakespeare's life and even less about his method of working, we shall never know the truth about his plays. They certainly contain some very elegant phrasing, clever plot devices and plenty of words never before seen in print, but as to whether Shakespeare invented them from a unique imagination or whether he simply took them from others around him is anyone's guess.

The best bet seems to be that Shakespeare probably took the lead role in devising the original drafts of the plays, but was open to collaboration from any source when it came to developing them into workable scripts for effective performances. He would have had to work closely with his fellow actors in rehearsals, thereby finding out where to edit, abridge, alter, reword and so on.

In turn, similar adjustments would have occurred in his absence, so that definitive versions of his plays never really existed. In effect Shakespeare was only responsible for providing the framework of plays, upon which others took liberties over time. This wasn't helped by the fact that the English language itself was not definitive at that time either. The consequence was that people took it upon themselves to spell words however they pleased or to completely change words and phrasing to suit their own preferences.

It is easy to see then, that Shakespeare's plays were always going to have lives of their own, mutating and distorting in detail like Chinese whispers. The culture of creative preservation was simply not established in Elizabethan England. Creative ownership of Shakespeare's plays was lost to him as soon as he released them into the consciousness of others. They saw nothing wrong with taking his ideas and running with them, because no one had ever suggested that one shouldn't, and Shakespeare probably regarded his work in the same way. His plays weren't sacrosanct works of art, they were templates for theatre folk to make their livings from, so they had every right to mould them into productions that drew in the crowds as effectively as possible. Shakespeare was like the helmsman of a sailing ship, steering the vessel but wholly reliant on the team work of his crew to arrive at the desired destination.

It seems that Shakespeare certainly had a natural gift, but the genius of his plays may be attributable to the collective efforts of Shakespeare and others. It is a rather satisfying notion to think that *his* plays might actually be the creative outpourings of the Elizabethan milieu in which Shakespeare immersed himself. That makes them important social documents as well as seminal works of the English language.

Money in Shakespeare's Day

It is extremely difficult, if not impossible, to relate the value of money in our time to its value in another age and to compare prices of commodities today and in the past. Many items *are* simply not comparable on grounds of quality or serviceability.

There was a bewildering variety of coins in use in Elizabethan England. As nearly all English and European coins were gold or silver, they had intrinsic value apart from their official value. This meant that foreign coins circulated freely in England and were officially recognized, for example the French crown (écu) worth about 30p (72 cents), and the Spanish ducat worth about 33p (79 cents). The following table shows some of the coins mentioned by Shakespeare and their relation to one another.

GOLD	British	American	SILVER	British	American
sovereign (heavy type)	£1.50	$3.60	shilling	10p	24c
sovereign (light type)	66p–£l	$1.58–$2.40	groat	1.5p	4c
angel royal	33p–50p	79c–$1.20			
noble	50p	$1.20			
crown	25p	60c			

A comparison of the following prices in Shakespeare's time with the prices of the same items today will give some idea of the change in the value of money.

ITEM	PRICE British	American	ITEM	PRICE British	American
beef, per lb.	0.5p	1c	cherries (lb.)	1p	2c
mutton, leg	7.5p	18c	7 oranges	1p	2c
rabbit	3.5p	9c	1 lemon	1p	2c
chicken	3p	8c	cream (quart)	2.5p	6c
potatoes (lb)	10p	24c	sugar (lb.)	£1	$2.40
carrots (bunch)	1p	2c	sack (wine) (gallon)	14p	34c
8 artichokes	4p	9c	tobacco (oz.)	25p	60c
1 cucumber	1p	2c	biscuits (lb.)	12.5p	30c

INTRODUCTION

Romeo and Juliet holds many attractions for a young audience, not least its simplicity of design. The action is straightforward, undiverted by sub-plots and minor themes, and this is achieved through its concentration on the two lovers who gather the play into a unity. All the characters contribute to the main action and push it towards its conclusion. This unelaborate quality of the play is reinforced by the tightness of the time-scheme – the drama spans only five days in mid-July. The compression of the action binds the structure closely and indicates the kind of simplicity it achieves. But this is not to say that the play lacks variety; on the contrary, it is full of movement, colour and vigour, and it is given life by the gallery of individually realised characters.

The Language of the Play

The modern reader will face certain difficulties in *Romeo and Juliet*. These difficulties consist not so much in the strangeness of the words or the structure of the sentences, as in grasping quickly the purposes for which the language is used as it is. The Elizabethans (as those who lived during the reign of Elizabeth I are called) were as adventurous in their use of words as they were physically. Shakespeare too, delighted in playing about with words. He aimed to delight his audience by clever manipulation of the language. The pun is used often throughout this play. To the Elizabethans the pun was a perfectly legitimate device for the expression of deep emotion. Our own use of the pun today is rather different. The Elizabethan audience liked to hear ordinary events described in elaborate and dignified language; when Benvolio speaks of getting up before sunrise he says:

> . . . an hour before the worshipped sun Peered
> forth the golden window of the east.

A third feature of the language of the play is its open bawdiness – it is full of verbal jokes about sex. Two of the play's liveliest characters, Mercutio and the Nurse, are scarcely on stage without making bawdy remarks. Mercutio favours the double meaning – his remarks *could* be taken to be quite innocent. The Nurse is quite simply coarse. Here we find the essential contrast to the freshness, purity and frankness of the lovers' sexuality, a very special quality of their love.

Characterization

The names Romeo and Juliet have come to epitomize passionate young love, so successful was Shakespeare in creating these characters through the power of poetry. They are quite different from each other. Romeo, seen first, is presented as the figure ever-present in Elizabethan poetry – a young man indulging himself in misery because he is rejected by the girl with whom he supposes himself in love. Through the elaborate and self-conscious words he speaks, we can gather that he has no real depth of feeling. His language becomes simpler and less artificial with the first words spoken to Juliet, though it is still somewhat contrived. Romeo, though young, is shown as a man of the world. But Juliet up to this point is presented as totally without emotional experience, imaginary or real. Told that she has a suitor, she says, in effect, that she will follow her mother's instructions. After the meeting with Romeo, however, she is transformed by the first arousal of her emotions, and in the balcony scene the two young people discover their true feelings. Romeo, released from playing with words about love, and Juliet, finding for the first time the world of sexual feeling, both speak directly to each other from the heart.

Following this scene, differences between the two become apparent again. Love, pure but sexually impassioned, is given superb expression in Juliet's soliloquy in Act II, Scene ii, and we are deeply struck by her emotional maturity. Romeo, caught up in the world of brawls and banishment, loses balance and becomes hysterical – he seems well short of heroic, though we do suffer for him when we see his condition momentarily through the Nurse's eyes: 'Ah, sir! Ah, sir. Well, death's the end of all' (Act III, Scene iii, line 92). Juliet bears her troubles more steadily, and with clear determination. Finally Romeo, when his mind is also resolved, speaks lines over what he supposes is Juliet's dead body, which raise him to the rare dignity of a tragic hero. The boy we met dies a man, and a few moments later the girl we met dies a woman. It is this process of growth that makes their characterization so masterly, and so justly famous.

Though Shakespeare spends more time on the characterization of the two young lovers than upon anyone else, the play has a number of other parts of great interest. One of these is Mercutio: witty, high-spirited and courageous, he can easily dominate the first half of the play. His wit finds expression in a bewildering dexterity with words, which entertained the Elizabethan audience by being full of sexual overtone. Though Shakespeare gives him this abundant sexuality, it is important for the interplay between the characters that he has evidently never been in love, and indeed scarcely seems able to understand that emotion – 'he jests at scars who never felt a wound' (Act II, Scene ii, line 1). Though nominally Italian, Mercutio is given the qualities of a young Elizabethan Englishman – note his scorn for 'strange flies', these 'fashion-mongers' who affect continental manners. It is because of his irritation at Tybalt, whom he sees as just such a person, that he meets his death. His removal from the scene, though its immediate cause is an accident, is therefore a direct result of his character.

Tybalt, though more slightly drawn, is still a convincing person. With him, high spirits become contemptuous bravado and a sense of family honour an overbearing arrogance, which is rebuked even by the head of the family himself. This portrait is made a little more attractive by the fact that Juliet and the Nurse both loved Tybalt. Shakespeare knows well that characterization may be enriched by letting the audience see a person through the eyes of others as well as through their own.

Playing Benvolio might strike an actor as being less exciting than portraying the other young men, but the skill shown in creating him is of the same order as in those other characters. Shakespeare needed someone against whom the extremes of Romeo and the fire and brilliance of Mercutio and Tybalt could be set off, someone who could present saner counsels. Within this framework, Benvolio is presented as sensible and restrained, but loyal and resourceful.

Among the older people in the play, Capulet and the Nurse stand out. Capulet is brilliantly portrayed. He likes to see himself as a benevolent man, an indulgent father and a genial host. He warns Paris that he will follow his daughter's own inclinations about the choice of a husband, and as a host he is generous enough to welcome the son of his old enemy to his accustomed feast. But Shakespeare shows another side to his character when he is crossed by Tybalt in Act 1, Scene v. His judgment is sound, but his language violent and intemperate. So it is that Capulet's later behaviour to Juliet is seen to be 'in character'. His language when faced with opposition from her in Act V, Scene iii, shows him as self-willed, insensitive, and brutal. Such a reaction at this point is vital to the development of the plot – as is the much slighter portrait of Lady Capulet as cold and unsympathetic. The Nurse, who attracts great comic actresses with one of the few plums Shakespeare provides for them, is equally alive. She is earthy and talkative, with a primitive sense of humour. It is consistent in such a character that she should have as little control over her emotions as she has over her tongue. She is warm and affectionate, and it may come as something of a shock when she advises Juliet to abandon Romeo. However, this too, is essential to the plot, and given her straightforward, unromantic ideas, is quite believable. Friar Lawrence, so important in the action of the play, is conventionally drawn. He moralizes, saying all that a religious man should say. He is not without touches of humour, though, and is shown to have a lively affection for his young friend Romeo. Towards the end of the play, Shakespeare perhaps loses interest in him as a character, and his actions are governed by the necessities of the plot.

Plot Chorus

ACT 1

It is generally no part of the intentions of a Tragedy to be original in its plot: such a work deals most frequently with a story that is well-known to the audience. So it is with *Romeo and Juliet*, and indeed Shakespeare straight away introduces a Chorus to tell us what the play is going to be about.

The action starts with a street brawl between servants of the two rival families, the Capulets and the Montagues. They are at first rather wary of one another, and fighting only begins when the Capulet pair see Benvolio coming, from whom they expect support. In fact, Benvolio responsibly tries to break up the fight, but Tybalt, far from heeding his call for help in subduing the riotous servants, joins in himself by attacking Benvolio. Some citizens of Verona, evidently weary of the quarrels between the two families, set upon them both impartially. When Capulet and Montague themselves arrive, they are only prevented from drawing swords on one another by their wives. The fighting is at its height when the Prince arrives. Having with some difficulty restored order, he threatens death to any member of either family found in the street disturbances in future. He leaves, taking Capulet with him, Montague remaining behind under instructions to attend the Prince later.

Montague and his wife, relieved that their son Romeo was not involved in the fray, inquire if Benvolio has seen him. It is agreed that he is in a strange and gloomy mood, and Benvolio promises to try to find out the reason. This he does easily enough when his friend joins him: Romeo is in love with a girl who will have nothing to do with him. He rejects Benvolio's advice to look elsewhere.

Capulet returns from his interview with the Prince, and is talking to Paris, who wishes to marry his daughter, Juliet. Capulet objects that she is too young for marriage, but nevertheless he encourages the young nobleman to woo her, adding that the choice of a husband lies entirely with the girl herself. (We shall see how far from the truth this really is later in the play). He then invites Paris to a feast he is holding at his house that night, where there will be many pretty girls with whom Paris may compare Juliet. He sends a servant off with a list of guests upon whom he must call to deliver the invitations to the feast, and leaves. The servant, who is unable to read, seeks the assistance of Romeo in understanding the list of names he has been given. It includes the name of Rosaline, the girl whom Romeo thinks he loves and Benvolio suggests that they go to the feast, so that Romeo can see that there are more attractive girls than Rosaline about. Romeo scorns such an idea, but agrees to go along. At this feast, a Masked Ball, 'gate-crashers' were acceptable, as long as they offered some entertainment to the other guests.

The third scene is given over entirely to the women. Lady Capulet is trying to tell Juliet that Paris wishes to marry her, but is constantly interrupted by the talkative Nurse.

Next, Romeo and Benvolio appear with their friend Mercutio, discussing the precise way they will make their entrance at the Masked Ball – shall they excuse their presence with a speech, or get straight on with their act, which it seems, is to be a dance? Romeo declares that he is not in the mood for dancing, and advises against their going to the ball, because of a dream he has had. From the banter that follows this emerges one of the most famous speeches in the play – Mercutio's entertaining account about Queen Mab. Romeo expresses forebodings that there will be some tragic consequences following the night's revels.

The first Act ends with the scene of the feast at Capulet's house. The Montague party is welcomed by Capulet, and take part in a dance, but Tybalt recognizes Romeo and, very angry at his presence, sends for his rapier with the intention of fighting. He is restrained by Capulet, who gets equally angry at Tybalt's arguing with him. Tybalt leaves, declaring that he will take some form of revenge on the hated Montague. During the dance, in which Romeo takes no part, he sees Juliet, and falls in love with her, and she with him. They kiss. When the visitors leave, she enquires from the Nurse who the young man that so attracted her is, and discovering that he is a Montague, realizes the impossible position that this, her first love, has put her in.

ACT II

At the start of the second Act, the Chorus reappears, telling us that Romeo is now in love with someone who returns his love, and that despite the fact that they cannot meet openly, they do contrive to do so in secret.

The first two scenes of this Act are in fact a continuous whole. (You will remember that the division of the play into 'Acts' and 'Scenes' is the work of editors, not of Shakespeare himself.) It is night. Romeo has separated himself from his friends on the way home from the ball, and they are looking for him. Mercutio pretends to try to make Romeo appear by means of a magical incantation, heavily spiced with sexual references. When he and Benvolio go off to bed, Romeo, who has been listening, comes out of hiding. He sees Juliet come out of a room on to her balcony, and hears her speaking about her love for him, despite the quarrel between their families, though wishing he could change his name, so that she might openly declare her love. He interrupts. She is at first frightened at being overheard, then quickly recognizes his voice, and expresses her fears for his safety, should her kinsmen discover him there. The scene then develops into a long exchange between the lovers commonly known as the 'first balcony scene'. The action of the play is advanced to the extent that Juliet promises that if Romeo wishes to marry her, she will come to him, and Romeo proposes to seek the aid of Friar Lawrence to achieve that end.

As dawn breaks, we see Friar Lawrence going about his business of collecting herbs for the making of medicines. Romeo arrives in great haste to ask the Friar to marry Juliet and himself. The Friar, though chiding the young man for his easily changed affections, agrees to do so in the hope that it may bring their two families together, and end the feud in Verona.

Benvolio, Mercutio and Romeo (now in high spirits) are all joking together. Their jesting, which becomes highly improper, is interrupted by the Nurse who is looking for Romeo (she does not know him) with a message from Juliet. She is mocked outrageously by Mercutio, but Romeo eventually gets her to understand that Juliet is to go to Confession at Friar Lawrence's cell that afternoon, where they will be married. His servant will later give the Nurse a rope-ladder which he will use to climb to his wife's room that night.

Juliet is impatiently awaiting the Nurse's return. When she does arrive, she spends some time teasing Juliet, before giving her Romeo's message. Juliet does as she is asked, and Friar Lawrence, after some warning to Romeo of the dangers of violent passion, marries them.

At this point, the play has had very much the nature of a romantic comedy (apart from several characters' forebodings), with much fun and laughter.

ACT III

The next scene, it is important to realize, starts at much the same time as Romeo and Juliet are being married. It is a very hot day – the kind of day on which, as Benvolio remarks, tempers may be lost. He and Mercutio, with some others of the house of Montague, are talking of this very subject, when Tybalt comes in looking for trouble. Mercutio is very ready to match him, and despite restraining words from Benvolio, they are about to fight when Romeo comes along, on his way from the secret marriage ceremony. Tybalt breaks off his quarrel with Mercutio to insult Romeo and to challenge him to a duel. Romeo, now of course a kinsman of the hot-tempered Capulet, turns aside the challenge with an enigmatic remark about the reason he now has to love Tybalt. Mercutio takes this as cowardice, starts a fight with Tybalt, and is fatally wounded when Romeo tries to part them. Tybalt goes out. Mercutio dies. Tybalt returns, and Romeo, furious at the death of his friend, attacks and kills him. Benvolio persuades the bewildered Romeo to run off, as a crowd of citizens, quickly followed by Montague and Capulet and their wives and then by the Prince, come in to see what is going on. Benvolio, called upon to explain what has happened, does his best to defend Romeo's conduct, whilst Lady Capulet demands revenge. The Prince, angry that someone of his own blood has now become a victim of the feud, passes sentence of immediate banishment from Verona on Romeo.

Meanwhile, Juliet is eagerly awaiting the coming of night, looking forward passionately to her first encounter with Romeo as her husband. The Nurse arrives with the terrible news of Romeo's banishment, given in a very confused way because of her distress. Juliet, at first torn between her love for Romeo and her horror that he has killed her cousin Tybalt, gradually realizes how terrible for her is her husband's banishment. The Nurse tells her that she knows where Romeo is, and that he will come to her that night, as planned, to take his farewell.

Friar Lawrence brings to Romeo, who is hiding in his cell, the news of his banishment. Romeo, maddened by grief at being parted from his wife of a few hours, pours out an hysterical torrent of words, and tries to stab himself. He is sternly rebuked by the Friar for unmanliness, then confronted by a plan that he should take refuge in nearby Mantua, while matters are sorted out so that he may return and resume his marriage. The Nurse, who is present during most of this, is deeply impressed by what seems to her the Friar's wisdom, and urges Romeo to make haste to Juliet, as it is getting very late.

There follows a short but very fateful scene, late at night, in which Capulet proposes that Juliet shall marry Paris almost at once, and tells his wife to see that the girl is informed of his decision.

It is now dawn on the following day (you will have noticed how very fast the action of this play moves). Romeo and Juliet have spent a brief night together, and she is at first reluctant to let him go. Romeo eventually climbs down the ladder, and no sooner have they said their unhappy goodbyes than Lady Capulet arrives. Supposing Juliet's tears to be for the death of Tybalt, she breaks what she imagines to be the happy news of the intended marriage to Paris. Juliet, knowing of the impossibility of this, passionately refuses. Capulet, upon entering and hearing of her refusal, rejects the pleas she makes on her knees for a delay, and declares in the most brutal terms that he will, if need be, drag her in a cart to her wedding the following Thursday. Left alone with her Nurse, Juliet seeks her help, only to be advised to forget about Romeo, and go ahead with marriage to the 'lovely gentleman',

Paris. Pretending to agree, but bitterly condemning the old woman as soon as she is gone, Juliet decides to seek help from the Friar and, if necessary, to die.

ACT IV

At the Friar's cell, after a brief and embarrassing encounter with Paris, who behaves to her in a gracious way, as her husband-to-be, Juliet tells the Friar she will kill herself unless he can find some way out of a bigamous marriage. Restraining her, he produces a plan: he will give her a drug (we now see the point of our first sight of the Friar collecting herbs) which will have the effect of making her appear dead for a period of nearly two days. She will be laid in the vault of the Capulet family, and the Friar himself will send a message to Mantua arranging for Romeo to get to her in the tomb just as consciousness is returning, and to take her away with him. Juliet agrees.

Back at the Capulet home, preparations are going ahead for a wedding feast. Capulet is told that Juliet has gone to confession, and when she returns and asks his pardon for her disobedience, he becomes extremely affable again, expresses his admiration for the good influence of the Friar, and decides to have the wedding brought forward by a day. He goes off to fetch the young bridegroom himself.

Juliet persuades the Nurse and her mother to leave her to herself in her bedroom. As she prepares to drink the drug, she fears that it might not work at all and then that it may be a poison. Terrified by a vision of Tybalt however, she drinks, and the drug takes immediate effect. The Nurse, coming to rouse Juliet for her wedding day, finds her apparently dead. Her screams bring others running in, including the parents, who join the Nurse in expressions of grief. The Friar arrives with Paris, seeks to calm the outbursts, and advises that, 'as the custom is', she shall be carried 'in her best array' to church and then to burial in the tomb.

ACT V

Romeo is in Mantua. He has had a dream which has left him happy. His servant arrives from Verona with news of Juliet's death and burial. Romeo, grief-stricken, determines, in spite of fate, to return to Verona and die there with his wife. He buys a poison from an apothecary, and sets off for Juliet's tomb.

Back in Verona, the messenger entrusted by Friar Lawrence with a letter of instructions for Romeo returns having been unable to deliver it. The Friar, realizing the dangers of Juliet's awaking alone in the vault, plans at once to go there and release Juliet and to keep her at his cell until he can get in touch with Romeo.

The final scene of the play takes place near and inside the tomb of the Capulets. First to arrive is Paris. He is spreading flowers before the tomb, when his page whistles a warning that someone is coming. It is Romeo with his servant. Dismissing the latter, he sets about breaking open the gates of the vault, but is interrupted by Paris, who had hidden himself. They fight. Paris is killed. Romeo grieves over the body of Juliet, kisses her for the last time, and drinks the poison he has brought with him. No sooner is he dead than Friar Lawrence arrives and discovers his body just as Juliet begins to awake. He tells her what has happened, tries to take her away. She refuses. The Friar, alarmed by the noise of the nightwatchmen, who have been brought to the scene, goes off, and Juliet discovering Romeo dead by her side, uses his dagger to kill herself. Almost at once, the vault begins to fill with people: the watchmen, who have found Friar Lawrence, and Romeo's servant, the Prince, and the Capulets and Montagues. All the story of past events emerges, and Capulet and Montague clasp hands over the bodies of their children – 'poor sacrifices of our enmity'.

Dramatic Structure

It is important to realize that the division into Acts and Scenes of a play by Shakespeare is not necessarily of much help in perceiving its dramatic structure, for such divisions are generally the work of later editors. The action of his plays is much more of a continuous flow, moving quite across the division into Scenes which you find in this text. A good production of the play ignores such arbitrary divisions when they do not accord with the actual dramatic structure of the piece.

Structurally, the play may usefully be regarded as falling into two parts. The first gives us the background of the family quarrel in Verona, but then is principally concerned with the courtship of Romeo and Juliet, and ends with their wedding. Despite some brief forebodings of evil to come, the immediate effect of this part as we watch it is that of comedy – it is dominated by merry and entertaining scenes with high-spirited young men, and by the development of love between Romeo and Juliet, with its apparently happy issue in their marriage. Immediately afterwards, in Act III, the mood changes. It is hot and we find 'the mad blood stirring'. Mercutio dies, Tybalt is killed, Romeo is banished, and it becomes clear to us what was meant in the Prologue by the phrase 'a pair of star-cross'd lovers'. Events move with speed to a tragic conclusion.

Within this broad framework, other structural patterns may be discerned. One is an alternation between scenes of a public nature, and those which are of a more private and intimate kind. This, of course, mirrors the interaction in the play between personal relationships, and family and group attitudes. This interaction lies at the very heart of the play, and provides the cause of the tragedy. Thus, the play begins with a very public scene, involving the heads of both quarrelling families, their kinsmen and servants, citizens of Verona, and their ruler himself. This occasion dissolves into a private encounter between

Benvolio and Lord and Lady Montague, thence into another between Capulet and Paris, and so to a third between three of the four women of the play. A noisy open air scene with the revellers on their way to the feast is then followed by the feast itself which, though in a private house, has something of the character of a crowded public occasion. The company disperses, and then comes a long intimate meeting in darkness and privacy, between the young lovers, and a brief look at their secret marriage. The second part of the play opens with the second big public scene, involving everyone, as before, including the citizens of Verona and their angry Prince. As before, this is followed by a series of more intimate scenes, but ones in which the fun and supreme happiness of those in the first part of play are replaced by anger, misunderstanding, misery and despair. The deaths of Romeo and Juliet finally call together once again families, citizens and the Prince for the third and last public occasion. The play ends with the public reconciliation, over the bodies of the young, of the quarrels of the old which brought about their deaths.

Other ways of looking at the dramatic structure of the play might concern themselves with the clash between young and old hinted at above, or with the handling of time in the play, or with the carefully placed juxtaposition of dramatic incidents. Or one might look at the different varieties of language in the play, from the essentially lyrical in which little dramatic action is intended, to the language which carries the drama forward.

The truth of the matter is, that for those who admire classical formality, Shakespeare's plays are likely to seem somewhat 'loose' in structure. He does not start out with a structure in mind, but lets one emerge, as the play develops. When we look at the completed work, as with *Romeo and Juliet*, we can find a number of ways of regarding the structure, none of them exclusive.

LIST OF CHARACTERS

Chorus

Escalus   Prince of Verona

Paris   a young nobleman, kinsman to the Prince

Montague ⎫ heads of two houses at variance
Capulet   ⎭ with each other

An Old Man   of the Capulet family

Romeo   son to Montague

Mercutio   kinsman to the Prince, and friend to Romeo

Benvolio   nephew to Montague, and friend to Romeo

Tybalt   nephew to Lady Capulet

Friar Lawrence ⎫ Franciscans
Friar John   ⎭

Balthasar   servant to Romeo

Sampson ⎫ servants to Capulet
Gregory ⎭

Peter   servant to Juliet's nurse

Abraham   servant to Montague

An Apothecary

Three Musicians

An Officer

Lady Montague wife to Montague

Lady Capulet wife to Capulet

Juliet   daughter to Capulet

Nurse   to Juliet

Citizens of Verona; *Gentlemen* and *Gentlewomen* of both houses; *Maskers*, *Torchbearers*, *Pages*, *Guards*, *Watchmen*, *Servants*, and *Attendants*

The Scene: Verona and Mantua

ACT I

THE PROLOGUE

This is an introduction to the play spoken by one of the actors and in this case he tells us, in general terms, what the plot of the play is going to be.

2. Verona a town in Italy.

3. 'Their old quarrel erupts into new violence.'

4. *civil blood* blood shed in fighting between people of the same town.

6. *star-cross'd* lovers who are ill-fated because of the influence of the stars. In Shakespeare's time it was widely believed that people's lives were affected by the position of the stars when they were born. This is why Shakespeare tells us right at the start, that the love of Romeo and Juliet will come to a tragic end, not because of their own faults but because it is destined to do so.

9. *death-mark'd* marked out for death. This phrase emphasizes the warning that they are doomed.

11. *but* except for.

12. *two hours' traffic* Elizabethan plays usually lasted about this time: the words were probably said briskly and there was no stage-shifting to waste time.

14. This means that whatever failings the play or performance has – the actors will try to make up for them by their hard work.

THE PROLOGUE

[Enter CHORUS.*]*

Two households, both alike in dignity,
In fair Verona, where we lay our scene,
From ancient grudge break to new mutiny,
Where civil blood makes civil hands unclean.
From forth the fatal loins of these two foes   5
A pair of star-cross'd lovers take their life;
Whose misadventur'd piteous overthrows
Doth with their death bury their parents' strife.
The fearful passage of their death-mark'd love,
And the continuance of their parents' rage,   10
Which, but their children's end, nought could remove,
Is now the two hours' traffic of our stage;
The which if you with patient ears attend,
What here shall miss, our toil shall strive to mend.

[Exit.]

SCENE I

Immediately the play begins properly, we begin to see the kind of picky playing around with words that is common in the play. Much of it here, spoken by the serving men is crude and vulgar.

1. *carry coals* do menial work.

2. *colliers* coal-miners. Gregory takes Sampson's phrase literally, when perhaps he just meant he didn't want to do dull and laborious jobs.

3. *choler* anger. The word puns backwards to *collier* and forwards to *collar* in line 4.

3. *draw* draw their swords. Gregory puns on this with the phrase: *draw your neck out of collar* in line 4.
4. *collar* hangman's noose.
5–10. There follows a series of puns on the word *move,* meaning in lines 5 and 7 'made angry', in lines 6 and 10 'given cause to', and in lines 8 and 9 'to change position'.

10–11. *take the wall* walk nearest the wall: an aggressive action, forcing anyone passing to walk nearest the road and as a result run the risk of being splashed with mud.
12–13. *goes to the wall* is pushed into an inferior position.

ACT ONE
Scene I

Verona. A public place

[Enter SAMPSON *and* GREGORY, *of the house of Capulet,
with swords and bucklers on.]*

Sampson
    Gregory, on my word, we'll not carry coals.
Gregory
    No, for then we should be colliers.
Sampson
    I mean, an we be in choler, we'll draw.
Gregory
    Ay, while you live, draw your neck out of collar.
Sampson
    I strike quickly, being moved. 5
Gregory
    But thou art not quickly moved to strike.
Sampson
    A dog of the house of Montague moves me.
Gregory
    To move is to stir, and to be valiant is to stand; there-
    fore, if thou art moved, thou run'st away.
Sampson
    A dog of that house shall move me to stand. I will take 10
    the wall of any man or maid of Montague's.
Gregory
    That shows thee a weak slave; for the weakest goes to
    the wall.
Sampson
    'Tis true; and therefore women, being the weaker
    vessels, are ever thrust to the wall; therefore I will 15
    push Montague's men from the wall and thrust his
    maids to the wall.

18. Gregory pretends to tell Sampson off saying that the quarrel is between men and that women are not involved.

23. *maidenheads* state of virginity.
24–5. Gregory and Sampson quibble on the word *sense,* meaning in line 24 'meaning' and in line 25 'feeling'.

26–7. Sampson says that he will make their women feel him as long as he can maintain an erection, and it's well known how effective he is at doing that!
29. *poor-John* dried hake, a very unappetising dish.

35. *Let us take the law of our sides* Let us make sure we are on the right side of the law. Gregory and Sampson are not really so bold as they like to pretend.
38. *bite my thumb* an insulting gesture at that time – the clicking of the thumbnail against the teeth.

Gregory
The quarrel is between our masters and us their men.
Sampson
'Tis all one; I will show myself a tyrant. When I have
fought with the men, I will be civil with the maids – I   20
will cut off their heads.
Gregory
The heads of the maids?
Sampson
Ay, the heads of the maids, or their maidenheads; take
it in what sense thou wilt.
Gregory
They must take it in sense that feel it.   25
Sampson
Me they shall feel while I am able to stand; and 'tis
known I am a pretty piece of flesh.
Gregory
'Tis well thou art not fish; if thou hadst, thou hadst
been poor-John. Draw thy tool; here comes two of the
house of Montagues.   30

[Enter two other SERVINGMEN, ABRAHAM *and* BALTHASAR.*]*

Sampson
My naked weapon is out; quarrel, I will back thee.
Gregory
How? turn thy back and run?
Sampson
Fear me not.
Gregory
No, marry; I fear thee!
Sampson
Let us take the law of our sides; let them begin.   35
Gregory
I will frown as I pass by, and let them take it as they
list.
Sampson
Nay, as they dare. I will bite my thumb at them, which
is disgrace to them if they bear it.

40–50. This exchange between the two 'gangs' seems fairly basic on the page, but the words come alive when spoken; Sampson's riposte, 'I do not bite my thumb at you, sir: but I bite my thumb, sir,' can be said sarcastically, mockingly, spitefully … in fact, in any number of ways that conveys the enmity between the two opposing groups on stage. It will be familiar to anyone who has seen gangs of young men in town centres 'staring each other out'.

53. Gregory urges Sampson to claim that Capulet is a better man than Montague; he feels it is safe to be bolder because he sees Tybalt coming, who he thinks will support them.

57. *swashing* swishing, sweeping.

Abraham
  Do you bite your thumb at us, sir?   40
Sampson
  I do bite my thumb, sir.
Abraham
  Do you bite your thumb at us, sir?
Sampson
  [Aside to GREGORY*]* Is the law of our side, if I say ay?
Gregory
  [Aside to SAMPSON*]* No.
Sampson
  No, sir, I do not bite my thumb at you, sir; but I bite   45
  my thumb, sir.
Gregory
  Do you quarrel, sir?
Abraham
  Quarrel, sir! No, sir.
Sampson
  But if you do, sir, I am for you. I serve as good a man
  as you.   50
Abraham
  No better?
Sampson
  Well. sir.

                    [Enter BENVOLIO.*]*

Gregory
  [Aside to SAMPSON*]* Say 'better'; here comes one of my
  master's kinsmen.
Sampson
  Yes, better, sir.
Abraham
  You lie.   55
Sampson
  Draw, if you be men. Gregory, remember thy swashing
  blow.

                    [They fight.]

60–6. Benvolio tries to stop the servants fighting; but when Tybalt enters, he forces Benvolio into a fight himself; so begins the 'new mutiny' of the Prologue.

60. *heartless hinds* a complicated pun *(hind* = deer and servant). Presumably the hind is to be regarded as a symbol of timidity. 'Heartless' here might suggest 'cowardly' (i.e without heart ...)

67. *bills, and partisans* long-handled weapons, such as pikes.

70. *A crutch, a crutch!* In the midst of the fighting, Lady Capulet's sarcasm, mocking her husband, 'Old' Capulet, whom she presumably thinks is too ancient for fighting in the street, provides an early idea of her sharp tongue. It also gives us a sense of how reason and normal behaviour go out of the window when long-standing hatred and grudges surface.
74. Like Lady Capulet, Lady Montague appears to be a peacemaker here, although whether out of embarrassment at her husband's behaviour, or out of genuine goodwill, is not clear.

Benvolio
    Part, fools *[Beats down their swords]*
    Put up your swords; you know not what you do.

[Enter TYBALT.*]*

Tybalt
    What, art thou drawn among these heartless hinds?   60
    Turn thee, Benvolio; look upon thy death.
Benvolio
    I do but keep the peace; put up thy sword,
    Or manage it to part these men with me.
Tybalt
    What, drawn, and talk of peace! I hate the word,
    As I hate hell, all Montagues, and thee.   65
    Have at thee, coward!

[They fight.]

*[Enter an officer, and three or four citizens with clubs
or partisans.]*

Officer
    Clubs, bills, and partisans! Strike; beat them down.
Citizens
    Down with the Capulets! Down with the Montagues!

[Enter OLD CAPULET *in his gown, and his wife.]*

Capulet
    What noise is this? Give me my long sword, ho!
Lady Capulet
    A crutch, a crutch! Why call you for a sword?   70
Capulet
    My sword, I say! Old Montague is come,
    And flourishes his blade in spite of me.

75–97. The Prince's speech is powerful and full of rhetoric and exaggerated language, but is also very realistic. Note how he is not listened to immediately ('Will they not hear?') and how he has to shout to make himself heard above the fighting ('What, ho!). We can imagine him surrounded by the brawlers on stage, who slowly become aware of his presence. The speech not only summarises for us what has happened previously, this being the last of three 'civil brawls' but demonstrates how the conflict between the two families, whose names are mentioned here again, comes from the slightest spark – in this case, an 'airy word'. The speech ends with all present being threatened with death if they cause trouble on the streets again.

76. *Profaners* abusers

76. *neighbour-stained* stained with the blood of neighbours.

78. *pernicious* wicked, malicious

81. *mistempered* used in a wrong cause.

86–9. The Prince says that the old citizens of Verona have had to intervene to break up the quarrels between the parties of Montague and Capulct.

87. *grave beseeming ornaments* the sober equipment of peaceful men.

89. *Canker'd ... canker'd* (1) age-stiffened; (2) malignant.

98. *abroach* open (a term usually applied to a barrel).

[Enter OLD MONTAGUE *and his* WIFE.*]*

Montague
    Thou villain Capulet! – Hold me not, let me go.
Lady Montague
    Thou shall not stir one foot to seek a foe.

[Enter PRINCE ESCALUS *with his* TRAIN.*]*

Prince
    Rebellious subjects, enemies to peace,   75
    Profaners of this neighbour-stained steel –
    Will they not hear? What, ho! you men, you beasts,
    That quench the fire of your pernicious rage
    With purple fountains issuing from your veins!
    On pain of torture, from those bloody hands   80
    Throw your mistempered weapons to the ground,
    And hear the sentence of your moved prince.
    Three civil brawls, bred of an airy word,
    By thee, old Capulet, and Montague,
    Have thrice disturbed the quiet of our streets   85
    And made Verona's ancient citizens
    Cast by their grave beseeming ornaments
    To wield old partisans, in hands as old,
    Canker'd with peace, to part your canker'd hate.
    If ever you disturb our streets again,   90
    Your lives shall pay the forfeit of the peace.
    For this time all the rest depart away.
    You, Capulet, shall go along with me;
    And, Montague, come you this afternoon,
    To know our farther pleasure in this case,   95
    To old Free-town, our common judgment-place.
    Once more, on pain of death, all men depart.

[Exeunt all but MONTAGUE, *his* WIFE, *and* BENVOLIO.*]*

Montague
    Who set this ancient quarrel new abroach?
    Speak, nephew; were you by when it began?

104–6. Benvolio speaks with contempt of Tybalt's showy behaviour, flinging his sword around in fancy movements but hitting only 'the winds'.

108. *on part and part* on either side.

111. *fray* street fight, battle.
112. Note that the tone of the language here changes from that of violence to a song-like, decorative style. Does this flag up the theme of love that will run alongside that of conflict?

119. *covert* shade, cover.
120. *measuring his affections by my own* 'judging his mood by what I know of my own.'
121. 'which at that time inclined me to be alone.'
123. 'followed my own inclination not to break in upon his desire to be alone.'

126. *augmenting* adding to.
129–31. An elaborate way of describing the sunrise, in keeping with the change in the style of the language mentioned in the note to line 112.

130. *Aurora* in Roman mythology, the goddess of the dawn.
131. *heavy* heavy-hearted.

Benvolio
    Here were the servants of your adversary   100
    And yours, close fighting ere I did approach.
    I drew to part them; in the instant came
    The fiery Tybalt, with his sword prepar'd;
    Which, as he breath'd defiance to my ears,
    He swung about his head and cut the winds,   105
    Who, nothing hurt withal, hiss'd him in scorn.
    While we were interchanging thrusts and blows,
    Came more and more, and fought on part and part,
    Till the Prince came, who parted either part.

Lady Montague
    O, where is Romeo? Saw you him to-day?   110
    Right glad I am he was not at this fray.

Benvolio
    Madam, an hour before the worshipp'd sun
    Peer'd forth the golden window of the east,
    A troubled mind drew me to walk abroad;
    Where, underneath the grove of sycamore   115
    That westward rooteth from this city side,
    So early walking did I see your son.
    Towards him I made; but he was ware of me
    And stole into the covert of the wood.
    I, measuring his affections by my own,   120
    Which then most sought where most might not be
        found,
    Being one too many by my weary self,
    Pursu'd my humour, not pursuing his,
    And gladly shunn'd who gladly fled from me.

Montague
    Many a morning hath he there been seen,   125
    With tears augmenting the fresh morning's dew,
    Adding to clouds more clouds with his deep sighs;
    But all so soon as the all-cheering sun
    Should in the farthest east begin to draw
    The shady curtains from Aurora's bed,   130
    Away from light steals home my heavy son,
    And private in his chamber pens himself,

134. *artificial night* We will learn shortly that his mood is due to his apparent 'love' for Rosaline, but the use of the word 'artificial' here implies, even now, that Romeo is indulging himself in this passion.

135. This mood suggests a gloomy outcome.

139. *importun'd* urged him to explain his behaviour.

141. *his own affections' counsellor* suggests that Romeo will be guided only by his own wishes, which are to keep his affairs very strictly to himself.

144. *sounding and discovery* submitting to questions, and answering them.

145. In the same way that if we can see the maggot or worm that eats away at a flower we can then deal with it, so we can help Romeo if we can find out the cause of his sorrow.

152–3. 'I hope that you will be so fortunate by staying behind as to get a true confession out of him.'

154. How do you think Romeo enters the stage here? Presumably, most actors would take what they have learned from the descriptions of him in his moody state, and he would enter in a gloomy fashion. Does he really not know the time of day, or is this just a pretence?

Shuts up his windows, locks fair daylight out,
And makes himself an artificial night.
Black and portentous must this humour prove,   135
Unless good counsel may the cause remove.

Benvolio
My noble uncle, do you know the cause?

Montague
I neither know it nor can learn of him.

Benvolio
Have you importun'd him by any means?

Montague
Both by myself and many other friends.   140
But he, his own affections' counsellor,
Is to himself – I will not say how true;
But to himself so secret and so close,
So far from sounding and discovery,
As is the bud bit with an envious worm,   145
Ere he can spread his sweet leaves to the air,
Or dedicate his beauty to the sun.
Could we but learn from whence his sorrows grow,
We would as willingly give cure as know.

[Enter ROMEO.]

Benvolio
See where he comes. So please you step aside;   150
I'll know his grievance or be much denied.

Montague
I would thou wert so happy by thy stay
To hear true shrift. Come, madam, let's away.

[Exeunt MONTAGUE and his wife.]

Benvolio
Good morrow, cousin.

Romeo
                        Is the day so young?

Benvolio
But new struck nine.

162. 'out of favour with the girl I'm in love with.'

163–4. 'Alas that love, which seems so attractive as an idea, turns out to be so harsh in reality.'

165. Alas that love, whose view is muffled ... Romeo is here referring to Cupid, the archer of love in Roman mythology who was always pictured as blind, but who is nevertheless able to get his own way with us (see pathways to his will).

167. *O me! What fray was here?* Romeo presumably notices the weapons lying on the ground and goes on to lament the social disorder in a series of contradictory phrases (oxymorons) such as 'brawling love' and 'loving hate'.The over-elaborate style of the language suits Romeo's present superficial form of romantic love.

178. 'at your being so heavy-hearted.'

Romeo

    Ay me! sad hours seem long.   155

    Was that my father that went hence so fast?

Benvolio

    It was. What sadness lengthens Romeo's hours?

Romeo

    Not having that which having makes them short.

Benvolio

    In love?

Romeo

    Out –   160

Benvolio

    Of love?

Romeo

    Out of her favour where I am in love.

Benvolio

    Alas that love, so gentle in his view,

    Should be so tyrannous and rough in proof!

Romeo

    Alas that love, whose view is muffled still,   165

    Should without eyes see pathways to his will!

    Where shall we dine? O me! What fray was here?

    Yet tell me not, for I have heard it all.

    Here's much to do with hate, but more with love.

    Why then, O brawling love! O loving hate!   170

    O anything, of nothing first create!

    O heavy lightness! serious vanity!

    Mis-shapen chaos of well-seeming forms!

    Feather of lead, bright smoke, cold fire, sick health!

    Still-waking sleep, that is not what it is!   175

    This love feel I, that feel no love in this.

    Dost thou not laugh?

Benvolio

                   No, coz, I rather weep.

Romeo

    Good heart, at what?

Benvolio

                      At thy good heart's oppression.

179. Romeo replies that this is the common effect of being in love. (The audience might contrast this superficial infatuation with the profound passion that Romeo will feel for Juliet after meeting her.)

180–2. 'I am weighed down by my own troubles, which will only be increased if you show distress.'

187. *discreet* discriminating – another forced paradox, since madness usually implies someone's inability to make wise decisions. In this speech Romeo continues to play with words and act the conventional part of the distracted lover.

188. *gall* bitterness, poison.

193. *in sadness* in all seriousness.

195. *sadly* seriously.

196. *in sadness* a pun, introducing the more modern meaning of 'unhappiness'.

197. Romeo goes on to say that, with this meaning, the word is an unfortunate one to use to a man who is sick, i.e. with love.

199. Benvolio's introduces the metaphor of firing arrows (*'I aimed so near ...'*) to explain that he has guessed why Romeo is so sad. This is appropriate as it fits with the idea of a lover being hit with Cupid's arrows, and Romeo immediately picks up on the connection.

201. *A right fair mark* an easily seen target.

203. *Dian's wit* she has the cleverness of Diana (the Roman goddess of chastity) in avoiding the temptations of love and remaining a virgin.

Romeo
Why, such is love's transgression.
Griefs of mine own lie heavy in my breast, 180
Which thou wilt propagate, to have it prest
With more of thine. This love that thou hast shown
Doth add more grief to too much of mine own.
Love is a smoke rais'd with the fume of sighs;
Being purg'd, a fire sparkling in lovers' eyes; 185
Being vex'd, a sea nourish'd with loving tears.
What is it else? A madness most discreet,
A choking gall, and a preserving sweet.
Farewell, my coz.

Benvolio
                    Soft! I will go along;
An if you leave me so, you do me wrong. 190

Romeo
Tut, I have lost myself; I am not here:
This is not Romeo, he's some other where,

Benvolio
Tell me in sadness who is that you love.

Romeo
What, shall I groan and tell thee?

Benvolio
                    Groan! Why, no;
But sadly tell me who. 195

Romeo
Bid a sick man in sadness make his will.
Ah, word ill urg'd to one that is so ill!
In sadness, cousin, I do love a woman.

Benvolio
I aim'd so near when I suppos'd you lov'd.

Romeo
A right good markman! And she's fair I love. 200

Benvolio
A right fair mark, fair coz, is soonest hit.

Romeo
Well, in that hit you miss: she'll not be hit
With Cupid's arrow. She hath Dian's wit,

206. *stay* give in to.

207. *bide* put up with.

208. She will not give up her virginity even for gold, capable of seducing saints.

210. Because she will have no children to continue her beauty after death (*store* = fertility, increase). This idea is restated in lines 213 and 214, and is a common one in Elizabethan poetry. Elizabethan ladies often wore black masks when they walked in public places.

211. *live chaste* remain a virgin/maid.

212–218. Romeo continues the idea of the waste of beauty: 'posterity' (the future) will never see her beauty repeated. The speech ends with a typically exaggerated statement from Romeo at this point – that he is 'dead' because his lover has rejected him.

229–30. Romeo says that looking at other women only heightens and emphasizes her beauty in his eyes. This would be ironic, but we don't actually know **who** Romeo is talking about at this point; the audience may be forgiven for thinking it is Juliet, whose name has been mentioned in the Prologue.

232. *I'll pay that doctrine* I'll teach you that lesson.

And in strong proof of chastity well arm'd,
From Love's weak childish bow she lives unharm'd.   205
She will not stay the siege of loving terms,
Nor bide th' encounter of assailing eyes,
Nor ope her lap to saint-seducing gold.
O, she is rich in beauty; only poor
That, when she dies, with beauty dies her store.   210

Benvolio
Then she hath sworn that she will still live chaste?

Romeo
She hath, and in that sparing makes huge waste;
For beauty, starv'd with her severity,
Cuts beauty off from all posterity.
She is too fair, too wise, wisely too fair,   215
To merit bliss by making me despair.
She hath forsworn to love, and in that vow
Do I live dead that live to tell it now.

Benvolio
Be rul'd by me: forget to think of her.

Romeo
O teach me how I should forget to think!   220

Benvolio
By giving liberty unto thine eyes.
Examine other beauties.

Romeo
                    'Tis the way
To call hers, exquisite, in question more.
These happy masks that kiss fair ladies' brows,
Being black, puts us in mind they hide the fair.   225
He that is strucken blind cannot forget
The precious treasure of his eyesight lost.
Show me a mistress that is passing fair,
What doth her beauty serve but as a note
Where I may read who pass'd that passing fair?   230
Farewell; thou canst not teach me to forget.

Benvolio
I'll pay that doctrine or else die in debt.

[Exeunt.]

37

SCENE II

It is clear at the beginning of this scene, that Capulet and Paris have been discussing the Duke's warning that the family quarrel between the Montagues and the Capulets must stop.

3. This is ironic, given that both men were extremely willing to join in the fight!

6. *my suit* Paris is evidently seeking to marry Juliet.

9. 'She is not yet fourteen.' In Shakespeare's day, it would have been quite normal for girls to marry young, especially in Mediterranean countries. Nevertheless, Capulet would prefer his daughter to be a couple of years older before she has a husband.

14. Capulet's other children are dead and buried and all his hopes are centred upon Juliet. Whilst this doesn't excuse his later behaviour, it does perhaps explain how much he has invested in her.
17. Capulet is saying that he is quite willing to fall in with Juliet's own decision; of course, he takes a very different view later on!

25. *Earth-treading stars* extremely pretty girls – goddesses on earth, as it were.
27. *well-apparell'd* prettily-dressed.

Scene II

A street

[Enter CAPULET, COUNTY PARIS, and the CLOWN, his servant.]

Capulet
But Montague is bound as well as I,
In penalty alike; and 'tis not hard, I think,
For men so old as we to keep the peace.
Paris
Of honourable reckoning are you both,
And pity 'tis you liv'd at odds so long.   5
But now, my lord, what say you to my suit?
Capulet
But saying o'er what I have said before:
My child is yet a stranger in the world,
She hath not seen the change of fourteen years;
Let two more summers wither in their pride   10
Ere we may think her ripe to be a bride.
Paris
Younger than she are happy mothers made.
Capulet
And too soon marr'd are those so early made.
Earth hath swallowed all my hopes but she;
She is the hopeful lady of my earth.   15
But woo her, gentle Paris, get her heart;
My will to her consent is but a part.
And, she agreed, within her scope of choice
Lies my consent and fair according voice.
This night I hold an old accustom'd feast,   20
Whereto I have invited many a guest,
Such as I love; and you among the store,
One more, most welcome, makes my number more.
At my poor house look to behold this night
Earth-treading stars that make dark heaven light.   25
Such comfort as do lusty young men feel
When well-apparell'd April on the heel

29. *fresh female buds* girls who have not yet blossomed into womanhood.

30. *Inherit* enjoy, receive as your own.

32-3. He says that Paris will that evening see Juliet among all the other girls and then he may, or may not, think her the best.

39-44. The servant, apparently a comically stupid figure here, gets into a muddle: it is the tailor who uses a yard, the shoemaker a last, the fisher a net and the painter a pencil.

44. He goes off to find a more educated person who can read the list for him.

45-50. Benvolio is again advising Romeo to find another girl for this will cure him of the pain of his present infatuation.

47. *holp* helped.

48. *languish* disease.

50. *rank* strong.

51. A plantain leaf was supposed to be a remedy for a sore shin; Romeo scornfully dismisses Benvolio's remedy for love by implying that love-sickness cannot be cured as easily as a cut shin.

Of limping winter treads, even such delight
Among fresh female buds shall you this night
Inherit at my house. Hear all, all see,   30
And like her most whose merit most shall be;
Which on more view of many, mine, being one,
May stand in number, though in reck'ning none.
Come, go with me. *[To* SERVANT, *giving him a paper]*
      Go sirrah, trudge about
Through fair Verona; find those persons out   35
Whose names are written there, and to them say
My house and welcome on their pleasure stay.

[Exeunt CAPULET *and* PARIS.]

Servant
    Find them out whose names are written here! It is
written that the shoemaker should meddle with his
yard and the tailor with his last, the fisher with his   40
pencil and the painter with his nets; but I am sent to
find those persons whose names are here writ, and can
never find what names the writing person hath here
writ. I must to the learned. In good time!

[Enter BENVOLIO *and* ROMEO.]

Benvolio
    Tut, man, one fire burns out another's burning,   45
One pain is lessened by another's anguish;
Turn giddy rand be holp by backward turning;
One desperate grief cures with another's languish.
Take thou some new infection to thy eye,
And the rank poison of the old will die.   50
Romeo
    Your plantain leaf is excellent for that.
Benvolio
    For what, I pray thee?
Romeo   185
          For your broken shin.
Benvolio
    Why, Romeo, art thou mad?

41

54. *but bound more than a madman is* it was an Elizabethan custom to keep madmen tied up and shut away. In *Twelfth Night* Malvolio is presumed mad and locked up until he finally persuades his tormentors that he has been unfairly treated.

58. Romeo deliberately chooses to misintepret the servant's words to fit his mood: 'I can see what my future is going to be by examining my present unhappiness.'
59. *without book* by listening to a teacher.

62. The simple-minded servant fails to understand Romeo's elaborate way of saying yes.
63. It is through this rather obvious device of getting Romeo to read the letter aloud (how else would the audience know the details?) that we learn who may be present at the party, and hear Rosaline's name mentioned. Romeo does not say anything when he reads Rosaline's name, although the actor playing him can, of course, react appropriately.

Romeo

Not mad, but bound more than a madman is;
Shut up in prison, kept without my food,   55
Whipt and tormented, and – God-den, good fellow.

Servant

God gi' go'den. I pray, sir, can you read?

Romeo

Ay, mine own fortune in my misery.

Servant

Perhaps you have learned it without book. But I pray,
can you read anything you see?   60

Romeo

Ay, if I know the letters and the language.

Servant

Ye say honestly; rest you merry!

Romeo

Stay, fellow; I can read.
[He reads the list] 'Signior Martino and his wife and
daughters; County Anseime and his beauteous sisters;   65
the lady widow of Vitruvio; Signior Placentio and his
lovely nieces; Mercutio and his brother Valentine;
mine uncle Capulet, his wife, and daughters; my fair
niece Rosaline and Livia; Signior Valentio and his
cousin Tybalt; Lucio and the lively Helena.' A fair   70
assembly. *[Gives back the paper]* Whither should they
come?

Servant

Up.

Romeo

Whither?

Servant

To supper. To our house.   75

Romeo

Whose house?

Servant

My master's.

Romeo

Indeed, I should have ask'd you that before.

81. *crush* try the quality by drinking it.

84. We learn that it is Rosaline who Romeo loves, or thinks he loves.

86. *unattainted* unprejudiced.

89–92. 'When my eyes are so faithless to my belief in the superiority of Rosaline, may they, like heretics who reject the true faith, be burnt.'
91. *And these* i.e. his eyes.
often drown'd i.e. with tears of sorrow.
94. 'You believed her to be beautiful because there was no one else around to compare her with' Benvolio sees through Romeo's infatuation.

97. *crystal scales* Romeo's two eyes.

100. *scant* scarcely.

102. *splendour of mine own* the splendour of Rosaline. Romeo says he'll go along, but not to find someone else, but just to enjoy looking at how much more beautiful Rosaline is than anyone else present.

Servant

    Now I'll tell you without asking: my master is the great
    rich Capulet; and if you be not of the house of 80
    Montagues, I pray come and crush a cup of wine. Rest
    you merry!

[Exit.]

Benvolio

    At this same ancient feast of Capulets
    Sups the fair Rosaline whom thou so loves,
    With all the admired beauties of Verona. 85
    Go thither, and with unattainted eye
    Compare her face with some that I shall show,
    And I will make thee think thy swan a crow.

Romeo

    When the devout religion of mine eye
    Maintains such falsehood, then turn tears to fires; 90
    And these, who, often drown'd, could never die,
    Transparent heretics, be burnt for liars!
    One fairer than my love! The all-seeing sun
    Ne'er saw her match since first the world begun.

Benvolio

    Tut, you saw her fair, none else being by, 95
    Herself pois'd with herself in either eye;
    But in that crystal scales let there be weigh'd
    Your lady's love against some other maid
    That I will show you shining at this feast,
    And she shall scant show well that now seems best. 100

Romeo

    I'll go along, no such sight to be shown,
    But to rejoice in splendour of mine own.

[Exeunt.]

SCENE III

2. The Nurse swears by her virginity at twelve years old – presumably she lost it soon afterwards!

8. *give leave awhile.* 'Leave us alone a moment'. What can we read into the fact that Juliet's mother immediately calls the Nurse back? Perhaps she's not that comfortable talking to her daughter about 'womanly matters', unlike the Nurse, who seems to revel in it!

14. *teen* sorrow; even the Nurse is punning, on the word 'fourteen'.

16. *Lammas-tide* 1st August.

18. Juliet's youth is stressed.

Scene III

Capulet's house

[Enter LADY CAPULET and NURSE.]

Lady Capulet
Nurse, where's my daughter? Call her forth to me.
Nurse
Now, by my maidenhead at twelve year old,
I bade her come. What, lamb! what, ladybird!
God forbid! Where's this girl? What, Juliet!

[Enter JULIET.]

Juliet
How now, who calls?   5
Nurse
Your mother.
Juliet
Madam, I am here. What is your will?
Lady Capulet
This is the matter. Nurse, give leave awhile,
We must talk in secret. Nurse, come back again;
I have remember'd me, thou's hear our counsel.   10
Thou knowest my daughter's of a pretty age.
Nurse
Faith, I can tell her age unto an hour.
Lady Capulet
She's not fourteen.
Nurse
　　　　　　　I'll lay fourteen of my teeth –
And yet, to my teen be it spoken, I have but four –
She's not fourteen. How long is it now   15
To Lammas-tide?
Lady Capulet
　　　　　　　A fortnight and odd days.
Nurse
Even or odd, of all days in the year,
Come Lammas Eve at night shall she be fourteen.

19–21. Susan was the Nurse's own daughter, born at the same time as Juliet and because of whom the Nurse was able to suckle Juliet. According to this, it appears she died in infancy.

27. The Nurse had put wormwood, a bitter herb, upon her nipple to discourage the baby from taking milk. This kind of detail is in keeping with the earthy character of the Nurse.

30. *Nay, I do bear a brain* 'My, I am clever.' The Nurse's pride in her memory and her prattling on and on give us a very vivid impression of a talkative woman.

32. *dug* nipple or breast.

33. *tetchy* cross.

34. *Shake, quoth the dove-house.* The Nurse weaned Juliet, as she has said, on the day of the earthquake, sitting by the dovehouse wall *(dove-house* a nesting place for doves usually on top of a pole). Evidently the earthquake occurred as she was sitting there and the dovehouse began to rock (she personifies the building, making it say 'shake'). Her fear of its collapse was sufficient to send her scuttling for safety, as she says: *'Twas no need, I trow. To bid me trudge.'*

37. *high-lone* quite alone, without support.

37. *by th' rood* by the Holy Cross on which Christ died.

39. *broke her brow* cut her forehead.

43. The husband says that when Juliet is grown-up, she will fall on her back under a lover rather than on her face. He appears to have been just as vulgar a character as the Nurse is.

44. *by my holidam* This was originally an oath sworn on holy relics, but had come to be thought of as a reference to the Virgin Mary.

40–49. One can imagine the Nurse saying these words accompanied by loud guffaws of laughter. Again, we are given the impression that the Nurse, more than Lady Capulet, knows Juliet well.

49. *stinted* stopped crying.

53. *it* the old form of 'its'.

54. *stone* testicle. (very large on a young cockerel, hence the metaphor – which is exactly the sort one would expect the Nurse to use).

Susan and she – God rest all Christian souls –
Were of an age. Well, Susan is with God; 20
She was too good for me. But, as I said,
On Lammas Eve at night shall she be fourteen;
That shall she, marry; I remember it well.
'Tis since the earthquake now eleven years;
And she was wean'd – I never shall forget it – 25
Of all the days of the year, upon that day;
For I had then laid wormwood to my dug,
Sitting in the sun under the dove-house wall;
My lord and you were then at Mantua.
Nay, I do bear a brain. But, as I said, 30
When it did taste the wormwood on the nipple
Of my dug, and felt it bitter, pretty fool,
To see it tetchy, and fall out with the dug!
Shake, quoth the dove-house. 'Twas no need, I trow,
To bid me trudge. 35
And since that time it is eleven years;
For then she could stand high-lone; nay, by th' rood,
She could have run and waddled all about;
For even the day before, she broke her brow;
And then my husband – God be with his soul! 40
'A was a merry man – took up the child.
'Yea,' quoth he 'dost thou fall upon thy face?
Thou wilt fall backward when thou hast more wit,
Wilt thou not, Jule?' And, by my holidam,
The pretty wretch left crying, and said 'Ay'. 45
To see, now, how a jest shall come about!
I warrant, an I should live a thousand years,
I never should forget it: 'Wilt thou not, Jule?' quoth he;
And, pretty fool, it stinted, and said 'Ay'.

Lady Capulet
Enough of this; I pray thee hold thy peace. 50
Nurse
Yes, madam. Yet I cannot choose but laugh
To think it should leave crying and say 'Ay'.
And yet, I warrant, it had upon it brow
A bump as big as a young cock'rel's stone –

62. *once* some day.

64. The first *Marry* is the common oath, meaning 'by the Virgin Mary'.
66. *dispositions* views, opinions.

67. 'It's an honour that I haven't thought about'.

69. Unusual modesty on the Nurse's part.

72–4. 'By my reckoning, you were already born when I was your age.'

77. *a man of wax* a perfect figure of a man.

82–93. Lady Capulet praises Paris, in an extended image, speaking of
him as if he were a fine book.

A perilous knock; and it cried bitterly. 55
'Yea,' quoth my husband 'fall'st upon thy face?
Thou wilt fall backward when thou comest to age;
Wilt thou not, Jule?' It stinted, and said 'Ay'.

Juliet

And stint thou too, I pray thee, nurse, say I.

Nurse

Peace, I have done. God mark thee to his grace! 60
Thou wast the prettiest babe that e'er I nurs'd;
An I might live to see thee married once,
I have my wish.

Lady Capulet

Marry, that 'marry' is the very theme
I came to talk of. Tell me, daughter Juliet, 65
How stands your dispositions to be married?

Juliet

It is an honour that I dream not of.

Nurse

An honour! Were not I thine only nurse,
I would say thou hadst suck'd wisdom from thy teat.

Lady Capulet

Well, think of marriage now. Younger than you, 70
Here in Verona, ladies of esteem,
Are made already mothers. By my count,
I was your mother much upon these years
That you are now a maid. Thus, then, in brief:
The valiant Paris seeks you for his love. 75

Nurse

A man, young lady! lady, such a man
As all the world – why, he's a man of wax.

Lady Capulet

Verona's summer hath not such a flower.

Nurse

Nay, he's a flower; in faith, a very flower.

Lady Capulet

What say you? Can you love the gentleman? 80
This night you shall behold him at our feast;
Read o'er the volume of young Paris' face,

84. *married lineament* features that set one another off well.

87. *margent* margin. His eyes are compared to a note in the margin of the book; this elaborate imagery does not seem to have very much meaning, except that possibly Lady Capulet means that one can read Paris' character by looking into his eyes.

88. *unbound* unmarried.

89. *a cover* a wife.

90–1. Just as the sea is proud of containing beautiful fish, so Juliet (the cover) should be proud to have the beautiful Paris (the book) as her husband. This seems a rather complicated additional metaphor!

92–3. That is, Juliet, as Paris' wife, would share the respect and status shown to him.

96. The Nurse cannot miss this opportunity for a bawdy jest; she means that women grow larger when they are pregnant.

98. 'I will be prepared to like him, if I find him attractive to look at.'

99–100. Juliet says dutifully that she will only commit herself as far as her mother allows or desires.

103. *in extremity* in utter confusion. Is this the same servant as before? It could well be given his panicky state!

105. *County* Count, i.e. Paris.

106. Inevitably, the Nurse's thoughts run to the pleasures of lovers in bed.

And find delight writ there with beauty's pen;
Examine every married lineament,
And see how one another lends content;   85
And what obscur'd in this fair volume lies
Find written in the margent of his eyes.
This precious book of love, this unbound lover,
To beautify him, only lacks a cover.
The fish lives in the sea, and 'tis much pride   90
For fair without the fair within to hide.
That book in many's eyes doth share the glory
That in gold clasps locks in the golden story;
So shall you share all that he doth possess,
By having him making yourself no less.   95

Nurse
No less! Nay, bigger; women grow by men.

Lady Capulet
Speak briefly, can you like of Paris' love?

Juliet
I'll look to like, if looking liking move;
But no more deep will I endart mine eye
Than your consent gives strength to make it fly.   100

[Enter a SERVANT.]

Servant
Madam, the guests are come, supper serv'd up, you
call'd, my young lady ask'd for, the nurse curs'd in the
pantry, and everything in extremity. I must hence to
wait; I beseech you, follow straight.

Lady Capulet
We follow thee. *[Exit SERVANT]* Juliet, the County stays. 105

Nurse
Go, girl, seek happy nights to happy days.

[Exeunt.]

SCENE IV

The young men are on their way to the Capulet's ball: they propose to push their way in uninvited wearing comic masks, which was an accepted social custom of the time. They also plan to give an entertainment of their own.

1–2. As was the custom at the time, they have prepared a short speech to be spoken as they go in, explaining their intrusion.

3. Benvolio, however, says that such speeches are out of date and unfashionable.

prolixity long-windedness.

4–6. It would appear that such speeches were sometimes spoken by a character dressed up, for instance, as a blind Cupid, and that sometimes the ladies were frightened by such an apparition.

4. *hoodwinked* blindfolded.

5. The Tartars were traditionally armed with lip-shaped bows, such as Cupid bore.

of lath of thin wood; meaning that this bow is only a stage prop, and not for actual use.

6. *crow-keeper* a boy employed to scare crows.

7–8. *no without-book prologue … entrance* an introductory speech made haltingly without a script and with much assistance from the prompter, the person who reminds or helps out an actor who has forgotten his words.

9. 'Let them think what they like of us.'

10. We shall dance a dance for them and then leave.

12. *heavy* heavy-hearted because of his love for Rosaline which she has not returned.

15. *soles … soul* a typical pun.

18–21. Mercutio and Romeo pun heavily on the words *soar* (fly), *sore* (painfully), *bound* (tied down) and *bound* (leap).

22. 'I am weighed down by the pain of love.'

23–4. Mercutio deliberately misunderstands Romeo's previous words and gives them a directly sexual meaning. He says that to perform the sexual act *(to sink in it)* Romeo must be a weight on the woman *(love)* lying underneath him.

Scene IV

A street

[Enter ROMEO, MERCUTIO, BENVOLIO, *with five or six
other* MASKERS; TORCH-BEARERS.*]*

Romeo
    What, shall this speech be spoke for our excuse?
    Or shall we on without apology?
Benvolio
    The date is out of such prolixity.
    We'll have no Cupid hoodwink'd with a scarf,
    Bearing a Tartar's painted bow of lath,   5
    Scaring the ladles like a crow-keeper;
    Nor no without-book prologue, faintly spoke
    After the prompter, for our entrance;
    But, let them measure us by what they will,
    We'll measure them a measure, and be gone.   10
Romeo
    Give me a torch; I am not for this ambling;
    Being but heavy, I will bear the light.
Mercutio
    Nay, gentle Romeo, we must have you dance.
Romeo
    Not I, believe me. You have dancing shoes
    With nimble soles: I have a soul of lead   15
    So stakes me to the ground I cannot move.
Mercutio
    You are a lover; borrow Cupid's wings
    And soar with them above a common bound.
Romeo
    I am too sore enpierced with his shaft
    To soar with his light feathers; and so bound   20
    I cannot bound a pitch above dull woe.
    Under love's heavy burden do I sink.
Mercutio
    And to sink in it should you burden love;
    Too great oppression for a tender thing.

27–8. Mercutio suggests that if Romeo feels the pain of love he should give vent to his sexual desire, and so relieve the pain through having sex!

29. *a case* a mask.

30. 'An (ugly) false face to cover my (ugly) real one.'

31. *curious* inquisitive; *quote* observe.

32. He points to the extravagant features of the mask with large, overhanging eyebrows, and says that it will do his blushing for him.

34. *betake him to his legs* start to dance.

35. *wantons* foolish people. Romeo, looking down from the pedestal of his 'romantic' obsession for Rosaline takes a rather snooty view of ordinary human enjoyment.

36. The floor of Capulet's hall would be covered with rushes. Romeo is refusing to dance and says that he will be a torchbearer instead.

37–9. He is guided by a well-known traditional saying *(grandsire phrase)* which has it that the onlooker sees the best of the game.

39. The surviving texts give different versions of this line and it is not clear what Shakespeare wrote: if he wrote *done* then the meaning would seem to be that Romeo thinks that now the entertainment is at its height he should go no further.

40. *dun's the mouse* proverbial phrase meaning 'keep quiet!': presumably the words used by a constable on watch.

41. A third layer of the pun on the word *done*. The name Dun alludes to a Christmas game in which a log, representing the horse Dun, was dragged out of the mud into the house. Mercutio is suggesting that he and his companions will be able to drag Romeo out of his condition of being in love.

42. *sir-reverence* save your reverence. Mercutio is being ironically respectful when he refers to love.

44. Romeo reminds Mercutio and the Elizabethan audience that it is not daytime but night-time. Shakespeare's audience would have watched the play in daylight and needed to be reminded of the hour.

44–5. Mercutio points out that they are wasting their torches by hanging about, as they would be by burning them by day.

46–7. He tells Romeo not to be too literal and to accept the meaning intended in his words. 'Accept the goodness of our intentions because, for every five occasions when understanding comes by that means, it comes only once through the workings of the intellect.'

48. *And* even if.

49. Presumably Romeo is about to relate a dream which warned them not to go to the ball, but he never gets the chance to tell it.

Romeo
    Is love a tender thing? It is too rough,   25
    Too rude, too boist'rous, and it pricks like thorn.
Mercutio
    If love be rough with you, be rough with love;
    Prick love for pricking, and you beat love down.
    Give me a case to put my visage in. *[Putting on a mask]*
    A visor for a visor! What care I   30
    What curious eye doth quote deformities?
    Here are the beetle brows shall blush for me.
Benvolio
    Come, knock and enter; and no sooner in
    But every man betake him to his legs.
Romeo
    A torch for me. Let wantons, light of heart,   35
    Tickle the senseless rushes with their heels;
    For I am proverb'd with a grandsire phrase;
    I'll be a candle-holder and look on;
    The game was ne'er so fair, and I am done.
Mercutio
    Tut, dun's the mouse, the constable's own word;   40
    If thou art Dun, we'll draw thee from the mire
    Of this sir-reverence love, wherein thou stickest
    Up to the ears. Come, we burn daylight, ho!
Romeo
    Nay, that's not so.
Mercutio
                I mean, sir, in delay
    We waste our lights in vain – like lights by day.   45
    Take our good meaning, for our judgment sits
    Five times in that ere once in our five wits.
Romeo
    And we mean well in going to this mask;
    But 'tis no wit to go.
Mercutio
                Why, may one ask?
Romeo
    I dreamt a dream to-night.

52. Romeo is punning on the word *lie.*

53. *Queen Mab* a name for the queen of the fairies. Fairies are, in English folk-lore, little creatures in human form, who possess magical powers, often used mischievously.

55. *agate* the stone used for signet-rings.

56. *alderman* local councillor.

57. *little atomies* tiny creatures.

59. *spinners' legs* spiders' legs.

61. *traces* harness.

64. *Her whip* She has a whip with a handle made of cricket's bone or legs and a lash of gossamer (i.e. a strand of spider's web).

65–6. This refers to a superstition that lazy girls had worms in their fingers.

68. *joiner* a craftsman who works in wood; the suggestion seems to be that coaches for the fairies were made from the empty shells of hazel-nuts dropped by squirrels or left by grubs after they had eaten the kernel.

69. *Time out o' mind* for longer than anyone can remember.

70. *in this state* like a state procession in which a queen rides in her state-coach.

72. *curtsies* bows by either sex.

75–6. The ladies' breaths smell of sweets: it is not clear why Mab should object to this and give them blisters on their lips.

78. *a suit* a formal request for favour at court.

79. *tithe-pig* part of the payment to a parson from his parishioners.

81. *a benefice* a living gained from being someone in charge of a church, such as a rector, vicar etc.

Mercutio

And so did I.   50

Romeo

Well, what was yours?

Mercutio

That dreamers often lie.

Romeo

In bed asleep, while they do dream things true.

Mercutio

O, then I see Queen Mab hath been with you.
She is the fairies' midwife, and she comes
In shape no bigger than an agate stone   55
On the fore-finger of an alderman,
Drawn with a team of little atomies
Athwart men's noses as they lie asleep;
Her waggon-spokes made of long spinners' legs,
The cover, of the wings of grasshoppers;   60
Her traces, of the smallest spider's web;
Her collars, of the moonshine's wat'ry beams;
Her whip, of cricket's bone; the lash, of film;
Her waggoner, a small grey-coated gnat,
Not half so big as a round little worm   65
Prick'd from the lazy finger of a maid.
Her chariot is an empty hazel-nut,
Made by the joiner squirrel or old grub,
Time out o' mind the fairies' coachmakers.
And in this state she gallops night by night   70
Through lovers' brains, and then they dream of love;
O'er courtiers' knees, that dream on curtsies straight;
O'er lawyers' fingers, who straight dream on fees;
O'er ladies' lips, who straight on kisses dream,
Which oft the angry Mab with blisters plagues, 75
Because their breaths with sweetmeats tainted are.
Sometimes she gallops o'er a courtier's nose,
And then dreams he of smelling out a suit;
And sometime comes she with a tithe-pig's tail,
Tickling a parson's nose as 'a lies asleep,   80
Then dreams he of another benefice.

84. *breaches* gaps smashed in the walls of besieged towns.
84. ambuscadoes ambushes.
84. *Spanish blades* swords from Spain were famous for their quality.

90. *bakes* hardens by sticking together. The fairies were suspected of tangling up the manes of horses.
92–4. There was a belief that certain spirits had sexual intercourse with sleeping humans; Mercutio puns on the words *bear* and *carriage*: *bear* meaning to bear children or to bear the weight of a lover upon them, and *of good carriage* meaning walking elegantly or well able to bear the weight of a lover.

100–3. Imagination changes its focus as readily as the wind changes direction. The wind is pictured as a lover who, being rejected by the *frozen ... north* angrily turns around and instead woos the *dew-dropping south*.

104. *blows us from ourselves* diverts us from our purpose, i.e. to go to the almost forgotten ball.
106–11. Romeo is worried that some as yet unknown consequence of the night's revels may bring about his early death.
107. *hanging in the stars* Romeo believes that his fate is hanging over him and that it is determined by the influences of the stars. This links back to the prologue, and, is heavily ironic.

Sometime she driveth o'er a soldier's neck,
And then dreams he of cutting foreign throats,
Of breaches, ambuscadoes, Spanish blades,
Of healths five fathoms deep; and then anon   85
Drums in his ear, at which he starts and wakes,
And, being thus frighted, swears a prayer or two,
And sleeps again. This is that very Mab
That plats the manes of horses in the night;
And bakes the elf-locks in foul sluttish hairs,   90
Which once untangled much misfortune bodes.
This is the hag, when maids lie on their backs,
That presses them and learns them first to bear,
Making them women of good carriage.
This is she –

Romeo

               Peace, peace, Mercutio peace!   95
Thou talk'st of nothing.

Mercutio

                 True, I talk of dreams,
Which are the children of an idle brain,
Begot of nothing but vain fantasy;
Which is as thin of substance as the air,
And more inconstant than the wind, who woos   100
Even now the frozen bosom of the north,
And, being anger'd, puffs away from thence,
Turning his side to the dew-dropping south.

Benvolio

This wind you talk of blows us from ourselves:
Supper is done, and we shall come too late.   105

Romeo

I fear, too early; for my mind misgives
Some consequence, yet hanging in the stars,
Shall bitterly begin his fearful date
With this night's revels and expire the term
Of a despised life clos'd in my breast,   110
By some vile forfeit of untimely death.
But He that hath the steerage of my course
Direct my sail! On, lusty gentlemen.

114. One of the company has a drum and they joyfully strike up the beat as they march off in a loose procession.

Benvolio
  Strike, drum.

  [They march about the stage. Exeunt.]

SCENE V

The servingmen are clearing the hall in preparation for the dance. The scene is one of brisk action.

2. *trencher* wooden plate. The complaint is that another servant, Potpan (a very appropriate name!) is not around to help clear away and do the washing-up.

5. *join-stools* a stool, properly made by a joiner.
5. *court-cubbert* a movable cabinet used to display plates.
7. *marchpane* marzipan, almond paste.
7–8. The servingman wants his girls let in by the back door.

13 *longer liver takes all* probably a throwaway line meaning 'whoever lives longest out of us will end up with all our possessions' or 'there's no point in worrying about the present, we're all going to die'!!

17–18. Capulet jokingly says that he will suspect any lady who refuses to dance of having corns on her feet.
18. *am I come near ye now?* Am I embarrassingly near the truth?

Scene V

Capulet's house

[Enter the MASKERS. SERVINGMEN *come forth with napkins.]*

First Servant
> Where's Potpan, that he helps not to take away? He
> shift a trencher! He scrape a trencher!

Second Servant
> When good manners shall lie all in one or two men's
> hands and they unwash'd too, 'tis a foul thing.

First Servant
> Away with the join-stools, remove the court-cubbert,   5
> look to the plate. Good thou, save me a piece of march-
> pane; and as thou loves me let the porter let in Susan
> Grindstone and Nell. Antony, and Potpan!

Second Servant
> Ay, boy, ready.

First Servant
> You are look'd for and call'd for, ask'd for and sought   10
> for, in the great chamber.

Third Servant
> We cannot be here and there too. Cheerly, boys!
> Be brisk a while, and the longer liver take all!
> *[SERVANTS retire]*

[Enter CAPULET, *with all the* GUESTS *and* GENTLE-
WOMEN *to the* MASKERS.*]*

Capulet
> Welcome, gentlemen! Ladies that have their toes
> Unplagu'd with corns will have a bout with you.   15
> Ah ha, my mistresses! which of you all
> Will now deny to dance? She that makes dainty,
> She I'll swear hath corns; am I come near ye now?
> Welcome, gentlemen! I have seen the day
> That I have worn a visor and could tell   20
> A whispering tale in a fair lady's ear,
> Such as would please. 'Tis gone, 'tis gone, 'tis gone!

24. *A hall, a hall!* Clear a space!

25. *turn the tables up* pack the tables away (like trestle tables in canteens).
27. this unlook'd for sport the presence of Romeo and his friends.

36. *elder* older.

38. *a ward* a person under the care of a guardian.
39–40. *which doth enrich the hand of yonder knight?* Juliet's beauty, as she is dancing with *yonder knight,* is thought of as adding glory to her companion.

44. *Ethiop* Ethiopian, but probably meaning here any black African.

48. *The measure* the dance.
49. Romeo hopes to dance with her, or at least touch her hand in greeting.

You are welcome, gentlemen. Come, musicians, play.
A hall, a hall! give room; and foot it, girls.

[Music plays, and they dance.]

More light, you knaves; and turn the tables up,   25
And quench the fire, the room is grown too hot.
Ah, sirrah, this unlook'd for sport comes well
Nay, sit, nay, sit, good cousin Capulet,
For you and I are past our dancing days.
How long is't now since last yourself and I   30
Were in a mask?

Second Capulet

        By'r Lady, thirty years.

Capulet

What, man? 'tis not so much, 'tis not so much.
'Tis since the nuptial of Lucentio,
Come Pentecost as quickly as it will,
Some five and twenty years; and then we mask'd.   35

Second Capulet

'Tis more, 'tis more: his son is elder, sir;
His son is thirty.

Capulet

        Will you tell me that?
His son was but a ward two years ago.

Romeo

[To a SERVANT*]* What lady's that which doth enrich
   the hand
Of yonder knight?   40

Servant

I know not, sir.

Romeo

O, she doth teach the torches to burn bright!
It seems she hangs upon the cheek of night
As a rich jewel in an Ethiop's ear –
Beauty too rich for use, for earth too dear!   45
So shows a snowy dove trooping with crows
As yonder lady o'er her fellows shows.
The measure done, I'll watch her place of stand,
And, touching hers, make blessed my rude hand.
          67

50. Romeo, having fallen in love at first sight with Juliet, seems to recognize it as an emotion different from his infatuation for Rosaline.

52. *by his voice* presumably Romeo has given himself away by not knowing Juliet.

54. *antic face* Romeo's mask.

55. *to fleer ... at our solemnity* to sneer in a mocking way at our respectful gathering.

64. *portly* well-mannered and dignified.

68. *disparagement* disrespect.

70. Capulet speaks very firmly to Tybalt whom we may suppose has made a gesture of disagreement. Again, Capulet does not feel it is right to quarrel with his unexpected guests from the other family. His attitude fits in with ancient rules of hospitality.

72. *An ill-beseeming semblance* an unsuitable expression.

73. *It fits* i.e. 'my expression is appropriate ...'

74–9. Capulet characteristically flies into a temper when he faces disagreement.

75. *goodman boy.* Boy is always a term of insult in Elizabethan usage, *goodman* meaning 'not a gentleman' adds to the insult.

75. *Go to* an expression of impatience.

Did my heart love till now? Forswear it, sight;   50
For I ne'er saw true beauty till this night.

Tybalt

This, by his voice, should be a Montague.
Fetch me my rapier, boy. What, dares the slave
Come hither, cover'd with an antic face,
To fleer and scorn at our solemnity?   55
Now, by the stock and honour of my kin,
To strike him dead I hold it not a sin.

Capulet

Why, how now, kinsman! Wherefore storm you so?

Tybalt

Uncle, this is a Montague, our foe;
A villain, that is hither come in spite   60
To scorn at our solemnity this night.

Capulet

Young Romeo, is it?

Tybalt

          'Tis he, that villain Romeo.

Capulet

Content thee, gentle coz, let him alone.
'A bears him like a portly gentleman;
And, to say truth, Verona brags of him   65
To be a virtuous and well-govern'd youth.
I would not for the wealth of all this town
Here in my house do him disparagement.
Therefore be patient, take no note of him;
It is my will; the which if thou respect,   70
Show a fair presence and put off these frowns,
An ill-beseeming semblance for a feast.

Tybalt

It fits, when such a villain is a guest.
I'll not endure him.

Capulet

          He shall be endur'd.
What, goodman boy! I say he shall. Go to;   75
Am I the master here or you? Go to.
You'll not endure him! God shall mend my soul!

79. *set cock-a-hoop* encourage disorder (it originally meant 'drink too much').

81. *saucy* insolent, rude.

82. *This trick may chance to scathe you* 'This behaviour will do you no good.'

84. *Well said, my hearts!* This is spoken to some dancers as they pass by, to give the impression that he is not upset.

84. *a princox* an impudent pup.

85. *More light, more light!* This is spoken to some servants.

86. *Cheerly my hearts!* This is spoken to some of the guests as Capulet moves away from Tybalt.

87–8. 'The conflict between my anger and the restraint which my uncle has forced upon me makes me tremble.' Tybalt's parting remark is an ominous prophecy of the outcome of Romeo's meeting with Juliet. It echoes Romeo's previous forebodings (see Act I, Scene iv, lines 106–11).

91–104. The first conversation between Romeo and Juliet is put into the form of a sonnet ending with the word *take.* In it Romeo represents his lips as pilgrims, visiting a holy shrine, Juliet's hand; she replies in a similar manner.

91. *profane* to treat irreverently what is holy.

92. *fine* penalty.

95. Juliet says that the touch of his hand is not rough but tender.

96. *mannerly devotion* devout behaviour, proper to a pilgrim.

98. She, accepting the position of a saint, puts the palm of her hand against his in a *holy palmers' kiss;* that is, the kind of kiss proper to pilgrims.

100. Juliet is gently rebuking Romeo for his suggestion made in the previous line, that he should kiss her. The emphasis falls on the word *pray'r.*

101–2. Romeo, addressing her as a saint, suggests that she should let his lips do what their hands are already doing, that is pressing together; and that she should grant this prayer of his in case he should lose his faith.

103. 'Saints do not take the initiative, but do respond to prayer'; she is now inviting him to take the kiss.

You'll make a mutiny among my guests!
You will set cock-a-hoop! You'll be the man!
Tybalt
Why, uncle, 'tis a shame.
Capulet
                    Go to, go to;   80
You are a saucy boy. Is't so, indeed?
This trick may chance to scathe you. I know what:
You must contrary me. Marry, 'tis time. –
Well said, my hearts! – You are a princox; go.
Be quiet, or – More light, more light! – For shame!   85
I'll make you quiet. What! – Cheerly, my hearts!
Tybalt
Patience perforce with wilful choler meeting
Makes my flesh tremble in their different greeting.
I will withdraw; but this intrusion shall,
Now seeming sweet, convert to bitt'rest gall.   90

[Exit.]

Romeo
[To JULIET*]* If I profane with my unworthiest hand
This holy shrine, the gentle fine is this:
My lips, two blushing pilgrims, ready stand
To smooth that rough touch with a tender kiss.
Juliet
Good pilgrim, you do wrong your hand too much,   95
Which mannerly devotion shows in this;
For saints have hands that pilgrims' hands do touch,
And palm to palm is holy palmers' kiss.
Romeo
Have not saints lips, and holy palmers too?
Juliet
Ay, pilgrim, lips that they must use in pray'r.   100
Romeo
O, then, dear saint, let lips do what hands do!
They pray; grant thou, lest faith turn to despair.
Juliet
Saints do not move, though grant for prayers' sake.

104. *Then move not.* Even in the most tender passages, Shakespeare still uses puns.

107. *O trespass sweetly urg'd!* 'This is a sin for which I am given the sweetest encouragement.'

108. *You kiss by th' book!* literally, in the proper way, according to the rules; she means no doubt that Romeo kisses her in a very agreeable way.

113. *withal* with.

115. *the chinks* money.
116. When Romeo discovers that the girl he has fallen in love with is a Capulet, he says that his life is in the hands of his enemy.

117. 'Leave now, while you're ahead and before things go wrong.'

120. *a trifling foolish banquet towards* 'light refreshments ready.'

Romeo
    Then move not while my prayer's effect I take.
    Thus from my lips by thine my sin is purg'd.   105

              [Kissing her.]

Juliet
    Then have my lips the sin that they have took.
Romeo
    Sin from my lips? O trespass sweetly urg'd!
    Give me my sin again.

              [Kissing her.]

Juliet
                        You kiss by th' book.
Nurse
    Madam, your mother craves a word with you.
Romeo
    What is her mother?
Nurse
                        Marry, bachelor,   110
    Her mother is the lady of the house,
    And a good lady, and a wise and virtuous.
    I nurs'd her daughter that you talk'd withal.
    I tell you, he that can lay hold of her
    Shall have the chinks.
Romeo
                        Is she a Capulet?   115
    O dear account! my life is my foe's debt.
Benvolio
    Away, be gone; the sport is at the best.
Romeo
    Ay, so I fear; the more is my unrest.
Capulet
    Nay, gentlemen, prepare not to be gone;
    We have a trifling foolish banquet towards.   120
    Is it e'en so? Why, then I thank you all;
    I thank you, honest gentlemen; good night.
    More torches here! *[Exeunt MASKERS]* Come on then,
        let's to bed.

132–3. Juliet says that she will die unmarried if she cannot have Romeo for a husband.

137. Juliet is regretting the fact that she has fallen in love with a Montague before knowing he was from that family.
138. *Prodigious* ominous.

Ah, sirrah, by my fay, it waxes late;
I'll to my rest.   125

[Exeunt all but JULIET *and* NURSE.*]*

Juliet
Come hither, nurse. What is yond gentleman?
Nurse
The son and heir of old Tiberio.
Juliet
What's he that now is going out of door?
Nurse
Marry, that I think be young Petruchio.
Juliet
What's he that follows there, that would not dance?   130
Nurse
I know not.
Juliet
Go ask his name. – If he be married,
My grave is like to be my wedding bed.
Nurse
His name is Romeo, and a Montague;
The only son of your great enemy,   135
Juliet
My only love sprung from my only hate!
Too early seen unknown, and known too late!
Prodigious birth of love it is to me,
That I must love a loathed enemy.
Nurse
What's this? What's this?
Juliet
                                   A rhyme I learnt even now   140
Of one I danc'd withal. *[One calls within '*JULIET*']*
Nurse
Anon, anon!
Come, let's away; the strangers all are gone.

[Exeunt.]

ACT II

THE PROLOGUE

It has been suggested that this linking sonnet does not have much purpose in the play, and indeed is often left out of performances. However, it does do the basic job of summarising where things have got to in the action.

1. *old desire* refers to Romeo's infatuation for Rosaline.

2. *young affection* refers to his new love for Juliet.

2. *gapes* longs to, with also the notion of gasping for.

3. *That fair* Rosaline.

4. *match'd* compared.

5. *again* not 'for a second time', but 'in return'.

6. Each is captivated by the other's looks.

7. foe suppos'd. Since Juliet is a Capulet, Romeo, a Montague, is expected to regard her as his enemy.

7. complain protest his love.

8. The image is taken from fishing and indicates that despite the attraction of love for Juliet, this particular situation is beset with dangerous traps.

14. 'Lessening the difficulties of their situation by the sweetness of their meeting.'

ACT TWO
Prologue

[Enter CHORUS.*]*

Now old desire doth in his death-bed lie,
And young affection gapes to be his heir;
That fair for which love groan'd for and would die,
With tender Juliet match'd, is now not fair.
Now Romeo is belov'd, and loves again,   5
Alike bewitched by the charm of looks;
But to his foe suppos'd he must complain,
And she steal love's sweet bait from fearful hooks.
Being held a foe, he may not have access
To breathe such vows as lovers use to swear;   10
And she as much in love, her means much less
To meet her new beloved any where.
But passion lends them power, time means, to meet,
Temp'ring extremities with extreme sweet.

[Exit.]

SCENE I

2. *dull earth* Romeo's own body.

2. *thy centre* Juliet. The centre means the centre of the earth, believed in Shakespeare's day to be also the centre of the universe.

6. *conjure* call up a spirit through magic. Mercutio means that he will cause Romeo to appear by means of magical spell. In calling upon Romeo, Mercutio gives him all the characteristics of the popular image of a lover: that is, he is moody, he sighs and he writes rhymes.

7. *humours* moods.

11. *gossip* crony.

12. *purblind* totally blind. Cupid the archer, son of Venus, the goddess of love, is always pictured as blind.

13. *Adam Cupid* Adam was a name given to good archers, after Adam Bell, a famous one.

14. A reference to an old ballad which tells of a king who was smitten by love for a beggar-maid; this was the handiwork of Cupid with his arrows.

16–17. Since Romeo does not appear, Mercutio pretends to think that he is dead and seeks to raise his spirit by referring to what is most sacred to him. i.e. Rosaline's body.

20. *demesnes* regions, i.e. sexual regions. Mercutio's indecencies start here, and this is the reason for Benvolio's saying (line 22) that if Romeo could hear this he would be angry. Mercutio replies that this would not annoy him, but it would certainly make him very angry if someone else were to have sexual intercourse with Rosaline.

Scene I

A lane by the wall of Capulet's orchard

[Enter ROMEO.*]*

Romeo
    Can I go forward when my heart is here?
    Turn back, dull earth, and find thy centre out.

    [He climbs the wall and leaps down within.]

    [Enter BENVOLIO *with* MERCUTIO.*]*

Benvolio
    Romeo! my cousin, Romeo! Romeo!
Mercutio
                          He is wise,
    And, on my life, hath stol'n him home to bed.
Benvolio
    He ran this way, and leapt this orchard wall.   5
    Call, good Mercutio.
Mercutio
                  Nay, I'll conjure too.
    Romeo! humours! madman! passion! lover!
    Appear thou in the likeness of a sigh;
    Speak but one rhyme and I am satisfied;
    Cry but 'Ay me!' pronounce but 'love' and 'dove';   10
    Speak to my gossip Venus one fair word,
    One nickname for her purblind son and heir,
    Young Adam Cupid, he that shot so trim
    When King Cophetua lov'd the beggar-maid!
    He heareth not, he stirreth not, he moveth not;   15
    The ape is dead, and I must conjure him.
    I conjure thee by Rosaline's bright eyes,
    By her high forehead and her scarlet lip,
    By her fine foot, straight leg, and quivering thigh,
    And the demesnes that there adjacent lie,   20
    That in thy likeness thou appear to us.

23–9. This speech is full of double meanings developing the humorous indecencies.

24. *To raise a spirit* to call up one of the dead or to cause an erection.

24. *his mistress' circle* the magic circle drawn by a conjurer, or the female genitals.

25. *Of some strange nature* of another man.

25–6. Letting the strange spirit stay until she had used another incantation to get rid of it; or until love making had finished.

29. 'I am only trying to make him appear' or 'I am trying to get him sexually excited.'

31. *humorous* damp.

34–8. The general sense of this passage is that Romeo, since he cannot fulfil his desire with Rosaline, will simply sit and wish that he could. This meaning is derived from the fact that *pop'rin pear* (the name comes from the place Poperinghe, in Flanders) was a crude term for the penis and *open et cetera* is a euphemism for a vulgar name of the medlar fruit, which suggests readiness for the sexual act.

36. *when they laugh alone* suggests that young ladies would only use the vulgar term for the medlar in their joking together in private.

39. *truckle bed* a low bed on small wheels/castors.

Benvolio
An if he hear thee, thou wilt anger him.
Mercutio
This cannot anger him: 'twould anger him
To raise a spirit in his mistress' circle
Of some strange nature, letting it there stand   25
Till she had laid it and conjur'd it down;
That were some spite. My invocation
Is fair and honest: in his mistress' name,
I conjure only but to raise up him.
Benvolio
Come, he hath hid himself among these trees   30
To be consorted with the humorous night:
Blind is his love, and best befits the dark.
Mercutio
If love be blind, love cannot hit the mark.
Now will he sit under a medlar tree,
And wish his mistress were that kind of fruit   35
As maids call medlars when they laugh alone.
O Romeo, that she were, O that she were
An open et cetera, thou a pop'rin pear!
Romeo, good night. I'll to my truckle bed;
This field-bed is too cold for me to sleep.   40
Come, shall we go?
Benvolio
                    Go, then; for 'tis in vain
To seek him here that means not to be found.

                [Exeunt.]

SCENE II

From his first line, we understand that Romeo has overheard the previous conversation.

1. 'It is easy for those who have never loved to make fun of a lover.'

6. *That thou her maid* Diana, the goddess of the moon, was also the protector of virgins, and Juliet, being a virgin, is imagined as her maid.
7–9. Romeo calls upon Juliet to cast off her virginity. He is already envisaging her as his wife.
8. *vestal livery* virginity. The priestesses of the Roman goddess Vesta were vowed to chastity.
13. *discourses* communicates.

16. *entreat* plead with.
17. *their spheres* the positions of the stars, which were thought to be fixed in hollow transparent concentric globes.

Scene II

Capulet's orchard

[Enter ROMEO.]

Romeo
    He jests at scars that never felt a wound.

[Enter JULIET above at a window.]

But, soft! What light through yonder window breaks
It is the east, and Juliet is the sun.
Arise, fair sun, and kill the envious moon,
Who is already sick and pale with grief   5
That thou her maid art far more fair than she.
Be not her maid, since she is envious;
Her vestal livery is but sick and green,
And none but fools do wear it; cast it off.
It is my lady; O, it is my love!   10
O that she knew she were!
She speaks, yet she says nothing. What of that?
Her eye discourses; I will answer it.
I am too bold, 'tis not to me she speaks;
Two of the fairest stars in all the heaven,   15
Having some business, do entreat her eyes
To twinkle in their spheres till they return.
What if her eyes were there, they in her head?
The brightness of her cheek would shame those
    stars,
As daylight doth a lamp; her eyes in heaven   20
Would through the airy region stream so bright
That birds would sing, and think it were not night.
See how she leans her cheek upon her hand!
O that I were a glove upon that hand,
That I might touch that cheek!

Juliet
                Ay me!

Romeo
                            She speaks.   25

33. wherefore art thou Romeo? 'Why are you a member of the Montague family?' Juliet is already aware that this will be a barrier to their love.

34–6. She wishes that Romeo could renounce his parentage, or if that cannot be, and yet he loves her, that she could renounce her own.

39. 'What you are really like has nothing to do with the fact that you are a Montague.'

46. owes owns.

47. doff remove (as one takes off clothes).

48–49. Romeo presumably makes himself known at this point, or at least speaks loudly enough for Juliet to hear. Her words suggest she can't see clearly yet as he is 'bescreen'd in night.'

53. counsel private thoughts.

O, speak again, bright angel, for thou art
As glorious to this night, being o'er my head,
As is a winged messenger of heaven
Unto the white-upturned wond'ring eyes
Of mortals that fall back to gaze on him,   30
When he bestrides the lazy-pacing clouds
And sails upon the bosom of the air.

Juliet

O Romeo, Romeo! wherefore art thou Romeo?
Deny thy father and refuse thy name;
Or, if thou wilt not, be but sworn my love,   35
And I'll no longer be a Capulet.

Romeo

[Aside] Shall I hear more, or shall I speak at this?

Juliet

'Tis but thy name that is my enemy;
Thou art thyself, though not a Montague.
What's Montague? It is nor hand, nor foot,   40
Nor arm, nor face, nor any other part
Belonging to a man. O, be some other name
What's in a name? That which we call a rose
By any other name would smell as sweet;
So Romeo would, were he not Romeo call'd,   45
Retain that dear perfection which he owes
Without that title. Romeo, doff thy name;
And for thy name, which is no part of thee,
Take all myself.

Romeo

                    I take thee at thy word:
Call me but love, and I'll be new baptiz'd;   50
Henceforth I never will be Romeo.

Juliet

What man art thou, that, thus bescreen'd in night,
So stumblest on my counsel?

Romeo

                    By a name
I know not how to tell thee who I am:
My name, dear saint, is hateful to myself,   55

61. *if either thee dislike* 'if either is displeasing to you.'

64. *And the place death ...* 'being found here would be fatal for you.'

68. Love makes a man bold enough to attempt anything that is possible however dangerous.

72. *sweet* affectionate, gracious.

76. *And but* so long as.
78. *prorogued* put off, delayed.

82–5. Romeo here uses an image that would spring naturally to the minds of the Elizabethans in an age when great voyages of exploration were taking place; he says that, though not an experienced sailor, he would undertake a voyage to the ends of the earth if Juliet were his prize.

Because it is an enemy to thee;
Had I it written, I would tear the word.

Juliet

My ears have yet not drunk a hundred words
Of thy tongue's uttering, yet I know the sound:
Art thou not Romeo, and a Montague?   60

Romeo

Neither, fair maid, if either thee dislike.

Juliet

How cam'st thou hither, tell me, and wherefore?
The orchard walls are high and hard to climb;
And the place death, considering who thou art,
If any of my kinsmen find thee here.   65

Romeo

With love's light wings did I o'erperch these walls,
For stony limits cannot hold love out;
And what love can do, that dares love attempt.
Therefore thy kinsmen are no stop to me.

Juliet

If they do see thee, they will murder thee.   70

Romeo

Alack, there lies more peril in thine eye
Than twenty of their swords; look thou but sweet,
And I am proof against their enmity.

Juliet

I would not for the world they saw thee here.

Romeo

I have night's cloak to hide me from their eyes; 75
And but thou love me, let them find me here.
My life were better ended by their hate
Than death prorogued wanting of thy love.

Juliet

By whose direction found'st thou out this place?

Romeo

By love, that first did prompt me to enquire;   80
He lent me counsel, and I lent him eyes.
I am no pilot; yet, wert thou as far
As that vast shore wash'd with the farthest sea,

85–106. This whole speech gives us a vivid and sympathetic picture of a young girl, very much in love, who is afraid of her behaviour being thought too *light* but who is nevertheless anxious to make her love known.

88. *Fain would I dwell on form* 'I should like to behave in a proper lady-like fashion.'

89. *but farewell compliment!* 'but away with the restraints of formality.'

92. *lovers' perjuries* lovers' lies.

93. *Jove.* The King of the gods used various disguises in his amorous adventures.

96. *perverse* deliberately difficult.

98. *too fond* too foolish.

99. *think my haviour light* 'think my behaviour too forward.'

101. *strange* reserved.

104–5. Do not believe that my showing my feelings is due to being too easy, or lacking seriousness.

109–10. The moon is thought *inconstant* because it visibly waxes and wanes.

114. 'I am like a heathen (i.e non-Christian) worshipper and you are my idol.'

I should adventure for such merchandise.

Juliet

Thou knowest the mask of night is on my face,   85
Else would a maiden blush bepaint my cheek
For that which thou hast heard me speak to-night.
Fain would I dwell on form, fain, fain deny
What I have spoke; but farewell compliment!
Dost thou love me? I know thou wilt say ay,   90
And I will take thy word; yet, if thou swear'st,
Thou mayst prove false; at lovers' perjuries
They say Jove laughs. O gentle Romeo,
If thou dost love, pronounce it faithfully.
Or, if thou think'st I am too quickly won,   95
I'll frown, and be perverse, and say thee nay,
So thou wilt woo; but else, not for the world.
In truth, fair Montague, I am too fond;
And therefore thou mayst think my haviour light;
But trust me, gentleman, I'll prove more true   100
Than those that have more cunning to be strange.
I should have been more strange, I must confess,
But that thou overheard'st, ere I was ware,
My true love's passion. Therefore pardon me,
And not impute this yielding to light love,   105
Which the dark night hath so discovered.

Romeo

Lady, by yonder blessed moon I vow,
That tips with silver all these fruit-tree tops –

Juliet

O, swear not by the moon, th' inconstant moon,
That monthly changes in her circled orb,   110
Lest that thy love prove likewise variable.

Romeo

What shall I swear by?

Juliet

           Do not swear at all;
Or, if thou wilt, swear by thy gracious self,
Which is the god of my idolatry,
And I'll believe thee.

116–20. Is Juliet worried by the suddenness of their love? Or is this already a shadow of what is to come?

117. *this contract* their vows to each other.

121–2. Their love which isn't yet developed, may become mature by their next meeting.

129. I wish I could give it to you again.

131. *frank* generous.

Romeo

                   If my heart's dear love –   115

Juliet

Well, do not swear. Although I joy in thee,
I have no joy of this contract to-night:
It is too rash, too unadvis'd, too sudden;
Too like the lightning, which doth cease to be
Ere one can say 'It lightens'. Sweet, good night!   120
This bud of love, by summer's ripening breath,
May prove a beauteous flow'r when next we meet.
Good night, good night! As sweet repose and rest
Come to thy heart as that within my breast!

Romeo

O, wilt thou leave me so unsatisfied?   125

Juliet

What satisfaction canst thou have to-night?

Romeo

Th' exchange of thy love's faithful vow for mine.

Juliet

I gave thee mine before thou didst request it;
And yet I would it were to give again.

Romeo

Wouldst thou withdraw it? For what purpose, love?   130

Juliet

But to be frank, and give it thee again.
And yet I wish but for the thing I have.
My bounty is as boundless as the sea,
My love as deep; the more I give to thee,
The more I have, for both are infinite.   135

[NURSE calls within.]

I hear some noise within. Dear love, adieu! –
Anon, good nurse! – Sweet Montague, be true.
Stay but a little, I will come again.

[Exit.]

139. *afeard* afraid.

141. *substantial* a part of real life.

143. *bent* inclination, feeling.

145. 'Through someone (a messenger) I'll find, who will come and see you'.
147–8. The tender humility of Juliet's love, as expressed in these lines is very beautiful.

Romeo
O blessed, blessed night! I am afeard,
Being in night, all this is but a dream,   140
Too flattering-sweet to be substantial.

[Re-enter JULIET *above.]*

Juliet
Three words, dear Romeo, and good night indeed.
If that thy bent of love be honourable,
Thy purpose marriage, send me word to-morrow.
By one that I'll procure to come to thee,   145
Where and what time thou wilt perform the rite;
And all my fortunes at thy foot I'll lay,
And follow thee, my lord, throughout the world.
Nurse
[Within] Madam!
Juliet
I come anon. – But if thou meanest not well,   150
I do beseech thee –
Nurse
[Within]   Madam!
Juliet
                          By and by, I come –
To cease thy suit, and leave me to my grief.
To-morrow will I send.
Romeo
                          So thrive my soul –
Juliet
A thousand times good night!

[Exit.]

Romeo
A thousand times the worse, to want thy light.   155
Love goes toward love as school-boys from their
     books;
But love from love, toward school with heavy looks.

[Re-enter JULIET *above.]*

159. *tassel-gentle* Tercel is the male peregrine falcon; *gentle,* meaning noble, applies equally to the bird and to Romeo. It was a popular Elizabethan sport to tame falcons and use them for hunting other birds. Juliet wishes that she could lure Romeo back as a falconer could his falcon.

160. Because she is under the authority of her family, she has to speak to Romeo in a whisper.

161. In Greek mythology the nymph Echo lived in a cave.

166. note the alliteration on the 's' of 'silver-sweet sound lovers' tongues.' emphasising the beautiful tone of lovers' language.

177. *I would have thee gone* I'd prefer you to have left (she is perhaps thinking of the danger of Romeo being found out).

178. *a wanton's bird* the remainder of Juliet's words are a reference to a selfish little girl who keeps a bird on the end of a bit of string, pulling it back whenever it tries to escape.

180. *gyves* fetters (chains or locks that go round the ankles).

Juliet

Hist! Romeo, hist! – O for a falc'ner's voice,
To lure this tassel-gentle back again!
Bondage is hoarse, and may not speak aloud; 160
Else would I tear the cave where Echo lies,
And make her airy tongue more hoarse than mine
With repetition of my Romeo's name.
Romeo!

Romeo

It is my soul that calls upon my name. 165
How silver-sweet sound lovers' tongues by night,
Like softest music to attending ears!

Juliet

Romeo!

Romeo

My dear?

Juliet

At what o'clock to-morrow
Shall I send to thee?

Romeo

By the hour of nine.

Juliet

I will not fail. 'Tis twenty years till then. 170
I have forgot why I did call thee back.

Romeo

Let me stand here till thou remember it.

Juliet

I shall forget, to have thee still stand there,
Rememb'ring how I love thy company.

Romeo

And I'll still stay, to have thee still forget, 175
Forgetting any other home but this.

Juliet

'Tis almost morning. I would have thee gone;
And yet no farther than a wanton's bird,
That lets it hop a little from her hand,
Like a poor prisoner in his twisted gyves, 180
And with a silk thread plucks it back again,

184. Unlike the wanton, Juliet would be in danger of killing Romeo with too much attention.
185–6. This delicate reluctance to part from one another gives us a very real and sensitive picture of two young lovers.

189. *ghostly father* spiritual adviser (presumably the Friar).
190. *dear hap* great good fortune.

So loving-jealous of his liberty.

Romeo

I would I were thy bird.

Juliet

                Sweet, so would I.

Yet I should kill thee with much cherishing.

Good night, good night! Parting is such sweet sorrow 185

That I shall say good night till it be morrow.

[Exit.]

Romeo

Sleep dwell upon thine eyes, peace in thy breast!

Would I were sleep and peace, so sweet to rest!

Hence will I to my ghostly father's cell,

His help to crave and my dear hap to tell.   190

[Exit.]

SCENE III

*Stage Direction. **Enter Friar Lawrence*** a friar is a member of one of the four orders of holy men who lived as beggars. One of his religious duties was to hear confessions (see line 55).

2. *Check'ring* making a pattern of light and shade.

3. *fleckel'd* dappled.

4. According to Greek mythology, Hyperion, the sun-god is the Titan here and rode his chariot across the sky each day.

5. *advance his burning eye* that is, rises higher in the sky.

7. *osier cage* a basket. The Friar is collecting herbs in order to make medicines.

8. *baleful* evil.

9–12. This complicated passage refers to Earth as the mother of Nature. It is both Nature's grave – dead plants return to the soil – and its womb – new seeds grow out of it to replace the old. Upon the *natural bosom* of the Earth – that is, on its surface – are to be found sucking *children of divers kind* – that is, plants in great variety. Many of the plants have *many virtues* or many uses – and there are none without some uses, all of them different. (It may be thought that Shakespeare's delight in playing with words here leads him into making the Friar sound dull and boring – or do you think the Friar is meant by Shakespeare to be rather pompous ?)

15. *mickle* great.

16. *stones* i.e. stones of fruits such as a plum stone.

19–20. 'However good and useful a plant or herb is originally, they can all be put to evil purposes by those who misuse them.'

23–6. The Friar holds up a flower. It contains within it, he says, that which if properly used *(smelt)* as a medicine, will cheer and stimulate but which if wrongly used *(tasted)* will poison and kill.

27. *such opposed kings* contrasting powers, grace and wilful desire, comparable to medicine and poison. (Has this remark, perhaps, some relevance to the play as a whole?)

29. Both the poisonous and the medicinal forces within the flower are extremely strong; it's also true that people suffer from similarly powerful forces, *rude will* (i.e. wild desires) and *grace* (i.e. the influence of God).

30. *canker* caterpillar.

Scene III

Friar Lawrence's cell

[Enter FRIAR LAWRENCE *with a basket.]*

Friar Lawrence
The gray-ey'd morn smiles on the frowning night,
Check'ring the eastern clouds with streaks of light;
And fleckel'd darkness like a drunkard reels
From forth day's path and Titan's fiery wheels.
Now, ere the sun advance his burning eye   5
The day to cheer and night's dank dew to dry,
I must up-fill this osier cage of ours
With baleful weeds and precious-juiced flowers.
The earth that's nature's mother is her tomb;
What is her burying grave, that is her womb.   10
And from her womb children of divers kind
We sucking on her natural bosom find;
Many for many virtues excellent,
None but for some, and yet all different.
O, mickle is the powerful grace that lies   15
In plants, herbs, stones, and their true qualities;
For nought so vile that on the earth doth live
But to the earth some special good doth give;
Nor aught so good but, strain'd from that fair use
Revolts from true birth, stumbling on abuse: 20
Virtue itself turns vice, being misapplied,
And vice sometime's by action dignified.
Within the infant rind of this weak flower
Poison hath residence, and medicine power;
For this, being smelt, with that part cheers each part; 25
Being tasted, slays all senses with the heart.
Two such opposed kings encamp them still
In man as well as herbs – grace and rude will;
And where the worser is predominant,
Full soon the canker death eats up that plant.   30

[Enter ROMEO.*]*

32. *early tongue.* Dawn is only just breaking, and the Friar is surprised that Romeo is about so early.

33. *distempered head* troubled mind.

47. *That's my good son.* The Friar is relieved to hear that Romeo has overcome his infatuation for Rosaline – but, of course, he does not know yet about Juliet!

51–2. *both our remedies … lies* 'You can heal both of us, because you are a priest.'

54. 'What I am asking for will benefit my foe as well as me.' ***The foe*** is, of course, Juliet.

55–6. The Friar fails to understand what Romeo is talking about – as well he may! – and tells him that an incomprehensible confession is likely to be given an absolution that is equally difficult to understand!

Romeo
Good morrow, father!
Friar Lawrence
                    Benedicite!
What early tongue so sweet saluteth me?
Young son, it argues a distempered head
So soon to bid good morrow to thy bed.
Care keeps his watch in every old man's eye,   35
And where care lodges sleep will never lie;
But where unbruised youth with unstuff'd brain
Doth couch his limbs, there golden sleep doth reign.
Therefore thy earliness doth me assure
Thou art uprous'd with some distemp'rature;   40
Or if not so, then here I hit it right –
Our Romeo hath not been in bed to-night.
Romeo
That last is true; the sweeter rest was mine.
Friar Lawrence
God pardon sin! Wast thou with Rosaline?
Romeo
With Rosaline, my ghostly father? No;   45
I have forgot that name, and that name's woe.
Friar Lawrence
That's my good son; but where hast thou been then?
Romeo
I'll tell thee ere thou ask it me again.
I have been feasting with mine enemy;
Where, on a sudden, one hath wounded me   50
That's by me wounded; both our remedies
Within thy help and holy physic lies.
I bear no hatred, blessed man, for, lo,
My intercession likewise steads my foe.
Friar Lawrence
Be plain, good son, and homely in thy drift;   55
Riddling confession finds but riddling shrift.
Romeo
Then plainly know my heart's dear love is set
On the fair daughter of rich Capulet.

67. *forsaken* rejected.

69. *brine* sea-water (meaning 'tears').

73. Compare Act I, Scene i, lines 126–7: **With tears augmenting the fresh morning's dew. Adding to clouds more clouds with his deep sighs.** The lover's sighs are thought of as forming a small cloud of droplets, which the sun would evaporate in due course.

81. *chid'st me* criticised me, told me off.

82. The Friar gently reminds Romeo that it is foolish infatuation he disapproves of, not love.
83. *bad'st me* requested that I.

87–8. 'She (Rosaline) knew that your love only spoke what it had learned by heart, without really understanding what the words were. That is, Romeo only talked about love without understanding what it was.

As mine on hers, so hers is set on mine;
And all combin'd, save what thou must combine   60
By holy marriage. When, and where, and how,
We met, we woo'd, and made exchange of vow,
I'll tell thee as we pass; but this I pray,
That thou consent to marry us to-day.

Friar Lawrence

Holy Saint Francis! What a change is here!   65
Is Rosaline, that thou didst love so dear,
So soon forsaken? Young men's love, then, lies
Not truly in their hearts, but in their eyes.
Jesu Maria, what a deal of brine
Hath wash'd thy sallow cheeks for Rosaline!   70
How much salt water thrown away in waste,
To season love, that of it doth not taste!
The sun not yet thy sighs from heaven clears,
Thy old groans yet ring in mine ancient ears;
Lo, here upon thy cheek the stain doth sit   75
Of an old tear that is not wash'd off yet.
If e'er thou wast thyself, and these woes thine,
Thou and these woes were all for Rosaline.
And art thou chang'd? Pronounce this sentence, then
Women may fall, when there's no strength in men.   80

Romeo

Thou chid'st me oft for loving Rosaline.

Friar Lawrence

For doting, not for loving, pupil mine.

Romeo

And bad'st me bury love.

Friar Lawrence

                Not in a grave
To lay one in, another out to have.

Romeo

I pray thee chide me not; her I love now   85
Doth grace for grace and love for love allow;
The other did not so.

Friar Lawrence

            O, she knew well

92. *rancour* hate.

Thy love did read by rote that could not spell.
But come, young waverer, come, go with me,
In one respect I'll thy assistant be;   90
For this alliance may so happy prove
To turn your households' rancour to pure love.

Romeo

O, let us hence; I stand on sudden haste.

Friar Lawrence

Wisely and slow; they stumble that run fast.

[Exeunt.]

SCENE IV

Mercutio is still unaware of Romeo's change of heart at the start of the scene, but the shadow of what is to come is present within a few lines of the conversation with the mention of Tybalt's challenge.

11–12. Romeo's answer will be as bold as the challenge.

15. *pin* the very centre of the target in archery (the 'bull's eye' was a piece of cloth fastened with a pin).

19. *Prince of Cats* Tybalt was the name of a Cat Prince in a fairy-tale. Pet cats are sometimes still called 'Tib').
20–1. *prick-song* a simple melody. In this whole passage, Mercutio is making fun of Tybalt's attention to the formalities of duelling. There was at the time a cult of this kind, originating on the Continent, regarded with contempt by some Englishmen who probably thought it was too elaborate and fussy.

Scene IV

A street

[Enter BENVOLIO and MERCUTIO.]

Mercutio
Where the devil should this Romeo be?
Came he not home to-night?

Benvolio
Not to his father's; I spoke with his man.

Mercutio
Why, that same pale hard-hearted wench, that Rosaline
Torments him so that he will sure run mad.   5

Benvolio
Tybalt, the kinsman to old Capulet,
Hath sent a letter to his father's house.

Mercutio
A challenge, on my life.

Benvolio
Romeo will answer it.

Mercutio
Any man that can write may answer a letter.   10

Benvolio
Nay, he will answer the letter's master, how he dares,
being dared.

Mercutio
Alas, poor Romeo, he is already dead: stabb'd with a
white wench's black eye; run through the ear with a
love-song; the very pin of his heart cleft with the   15
blind bow-boy's butt-shaft. And is he a man to
encounter Tybalt?

Benvolio
Why, what is Tybalt?

Mercutio
More than Prince of Cats. O, he's the courageous
captain of compliments. He fights as you sing prick-   20
song: keeps time, distance, and proportion; he rests

23. *button* that is, on his opponent's shirt; a skilful fencer was supposed to be able to touch any particular button at will. Mercutio probably favoured the more traditional form of fighting with the long-sword.

24. *the very first house* of the highest rank.

25. *the first and second cause* the formal parts of the process – the initial taking of offence and then the issuing of a challenge.

25. *passado* a lunge with foot forward.

26. *the punto reverse* backhanded cut.

26. *the hay!* the final thrust.

28. *affecting fantasticoes* those who put on very extravagant behaviour. People of this sort often also spoke with an affected accent and Mercutio mimics this in the next line.

33–4. *who stand so much on the new form* who pay so much attention to the new manners (compare the modern English phrase, 'good form' meaning 'the proper way to behave'). Note also the word-play *on form* and *bench*.

35. *their bones, their bones* pun on the French word 'bon' meaning 'good'.

37. *Without his roe* with only half his name, therefore only half himself or looking exhausted like a fish that has spawned.

38. *numbers* verses.

39. *to his lady* compared with Rosaline; it must be remembered that Mercutio still thinks that Romeo is in love with that girl.

39. *Petrarch* a famous Italian poet whose beloved was called Laura.

40–2. Mercutio goes on to mock Romeo, and imagines him thinking that a number of famous beauties. Dido, Cleopatra, Helen, Hero and Thisbe were nothing when compared with Rosaline.

42. *hildings and harlots* immoral women.

46–92. The rapidity of movement and wit in the next fifty lines is most bewildering; it must have given great delight to the Elizabethan audience. The most important points are explained below.

47. *The slip, sir* (1) as in the modern expression 'to give someone the slip'; (2) a fake coin.

his minim rests, one, two, and the third in your bosom;
the very butcher of a silk button, a duellist, a duellist;
a gentleman of the very first house, of the first and
second cause. Ah, the immortal passado! the punto   25
reverse I the hay! –

Benvolio

The what?

Mercutio

The pox of such antic, lisping, affecting fantasticoes;
these new tuners of accent! – 'By Jesu, a very good
blade! a very tall man! a very good whore!' Why, is   30
not this a lamentable thing, grandsire, that we should
be thus afflicted with these strange flies, these fashion-
mongers, these pardon me's, who stand so much on
the new form that they cannot sit at ease on the old
bench? O, their bones, their bones!   35

[Enter ROMEO.]

Benvolio

Here comes Romeo, here comes Romeo.

Mercutio

Without his roe, like a dried herring. O flesh, flesh,
how art thou fishified! Now is he for the numbers
that Petrarch flow'd in; Laura, to his lady, was a kitchen-
wench – marry, she had a better love to berhyme her;   40
Dido, a dowdy; Cleopatra, a gipsy; Helen and Hero,
hildings and harlots; Thisbe, a gray eye or so, but not
to the purpose – Signior Romeo, bon jour! There's a
French salutation to your French slop. You gave us the
counterfeit fairly last night.   45

Romeo

Good morrow to you both. What counterfeit did I give
you?

Mercutio

The slip, sir, the slip; can you not conceive?

Romeo

Pardon, good Mercutio; my business was great, and
in such a case as mine a man may strain courtesy.   50

56. *the very pink* perfection.

59. *pump* shoe.
59. *flower'd* ornamented with punched holes.

64. *faints.* This is an old form of the third person plural of a verb, which was still sometimes used in Shakespeare's time.
65. *Swits and spurs … or I'll cry a match* 'Keep it going, keep it going, or I'll say I've won.' *(Swits and spurs* means 'with switch (whip) and spurs'; i.e. 'flat out.')
66. *the wild-goose chase* a frantic cross-country race in which whoever takes the lead has to be followed by the others.
68–9. *Was I with you there for the goose!* 'Did I keep up with you on the chase?' i.e. the contest of wit.

70–1. 'I have never known you in any company when you were not playing the fool.'

Mercutio

That's as much as to say, such a case as yours constrains
a man to bow in the hams.

Romeo

Meaning, to curtsy.

Mercutio

Thou hast most kindly hit it.

Romeo

A most courteous exposition.   55

Mercutio

Nay, I am the very pink of courtesy.

Romeo

Pink for flower.

Mercutio

Right.

Romeo

Why, then is my pump well flower'd.

Mercutio

Sure wit! Follow me this jest now till thou hast worn   60
out thy pump, that, when the single sole of it is worn,
the jest may remain, after the wearing, solely singular.

Romeo

O single-sol'd jest, solely singular for the singleness!

Mercutio

Come between us, good Benvolio; my wits faints.

Romeo

Swits and spurs, swits and spurs; or I'll cry a match.   65

Mercutio

Nay, if our wits run the wild-goose chase, I am done;
for thou hast more of the wild goose in one of thy
wits than, I am sure, I have in my whole five. Was I
with you there for the goose?

Romeo

Thou wast never with me for anything when thou wast   70
not there for the goose.

Mercutio

I will bite thee by the ear for that jest.

77. *cheveril* kid-leather. Mercutio says that Romeo is flogging the joke too far.

79–80. Far from giving up, Romeo picks up the word *broad,* and calls Mercutio *a broad goose,* i.e. a jester given to 'broad' (improper) jokes.

84. *natural* idiot.
85. *bauble* (1) the stick carried by a jester; (2) penis.
86. Benvolio intervenes because he sees that Mercutio is becoming wildly improper again.

87. *against the hair* against my wishes.
88. *thy tale large* (1) 'your story improper'; (2) 'your penis large'.
89–91. As in the previous speech, Mercutio's lines have two levels of meaning, one proper, one improper. (1) 'You are wrong: I would have made my story short, for I had come to the end of it and did not intend to continue further with the argument.' (2) 'You are wrong; I'd have made my penis small again, for I had thrust as deep as I could and meant to withdraw.'

94. *a shirt and a smock* a man and a woman.

Romeo

Nay, good goose, bite not.

Mercutio

Thy wit is a very bitter sweeting; it is a most sharp
sauce. 75

Romeo

And is it not then well serv'd in to a sweet goose?

Mercutio

O, here's a wit of cheveril, that stretches from an inch
narrow to an ell broad!

Romeo

I stretch it out for that word 'broad', which, added to
the goose, proves thee far and wide a broad goose 80

Mercutio

Why, is not this better now than groaning for love?
Now art thou sociable, now art thou Romeo; now art
thou what thou art by art as well as by nature; for this
drivelling love is like a great natural that runs lolling
up and down to hide his bauble in a hole. 85

Benvolio

Stop there, stop there.

Mercutio

Thou desirest me to stop in my tale against the hair.

Benvolio

Thou wouldst else have made thy tale large.

Mercutio

O, thou art deceived: I would have made it short; for
I was come to the whole depth of my tale, and meant 90
indeed, to occupy the argument no longer.

Romeo

Here's goodly gear!

[Enter NURSE and her man, PETER.]

Mercutio

A sail, a sail!

Benvolio

Two, two; a shirt and a smock.

101. *God ye good den* Mercutio corrects the Nurse and says 'Good evening'. The Elizabethans said 'Good evening' when we would say 'Good afternoon'. As soon as the Nurse arrives, Mercutio starts to poke fun at her.

104. *the prick of noon* the very point of noon, but the word also carries its modern sexual meaning.

105. The Nurse, of course, understands Mercutio's impropriety and appears to be shocked (although her earlier 'earthiness' may suggest she is not as shocked as she seems).

107. *mar* harm.

Nurse

Peter! 95

Peter

Anon.

Nurse

My fan, Peter.

Mercutio

Good Peter, to hide her face; for her fan's the fairer
face.

Nurse

God ye good morrow, gentlemen. 100

Mercutio

God ye good den, fair gentlewoman.

Nurse

Is it good den?

Mercutio

'Tis no less, I tell ye; for the bawdy hand of the dial
is now upon the prick of noon.

Nurse

Out upon you! What a man are you? 105

Romeo

One, gentlewoman, – that God hath made himself to
mar.

Nurse

By my troth, it is well said. 'For himself to mar'
quoth 'a! Gentlemen, can any of you tell me where I
may find the young Romeo? 110

Romeo

I can tell you; but young Romeo will be older when
you have found him than he was when you sought
him. I am the youngest of that name, for fault of a
worse.

Nurse

You say well. 115

Mercutio

Yea, is the worst well? Very well took, i' faith; wisely,
wisely.

119. 'If you are him, I'd like to speak to you privately'.

119–20. Benvolio and Mercutio pretend to think that the Nurse is a prostitute inviting Romeo to her house.

120. *So ho!* a huntsman's cry on sighting the quarry; hence Romeo's next line.

122. *hare* (1) the game that has been sighted and will be hunted; (2) a prostitute. Mercutio's song is an elaborate playing with the word *hare* in its double meaning, and the word *hoar* (whore) similarly.

136. *ropery* offensive jokes.

140. *An'a* If he.

Nurse
    If you be he, sir, I desire some confidence with you.
Benvolio
    She will indite him to some supper.
Mercutio
    A bawd, a bawd, a bawd! So ho!   120
Romeo
    What hast thou found?
Mercutio
    No hare, sir; unless a hare, sir, in a lenten pie, that
        is something stale and hoar ere it be spent.

        [He walks by them and sings.]

            An old hare hoar,
            And an old hare hoar,   125
        Is very good meat in Lent;
            But a hare that is hoar
            Is too much for a score,
        When it hoars ere it be spent.

    Romeo, will you come to your father's? We'll to   130
    dinner thither.
Romeo
    I will follow you.
Mercutio
    Farewell, ancient lady; farewell, *[sings]* lady, lady,
        lady.

        [Exeunt MERCUTIO and BENVOLIO.]

Nurse
    I pray you, sir, what saucy merchant was this that was 135
    so full of his ropery?
Romeo
    A gentleman, nurse, that loves to hear himself talk,
    and will speak more in a minute than he will stand
    to in a month.
Nurse
    An 'a speak anything against me, I'll take him down 140

143–4. *flirt-gills* and *skainsmates* loose women.

154–5. *fool's paradise* seduction.

157. *deal double* mistreat, trick.

169. *shrift* confession and absolution.

an 'a were lustier than he is, and twenty such Jacks;
and if I cannot, I'll find those that shall. Scurvy knave!
I am none of his flirt-gills; I am none of his skainsmates.
And thou must stand by too, and suffer every knave
to use me at his pleasure? 145

Peter

I saw no man use you at his pleasure; if I had, my
weapon should quickly have been out, I warrant you.
I dare draw as soon as another man, if I see occasion
in a good quarrel, and the law on my side.

Nurse

Now, afore God, I am so vex'd that every part about 150
me quivers. Scurvy knave! – Pray you, sir, a word;
and as I told you, my young lady bid me enquire you
out; what she bid me say I will keep to myself. But
first let me tell ye, if ye should lead her in a fool's
paradise, as they say, it were a very gross kind of 155
behaviour, as they say; for the gentlewoman is young;
and, therefore, if you should deal double with her,
truly it were an ill thing to be offer'd to any gentlewoman, and very weak dealing.

Romeo

Nurse, commend me to thy lady and mistress. I protest 160
unto thee –

Nurse

Good heart, and, i' faith, I will tell her as much. Lord,
Lord! she will be a joyful woman.

Romeo

What wilt thou tell her, nurse? Thou dost not mark
me. 165

Nurse

I will tell her, sir, that you do protest; which, as I take
it, is a gentleman-like offer.

Romeo

Bid her devise
Some means to come to shrift this afternoon;
And there she shall at Friar Lawrence' cell 170
Be shriv'd and married. Here is for thy pains.

177. *a tackled stair* a rope ladder.
178. *high top-gallant* a small extra mast fixed on the top of the main-mast in a sailing-ship.
179. *my convoy* my means of getting where I need to go.
180. *quit* reward.

186. 'Two can keep a secret if one is done away with.'

189. *prating* chattering.
190–1. *fain lay knife aboard* claim her for his own, like a pirate.
191. *had as lief* would rather.

194. *clout* a cloth.
195. *versal* universal.

197. *an R* this was commonly called *the dog's name,* the sound resembling a growl.

Nurse
  No, truly, sir; not a penny.
Romeo
  Go to; I say you shall.
Nurse
  This afternoon, sir? Well, she shall be there.
Romeo
  And stay, good nurse – behind the abbey wall   175
  Within this hour my man shall be with thee,
  And bring thee cords made like a tackled stair;
  Which to the high top-gallant of my joy
  Must be my convoy in the secret night.
  Farewell; be trusty, and I'll quit thy pains.   180
  Farewell; commend me to thy mistress.
Nurse
  Now God in heaven bless thee! –
  Hark you, sir.
Romeo
  What say'st thou, my dear nurse?
Nurse
  Is your man secret? Did you ne'er hear say   185
  Two may keep counsel, putting one away?
Romeo
  I warrant thee my man's as true as steel.
Nurse
  Well, sir. My mistress is the sweetest lady – Lord, Lord!
  when 'twas a little prating thing! O, there is a nobleman
  in town, one Paris, that would fain lay knife aboard; 190
  but she, good soul, had as lief see a toad, a very toad,
  as see him. I anger her sometimes, and tell her that
  Paris is the properer man; but, I'll warrant you, when
  I say so she looks as pale as any clout in the versal
  world. Doth not rosemary and Romeo begin both with 195
  a letter?
Romeo
  Ay, nurse; what of that? Both with an R.
Nurse
  Ah, mocker! that's the dog's name. R is for the – no,

200. *prettiest sententious* prettiest sayings. What they were we never learn as Romeo departs having had enough of the Nurse's talk. (The Nurse probably meant 'sentences'.)

205. *Before and apace* 'Go in front of me and quickly.'

I know it begins with some other letter. And she hath
the prettiest sententious of it, of you and rosemary, 200
that it would do you good to hear it.

Romeo

Commend me to thy lady.

Nurse

Ay, a thousand times. – Peter!

Peter

Anon.

Nurse

[*Handing him her fan*] Before and apace.   205

[Exeunt.]

SCENE V

6. *louring* threatening.

7. Love here means Venus, whose chariot was drawn by swift-winged doves.

14. *bandy* get her to him and back again quickly.

16. This line reflects one of the main themes of the play: that is, the conflict between the generations.

Scene V

Capulet's orchard

[Enter JULIET.]

Juliet

    The clock struck nine when I did send the nurse;
In half an hour she promis'd to return.
Perchance she cannot meet him – that's not so.
O, she is lame! Love's heralds should be thoughts,
Which ten times faster glide than the sun's beams   5
Driving back shadows over louring hills;
Therefore do nimble-pinion'd doves draw Love,
And therefore hath the wind-swift Cupid wings.
Now is the sun upon the highmost hill
Of this day's journey; and from nine till twelve   10
Is three long hours, yet she is not come.
Had she affections and warm youthful blood,
She would be as swift in motion as a ball;
My words would bandy her to my sweet love,
And his to me.   15
But old folks – many feign as they were dead;
Unwieldy, slow, heavy, and pale as lead.

[Enter NURSE and PETER.]

    O God, she comes! O honey nurse, what news?
Hast thou met with him? Send thy man away.

Nurse

    Peter, stay at the gate.   20

[Exit PETER.]

Juliet

    Now, good sweet nurse – O Lord, why look'st thou
        sad?
Though news be sad, yet tell them merrily;
If good, thou shamest the music of sweet news
By playing it to me with so sour a face.

26. *What a jaunce ...* 'What a jaunt/trip!'

36. *I'll stay the circumstance* 'I'll wait for details.'

38. *simple* foolish.
38–45. In this speech, the Nurse is being deliberately ambiguous; it is to be noted that throughout this scene she is teasing Juliet by delaying.

43. *flower of courtesy* the perfect example of a courteous man.

48–65. This interchange between the Nurse and Juliet is full of dramatic tension and humour as the Nurse continues to find excuses not to tell Juliet her news, or deliberately changes the subject to keep her waiting.
51. *beshrew* curse.

Nurse
    I am aweary, give me leave a while: 25
    Fie, how my bones ache! What a jaunce have I had!
Juliet
    I would thou hadst my bones and I thy news.
    Nay, come, I pray thee speak; good, good nurse, speak.
Nurse
    Jesu, what haste? Can you not stay a while?
    Do you not see that I am out of breath?   30
Juliet
    How art thou out of breath, when thou hast breath
    To say to me that thou art out of breath?
    The excuse that thou dost make in this delay
    Is longer than the tale thou dost excuse.
    Is thy news good or bad? Answer to that;   35
    Say either, and I'll stay the circumstance.
    Let me be satisfied, is't good or bad?
Nurse
    Well, you have made a simple choice; you know not
    how to choose a man. Romeo! no, not he; though his
    face be better than any man's, yet his leg excels all   40
    men's; and for a hand, and a foot, and a body, though
    they be not to be talk'd on, yet they are past compare.
    He is not the flower of courtesy, but I'll warrant him
    as gentle as a lamb. Go thy ways, wench; serve God.
    What, have you din'd at home?   45
Juliet
    No, no. But all this did I know before.
    What says he of our marriage? What of that?
Nurse
    Lord, how my head aches! What a head have I!
    It beats as it would fall in twenty pieces.
    My back a t' other side – ah, my back, my back!   50
    Beshrew your heart for sending me about
    To catch my death with jauncing up and down!
Juliet
    I' faith, I am sorry that thou art not well.
    Sweet, sweet, sweet nurse, tell me, what says my love?

WILLIAM SHAKESPEARE

62. *Marry, come up* an indignant expression.
63. *poultice* a heated application of various substances such as mustard and linseed placed on the skin to fight infection or improve circulation.

65. *Here's such a coil!* 'What a state of things!'

70. Juliet is blushing.

74. *a bird's nest* Juliet's bedroom.
75–6. The Nurse again makes a crude joke, this time about wedding nights.

Nurse

Your love says like an honest gentleman, and a cour-   55
teous, and a kind, and a handsome, and, I warrant, a
virtuous – Where is your mother?

Juliet

Where is my mother! Why, she is within;
Where should she be? How oddly thou repliest!
'Your love says like an honest gentleman,   60
Where is your mother?'

Nurse

O God's lady dear!
Are you so hot? Marry, come up, I trow;
Is this the poultice for my aching bones?
Henceforward, do your messages yourself.

Juliet

Here's such a coil! Come, what says Romeo?   65

Nurse

Have you got leave to go to shrift to-day?

Juliet

I have.

Nurse

Then hie you hence to Friar Lawrence' cell;
There stays a husband to make you a wife.
Now comes the wanton blood up in your cheeks;   70
They'll be in scarlet straight at any news.
Hie you to church; I must another way,
To fetch a ladder, by the which your love
Must climb a bird's nest soon when it is dark.
I am the drudge, and toil in your delight;   75
But you shall bear the burden soon at night.
Go; I'll to dinner; hie you to the cell.

Juliet

Hie to high fortune! Honest nurse, farewell.

[Exeunt.]

SCENE VI

1–2. The Friar is asking for a blessing upon the marriage that he is about to celebrate. In the next two speeches, both in Romeo's defiance of death and in the Friar's warning about the possible consequences of such an all-consuming passion, we get a sense of the tragedy coming on.

4. *countervail* cancel out.

11–12. It is in the nature of the exquisite flavour of the *sweetest honey*, that it soon fades; in the same way, a love that is too-violent will quickly die.

18–20. 'A lover could ride upon the spider's threads that sway in the summer air and yet not fall, so empty are the pleasures of this world, of which passion is but one.'

Scene VI

Friar Lawrence's cell

[Enter FRIAR LAWRENCE and ROMEO.]

Friar Lawrence
So smile the heavens upon this holy act
That after-hours with sorrow chide us not!
Romeo
Amen, amen! But come what sorrow can,
It cannot countervail the exchange of joy
That one short minute gives roe in her sight.   5
Do thou but close our hands with holy words,
Then love-devouring death do what he dare;
It is enough I may but call her mine.
Friar Lawrence
These violent delights have violent ends,
And in their triumph die; like fire and powder,   10
Which, as thy kiss, consume. The sweetest honey
Is loathsome in his own deliciousness,
And in the taste confounds the appetite.
Therefore love moderately: long love doth so;
Too swift arrives as tardy as too slow.   15

[Enter JULIET.]

Here comes the lady. O, so light a foot
Will ne'er wear out the everlasting flint.
A lover may bestride the gossamer
That idles in the wanton summer air
And yet not fall, so light is vanity.   20
Juliet
Good even to my ghostly confessor.
Friar Lawrence
Romeo shall thank thee, daughter, for us both.
Juliet
As much to him, else is his thanks too much.

26. To blazon it to describe it fittingly.

30–1. 'A true understanding (of the happiness of their love) is best judged by the feeling itself rather than the expression of it.'

32. 'Only those whose love is measured in small amounts can give an adequate summary of it.'

Romeo

    Ah, Juliet, if the measure of thy joy
    Be heap'd like mine, and that thy skill be more   25
    To blazon it, then sweeten with thy breath
    This neighbour air, and let rich music's tongue
    Unfold the imagin'd happiness that both
    Receive in either by this dear encounter.

Juliet

    Conceit, more rich in matter than in words,   30
    Brags of his substance, not of ornament.
    They are but beggars that can count their worth;
    But my true love is grown to such excess
    I cannot sum up sum of half my wealth.

Friar Lawrence

    Come, come with me, and we will make short work;   35
    For, by your leaves, you shall not stay alone
    Till holy church incorporate two in one.

[Exeunt.]

ACT III SCENE I

This pivotal scene can be seen as the turning point on the path to the play's tragic conclusion. We have not seen the Capulet and Montague young men together since the opening brawl, except in the restricted setting of the Capulet dance, and have been waiting for their inevitable clash.

1–4. Once again there is a sense of foreboding; Benvolio fears there may be trouble.

8. *by the operation ... cup* 'under the influence of two glasses of wine.'
9. *drawer* barman.

11–13. 'Come, come, you are as hot-tempered as any man in Italy, and as quick to become angry under provocation as you are ready to be provoked.'

22. *meat* food.
23. *addle* rotten.

ACT THREE
Scene I

A public place

[Enter MERCUTIO, BENVOLIO, PAGE, *and* SERVANTS.*]*

Benvolio
>I pray thee, good Mercutio, let's retire.
>The day is hot, the Capulets abroad,
>And if we meet we shall not scape a brawl;
>For now, these hot days, is the mad blood stirring.

Mercutio
>Thou art like one of these fellows that, when he enters   5
>the confines of a tavern, claps me his sword upon the
>table, and says 'God send me no need of thee!' and
>by the operation of the second cup draws him on the
>drawer, when, indeed, there is no need.

Benvolio
>Am I like such a fellow?   10

Mercutio
>Come, come, thou art as hot a Jack in thy mood as
>any in Italy; and as soon moved to be moody, and as
>soon moody to be moved.

Benvolio
>And what to?

Mercutio
>Nay, an there were two such, we should have none   15
>shortly, for one would kill the other. Thou! why,
>thou wilt quarrel with a man that hath a hair more
>or a hair less in his beard than thou hast. Thou wilt
>quarrel with a man for cracking nuts, having no other
>reason but because thou hast hazel eyes. What eye but   20
>such an eye would spy out such a quarrel? Thy head
>is as full of quarrels as an egg is full of meat; and yet
>thy head hath been beaten as addle as an egg for quar-
>relling. Thou hast quarrell'd with a man for coughing

31. fee simple absolute legal possession.
31–2. of my life for an hour and a quarter the period for which so argumentative a man might expect to survive.

40. apt ready, suitable.
41. occasion opportunity.

43. consortest belong to a company of travelling minstrels. Naturally Mercutio lakes such a suggestion as an insult.
44–7. Mercutio picks up this term and flings it back at Tybalt, playing with the words **discords** and **fiddlestick**.

46. Here's my fiddlestick he lays his hand on his sword.
47. Zounds 'God's wounds', a violent oath.

48. 'We're talking in a very public place...'

in the street, because he hath wakened thy dog that   25
hath lain asleep in the sun. Didst thou not fall out
with a tailor for wearing his new doublet before Easter?
With another for tying his new shoes with old riband?
And yet thou wilt tutor me from quarrelling!

Benvolio

An I were so apt to quarrel as thou art, any man   30
should buy the fee simple of my life for an hour and
a quarter.

Mercutio

The fee simple! O simple!

[Enter TYBALT and OTHERS.]

Benvolio

By my head, here comes the Capulets.

Mercutio

By my heel, I care not.   35

Tybalt

Follow me close, for I will speak to them.

Gentlemen, good den; a word with one of you.

Mercutio

And but one word with one of us? Couple it with
something; make it a word and a blow.

Tybalt

You shall find me apt enough to that, sir, an you will   40
give me occasion.

Mercutio

Could you not take some occasion without giving?

Tybalt

Mercutio, thou consortest with Romeo.

Mercutio

Consort! What, dost thou make us minstrels? An thou
make minstrels of us, look to hear nothing but   45
discords. Here's my fiddlestick; here's that shall make
you dance. Zounds, consort!

Benvolio

We talk here in the public haunt of men;

55–6. Mercutio takes the word *man* to mean servant, and retorts that Romeo will only be Tybalt's follower when he goes after him to a duelling place *(field)*.

61. *appertaining rage* the anger which would normally be the natural response to such an insult. Why does Romeo, who is not a coward, refuse Tybalt's challenge?

64. *Boy;* an insult in Elizabethan times.

67. *devise* realize.

71. Mercutio is clearly ashamed by Romeo not rising to Tybalt's challenge and sees it as dishonouring the Montague name.
72. *Alla staccato* an Italian expression in fencing used here as a nickname for Tybalt, referring as Mercutio had done previously (Act II, Scene iv, line 2) to Tybalt's reputation as a keen fencer.

Either withdraw unto some private place,
Or reason coldly of your grievances,   50
Or else depart; here all eyes gaze on us.
Mercutio
Men's eyes were made to look, and let them gaze;
I will not budge for no man's pleasure, I.

[Enter ROMEO.]

Tybalt
Well, peace be with you, sir. Here comes my man.
Mercutio
But I'll be hang'd, sir, if he wear your livery.   55
Marry, go before to field, he'll be your follower;
Your worship in that sense may call him man.
Tybalt
Romeo, the love I bear thee can afford
No better term than this: thou art a villain.
Romeo
Tybalt, the reason that I have to love thee   60
Doth much excuse the appertaining rage
To such a greeting. Villain am I none;
Therefore, farewell; I see thou know'st me not.
Tybalt
Boy, this shall not excuse the injuries
That thou hast done me; therefore turn and draw.   65
Romeo
I do protest I never injur'd thee,
But love thee better than thou canst devise
Till thou shalt know the reason of my love;
And so, good Capulet – which name I tender
As dearly as mine own – be satisfied.   70
Mercutio
O calm, dishonourable, vile submission!
Alla stoccata carries it away. *[Draws]*
Tybalt, you rat-catcher, will you walk?
Tybalt
What wouldst thou have with me?

77. *dry-beat* beat up.
78. *pilcher* scabbard.

81. An invitation to start the fight.

83. *passado* thrust with a sword (is Mercutio mocking Tybalt's fancy fencing moves?)

89. *a* on.
89. *I am sped* 'I am done for.'

96. *a grave man* even when dying, Mercutio makes a pun.

Mercutio

Good King of Cats, nothing but one of your nine   75
lives; that I mean to make bold withal, and, as you
shall use me hereafter, dry-beat the rest of the eight.
Will you pluck your sword out of his pilcher by the
ears? Make haste, lest mine be about your ears ere it
be out.   80

Tybalt

I am for you. *[Draws]*

Romeo

Gentle Mercutio, put thy rapier up.

Mercutio

Come, sir, your passado. *[They fight]*

Romeo

Draw, Benvolio; beat down their weapons.
Gentlemen, for shame, forbear this outrage!   85
Tybalt! Mercutio! the Prince expressly hath
Forbid this bandying in Verona streets.

*[TYBALT under ROMEO'S arm thrusts MERCUTIO in, and
flies with his friends.]*

Mercutio

                                I am hurt.
A plague a both your houses! I am sped.
Is he gone and hath nothing?

Benvolio

                         What, art thou hurt?   90

Mercutio

Ay, ay, a scratch, a scratch; marry, 'tis enough.
Where is my page? Go, villain, fetch a surgeon.

[Exit PAGE.]

Romeo

Courage, man; the hurt cannot be much.

Mercutio

No, 'tis not so deep as a well, nor so wide as a church
door, but 'tis enough, 'twill serve. Ask for me tomorrow,   95
and you shall find me a grave man. I am peppered, I

99–100. *fights by the book of arithmetic* fights according to the moves in a fencing manual.

107. *near ally* close relative.

112. *effeminate* like a woman (i.e without aggression).
113. Romeo speaks of himself as a sword, the hardness and resilience *(temper)* of which has been softened.

117. 'This day's misfortune casts a sense of foreboding over the days to come.'

121. *Away to respective lenity* 'Goodbye to respect and gentleness' – *respective* may refer to Romeo's respect for the Prince's order about street-fighting or to his regard for the fact that. by his marriage to Juliet, Tybalt is now his kinsman. By saying 'away', he means he is rejecting these things in order to revenge Mercutio's death.

warrant, for this world. A plague a both your houses!
Zounds, a dog, a rat, a mouse, a cat, to scratch a man
to death! A braggart, a rogue, a villain, that fights by
the book of arithmetic! Why the devil came you 100
between us? I was hurt under your arm.

Romeo

I thought all for the best.

Mercutio

Help me into some house, Benvolio, or I shall faint.
A plague a both your houses!
They have made worms' meat of me. 105
I have it, and soundly too – Your houses!

[Exeunt MERCUTIO and BENVOLIO.]

Romeo

This gentleman, the Prince's near ally,
My very friend, hath got this mortal hurt
In my behalf; my reputation stain'd
With Tybalt's slander – Tybalt, that an hour 110
Hath been my cousin. O sweet Juliet,
Thy beauty hath made me effeminate,
And in my temper soften'd valour's steel!

[Re-enter BENVOLIO.]

Benvolio

O Romeo, Romeo, brave Mercutio is dead!
That gallant spirit hath aspir'd the clouds, 115
Which too untimely here did scorn the earth.

Romeo

This day's black fate on moe days doth depend;
This but begins the woe others must end.

[Re-enter TYBALT.]

Benvolio

Here comes the furious Tybalt back again.

Romeo

Alive in triumph and Mercutio slain! 120
Away to heaven respective lenity,

122. *conduct* guide.

134. Romeo's remark makes us aware of Fate's sudden re-entry into the drama.

Stage Direction. *Enter citizens.* On the printed page this seems very sudden, but on the stage the fight would last some time and people would have gathered at the sound of the disturbance.

135–6. The citizen, very responsibly, in view of the Prince's order attempts to arrest Benvolio.

And fire-ey'd fury be my conduct now!
Now, Tybalt, take the 'villain' back again
That late thou gav'st me; for Mercutio's soul
Is but a little way above our heads,   125
Staying for thine to keep him company.
Either thou or I, or both, must go with him.

Tybalt

Thou, wretched boy, that didst consort him here,
Shall with him hence.

Romeo

      This shall determine that,

[They fight: TYBALT falls.]

Benvolio

Romeo, away, be gone.   130
The citizens are up, and Tybalt slain.
Stand not amaz'd. The Prince will doom thee death
If thou art taken. Hence, be gone, away!

Romeo

O, I am fortune's fool!

Benvolio

      Why dost thou stay?

[Exit ROMEO. Enter CITIZENS.]

First Citizen

Which way ran he that kill'd Mercutio?   135
Tybalt, that murderer, which way ran be?

Benvolio

There lies that Tybalt.

First Citizen

     Up, sir, go with me;
I charge thee in the Prince's name, obey.

[Enter PRINCE, attended: MONTAGUE. CAPULET, their
WIVES, and all.]

Prince

Where are the vile beginners of this fray?

140–1. *discover all The unlucky manage of this fatal brawl* 'tell you all about what happened in this fight.'

150–1. *bid him bethink* asked him to consider.
152. *nice* insignificant.

155. *unruly spleen* violent anger.

161. *dexterity* nimble movement.

169. *entertain'd* thought of.

Benvolio
   O noble Prince, I can discover all   140
   The unlucky manage of this fatal brawl:
   There lies the man, slain by young Romeo,
   That slew thy kinsman, brave Mercutio.

Lady Capulet
   Tybalt, my cousin! O my brother's child!
   O Prince! O husband! O, the blood is spill'd   145
   Of my dear kinsman! Prince, as thou art true,
   For blood of ours shed blood of Montague.
   O cousin, cousin!

Prince
   Benvolio, who began this bloody fray?

Benvolio
   Tybalt, here slain, whom Romeo's hand did slay;   150
   Romeo that spoke him fair, bid him bethink
   How nice the quarrel was, and urg'd withal
   Your high displeasure. All this, uttered
   With gentle breath, calm look, knees humbly bow'd
   Could not take truce with the unruly spleen   155
   Of Tybalt, deaf to peace, but that he tilts
   With piercing steel at bold Mercutio's breast;
   Who, all as hot, turns deadly point to point,
   And, with a martial scorn, with one hand beats
   Cold death aside, and with the other sends   160
   It back to Tybalt, whose dexterity
   Retorts it. Romeo he cries aloud
   'Hold, friends! friends, part!' and, swifter than his
      tongue,
   His agile arm beats down their fatal points,
   And 'twixt them rushes; underneath whose arm   165
   An envious thrust from Tybalt hit the life
   Of stout Mercutio; and then Tybalt fled;
   But by and by comes back to Romeo,
   Who had but newly entertain'd revenge,
   And to't they go like lightning; for ere I   170
   Could draw to part them was stout Tybalt slain;
   And as he fell did Romeo turn and fly.

187. *My blood* 'one of my family', that is, Mercutio.
188. *amerce* punish.

194. *attend our will* this is an order to Capulet and Montague themselves to come and hear judgement and the details of the fine at Court.

This is the truth, or let Benvolio die.

Lady Capulet
He is a kinsman to the Montague,
Affection makes him false, he speaks not true;   175
Some twenty of them fought in this black strife,
And all those twenty could but kill one life.
I beg for justice, which thou. Prince, must give:
Romeo slew Tybalt, Romeo must not live.

Prince
Romeo slew him; he slew Mercutio.   180
Who now the price of his dear blood doth owe?

Montague
Not Romeo, Prince; he was Mercutio's friend;
His fault concludes but what the law should end,
The life of Tybalt.

Prince
                    And for that offence,
Immediately we do exile him hence.   185
I have an interest in your hate's proceeding,
My blood for your rude brawls doth lie a-bleeding;
But I'll amerce you with so strong a fine
That you shall all repent the loss of mine.
I will be deaf to pleading and excuses,   190
Nor tears nor prayers shall purchase out abuses;
Therefore use none. Let Romeo hence in haste,
Else when he is found that hour is his last.
Bear hence this body, and attend our will:
Mercy but murders, pardoning those that kill.   195

                    [Exeunt.]

SCENE II

In this beautiful speech, we begin to understand the fullness of Juliet's love, which seems so much more than just girlish excitement. She desires the act of love, not just for the physical pleasure, but because it represents for her the pinnacle of marriage. It is to be a supreme experience, something quite different from the subject of the Nurse's crudities. The lines are all the more moving, because we realize that the lovers will meet only to be parted again as a result of Romeo's exile.

1–2. Shakespeare again uses the mythological image of the sun as the fiery chariot of the Greek god Phoebus.

3. *Phaethon* in Greek mythology, Phoebus' son, who one day stole his father's chariot and found himself unable to control the horses properly.

6. *runaways' eyes may wink* *wink* means shut; the meaning *of runaways'* is unclear, but has often been interpreted as meaning, 'people who would spy on lovers'.

8. *amorous rites* acts of love and passion.

12–13. Although Juliet will surrender herself to Romeo and both will give up their virginity (in this they will *lose*, the stakes being their *stainless maidenhoods)* she will gain a longed-for experience (a *winning match)* the consummation of their love.

14–16. 'Hide the blushes of a girl, who has never known a man sexually, with the darkness of night, until my new and unfamiliar passion is able to accept the act of love as pure and right.'

17. *thou day in night* Romeo is the day; his presence will shine out against the darkness.

25. *garish* colourful (in a crude or exaggerated way).

26–8. The *mansion* she has bought is Romeo; she has also been sold to him in a mutual exchange through their marriage vows, and she sees the sexual act as a fulfilment of the contract, for which she is longing.

Scene II

Capulet's orchard

[Enter JULIET.*]*

Juliet

Gallop apace, you fiery-footed steeds
Towards Phoebus' lodging; such a waggoner
As Phaethon would whip you to the west,
And bring in cloudy night immediately.
Spread thy close curtain, love-performing night,   5
That runaways' eyes may wink, and Romeo
Leap to these arms, untalk'd of and unseen,
Lovers can see to do their amorous rites
By their own beauties; or if love be blind,
It best agrees with night. Come, civil night,   10
Thou sober-suited matron, all in black,
And learn me how to lose a winning match,
Play'd for a pair of stainless maidenhoods;
Hood my unmann'd blood, bating in my cheeks,
With thy black mantle, till strange love, grown bold,   15
Think true love acted simple modesty.
Come, night; come, Romeo; come, thou day in night
For thou wilt lie upon the wings of night
Whiter than new snow on a raven's back.
Come, gentle night, come, loving black-brow'd night,   20
Give me my Romeo; and, when he shall die,
Take him and cut him out in little stars,
And he will make the face of heaven so fine
That all the world will be in love with night,
And pay no worship to the garish sun.   25
O, I have bought the mansion of a love,
But not possess'd it; and though I am sold,
Not yet enjoy'd. So tedious is this day
As is the night before some festival
To an impatient child that hath new robes,   30
And may not wear them. O, here comes my nurse,

33. *eloquence* fluent and beautiful speech.

34. In this line, the irony that has been running through the speech reaches its climax, for we can guess the news that the Nurse is bringing.

37. The Nurse is as incomprehensible in her grief as she was in her gossip, and accidentally misleads Juliet into thinking that Romeo is dead.

43–51. This speech is one of the most difficult for a modern audience to understand, as even in her deepest grief, Juliet indulges in a series of complicated puns. It must be realized, however, that for an Elizabethan audience there would be nothing dramatically strange in this. The meaning becomes easier to understand if the word *I* in lines 45 and 46 and the third *I* in line 48 are replaced by 'Ay', meaning 'Yes'. What Juliet is saying is if the answer to the question 'Hath Romeo slain himself?' is 'Ay' (yes) then the simple effect of that vowel sound will be worse to her than the murderous look from the 'eye' of the mythological creature, the 'cockatrice.'

47. *cockatrice* a mythological creature, hatched by a serpent from a cock's egg, supposed to kill by looking at you.

51. *weal* happiness.

54. *corse* corpse.

56. *swounded* swooned, fainted

[Enter NURSE *with cords.]*

And she brings news; and every tongue that speaks
But Romeo's name speaks heavenly eloquence.
Now, nurse, what news? What hast thou there? The
    cords
That Romeo bid thee fetch?

Nurse

                  Ay, ay, the cords.   35

[Throws them down.]

Juliet

Ay, me! what news? Why dost thou wring thy hands?

Nurse

Ah, well-a-day! he's dead, he's dead, he's dead.
We are undone, lady, we are undone.
Alack the day! he's gone, he's kill'd, he's dead.

Juliet

Can heaven be so envious?

Nurse

                Romeo can,   40
Though heaven cannot. O Romeo, Romeo!
Who ever would have thought it? Romeo!

Juliet

What devil art thou that dost torment me thus?
This torture should be roar'd in dismal hell.
Hath Romeo slain himself? Say thou but 'I'   45
And that bare vowel I shall poison more
Than the death-darting eye of cockatrice.
I am not I if there be such an 'I';
Or those eyes shut that makes thee answer 'I'.
If he be slain, say 'I'; or if not, 'No';   50
Brief sounds determine of my weal or woe.

Nurse

I saw the wound, I saw it with mine eyes –
God save the mark! – here on his manly breast.
A piteous corse, a bloody piteous corse;
Pale, pale as ashes, all bedaub'd in blood,   55
All in gore-blood. I swounded at the sight.

57. *poor bankrupt* her heart is bankrupt because she has spent all its love on Romeo *(bought the mansion of a love)*, who is now, she thinks, dead.

59. *Vile earth* her body. She wants to die.

60. *bier* platform for a coffin.

67. *dreadful trumpet* the last trumpet, which will sound when the world ends.

73–85. In this speech, Juliet, shocked by the news that Romeo has killed Tybalt, is horrified that someone who seemed so fine a man should be a murderer. She uses a series of paradoxes in which inward character is contrasted with outward appearance.

81. *bower* hide in a bower, enclose.

82–3. Compare these lines with Lady Capulet's image of Paris in Act I, Scene iii, lines 83–9.

Juliet

    O, break, my heart! poor bankrupt, break at once!
    To prison, eyes: ne'er look on liberty.
    Vile earth, to earth resign; end motion here;
    And thou and Romeo press one heavy bier!   60

Nurse

    O Tybalt, Tybalt, the best friend I had!
    O courteous Tybalt! honest gentleman!
    That ever I should live to see thee dead!

Juliet

    What storm is this that blows so contrary?
    Is Romeo slaughter'd, and is Tybalt dead?   65
    My dearest cousin and my dearer lord?
    Then, dreadful trumpet, sound the general doom;
    For who is living if those two are gone?

Nurse

    Tybalt is gone, and Romeo banished;
    Romeo that kill'd him, he is banished.   70

Juliet

    O God! Did Romeo's hand shed Tybalt's blood?

Nurse

    It did, it did; alas the day, it did!

Juliet

    O serpent heart, hid with a flow'ring face!
    Did ever dragon keep so fair a cave?
    Beautiful tyrant! fiend angelical!
    Dove-feather'd raven! wolfish-ravening lamb!
    Despised substance of divinest show!
    Just opposite to what thou justly seem'st,
    A damned saint, an honourable villain!
    O nature, what hadst thou to do in hell,   80
    When thou didst bower the spirit of a fiend
    In mortal paradise of such sweet flesh?
    Was ever book containing such vile matter
    So fairly bound? O, that deceit should dwell
    In such a gorgeous palace!

Nurse

                    There's no trust,   85

86. *perjur'd* sworn falsely.
87. *dissemblers* deceivers.
88. *aqua vitae* brandy or some other strong drink.

90–4. In this speech, by contrast, Juliet's love re-awakens and she scolds the Nurse for speaking ill of Romeo.

98–9. 'Who will stand up for Romeo, if I, his newly-married wife, do not?'

102–4. Juliet tells her tears to dry up, for they should signify sorrow, but hers are mistakenly falling over joyous news; that is, that Romeo is still alive.
103. *tributary* paying a tribute (usually money to a ruler).

109. *fain* gladly.

116–120. 'If sadness delights in or finds it necessary to be accompanied by other sorrows, why could not the news of Tybalt's death have been followed by the death of my father or mother, or both, which might have caused me conventional grief?'

No faith, no honesty in men; all perjur'd,
All forsworn, all naught, all dissemblers.
Ah, where's my man? Give me some aqua vitae.
These griefs, these woes, these sorrows, make me old.
Shame come to Romeo!

Juliet

                    Blister'd be thy tongue   90
For such a wish! He was not born to shame:
Upon his brow shame is asham'd to sit;
For 'tis a throne where honour may be crown'd
Sole monarch of the universal earth.
O, what a beast was I to chide at him!   95

Nurse

Will you speak well of him that kill'd your cousin?

Juliet

Shall I speak ill of him that is my husband?
Ah, poor my lord, what tongue shall smooth thy name,
When I, thy three-hours wife, have mangled it?
But wherefore, villain, didst thou kill my cousin?   100
That villain cousin would have kill'd my husband.
Back, foolish tears, back to your native spring;
Your tributary drops belong to woe,
Which you, mistaking, offer up to joy.
My husband lives that Tybalt would have slain,   105
And Tybalt's dead that would have slain my husband.
All this is comfort; wherefore weep I then?
Some word there was, worser than Tybalt's death,
That murder'd me; I would forget it fain,
But, O, it presses to my memory   110
Like damned guilty deeds to sinners' minds:
'Tybalt is dead, and Romeo banished'.
That 'banished', that one word 'banished',
Hath slain ten thousand Tybalts. Tybalt's death
Was woe enough, if it had ended there;   115
Or if sour woe delights in fellowship
And needly will be rank'd with other griefs,
Why followed not, when she said 'Tybalt's dead',
Thy father or thy mother, nay, or both,

121. 'But coming after Tybalt's death...' Are the expressions of Juliet's grief excessive?

132. *beguil'd* fooled.

134–7. Evidently, at this point Juliet does not expect Romeo to be able to visit her at all, and fears that she will never consummate her marriage, as she has been longing to do. She can see no life without Romeo and is resigned to die a virgin.

139. *wot* know.

Which modern lamentation might have mov'd?   120
But, with a rear-ward following Tybalt's death,
'Romeo is banished'– to speak that word
Is father, mother, Tybalt, Romeo, Juliet,
All slain, all dead. 'Romeo is banished' –
There is no-end, no limit, measure, bound,   125
In that word's death; no words can that woe sound.
Where is my father and my mother, nurse?

Nurse

Weeping and wailing over Tybalt's corse.
Will you go to them? I will bring you thither.

Juliet

Wash they his wounds with tears! Mine shall be
   spent,   130
When theirs are dry, for Romeo's banishment.
Take up those cords. Poor ropes, you are beguil'd,
Both you and I, for Romeo is exil'd;
He made you for a highway to my bed,
But I, a maid, die maiden-widowed.   135
Come, cords; come, nurse; I'll to my wedding-bed;
And death, not Romeo, take my maidenhead!

Nurse

Hie to your chamber; I'll find Romeo
To comfort you. I wot well where he is.
Hark ye, your Romeo will be here at night.   140
I'll to him; he is hid at Lawrence' cell.

Juliet

O, find him! give this ring to my true knight,
And bid him come to take his last farewell.

[Exeunt.]

SCENE III

1. *fearful* full of fear.
2–3. The Friar speaks of misfortune as being in love with Romeo; and he repeats the image by saying Romeo is married to disaster.

4. *doom* judgement.
9. Like Juliet, Romeo indulges in word-play at a moment of strong emotion.
doomsday here means 'death' (for Romeo) but literally it is the day on which the Last Judgement by God will occur, often associated with the end of the world.
18. *purgatory* in religious myth a place of suffering and torment.

Scene III

Friar Lawrence's cell

[Enter FRIAR LAWRENCE.]

Friar Lawrence
Romeo, come forth; come forth, thou fearful man;
Affliction is enamour'd of thy parts,
And thou art wedded to calamity.

[Enter ROMEO.]

Romeo
Father, what news? What is the Prince's doom?
What sorrow craves acquaintance at my hand   5
That I yet know not?
Friar Lawrence
Too familiar
Is my dear son with such sour company;
I bring thee tidings of the Prince's doom.
Romeo
What less than doomsday is the Prince's doom?
Friar Lawrence
A gentler judgment vanish'd from his lips –   10
Not body's death, but body's banishment.
Romeo
Ha, banishment! Be merciful, say 'death';
For exile hath more terror in his look,
Much more than death. Do not say 'banishment'.
Friar Lawrence
Here from Verona art thou banished.   15
Be patient, for the world is broad and wide.
Romeo
There is no world without Verona walls,
But purgatory, torture, hell itself.
Hence banished is banish'd from the world,
And world's exile is death. Then 'banished'   20
Is death mis-term'd; calling death 'banished',

24. *unthankfulness* ingratitude.

26. *rush'd aside* brushed aside.

29–51. The extraordinary violence of Romeo's grief matches that of Juliet.

35. *carrion flies* flies that live off rotting meat or flesh.

39. Juliet's lips are thought of as blushing because they touch each other.

48–51. 'How do you, being a man of good, my spiritual adviser and someone I confess my sins to – as well as my friend – have the heart to injure me with the word 'banished'?'

52. *fond* foolish.

Thou cut'st my head off with a golden axe,
And smil'st upon the stroke that murders me.

Friar Lawrence

O deadly sin! O rude unthankfulness!
Thy fault our law calls death; but the kind Prince,   25
Taking thy part, hath rush'd aside the law,
And turn'd that black word death to banishment.
This is dear mercy, and thou seest it not.

Romeo

'Tis torture, and not mercy; heaven is here
Where Juliet lives, and every cat, and dog,   30
And little mouse, every unworthy thing,
Live here in heaven and may look on her;
But Romeo may not. More validity,
More honourable state, more courtship lives
In carrion flies than Romeo. They may seize   35
On the white wonder of dear Juliet's hand,
And steal immortal blessing from her lips;
Who, even in pure and vestal modesty,
Still blush, as thinking their own kisses sin;
But Romeo may not – he is banished.   40
This may flies do, when I from this must fly;
They are free men, but I am banished.
And sayest thou yet that exile is not death?
Hadst thou no poison mix'd, no sharp-ground knife,
No sudden mean of death, though ne'er so mean,   45
But 'banished' to kill me – 'banished'?
O friar, the damned use that word in hell;
Howling attends it; how hast thou the heart,
Being a divine, a ghostly confessor,
A sin-absolver, and my friend profess'd,   50
To mangle me with that word 'banished'?

Friar Lawrence

Thou fond mad man, hear me a little speak.

Romeo

O, thou wilt speak again of banishment.

Friar Lawrence

I'll give thee armour to keep off that word;

163

55. 'A philosophical outlook can make even misfortune tolerable.'

59. *Displant* remove, move.

63. 'Let me discuss your situation with you.'

72–3. A far-fetched image (suggesting the 'mist' created by groans and moans might hide Romeo), but possibly, in a way, appropriate given his current state.

74–8. We must try to visualize this on stage: the flustered Friar is trying to persuade Romeo to hide himself, and, at the same time, is seeking to discover who is outside.

Adversity's sweet milk, philosophy, 55
To comfort thee, though thou art banished.
Romeo
Yet 'banished'? Hang up philosophy;
Unless philosophy can make a Juliet,
Displant a town, reverse a prince's doom,
It helps not, it prevails not. Talk no more. 60
Friar Lawrence
O, then I see that madmen have no ears.
Romeo
How should they, when that wise men have no eyes.
Friar Lawrence
Let me dispute with thee of thy estate.
Romeo
Thou canst not speak of that thou dost not feel.
Wert thou as young as I, Juliet thy love, 65
An hour but married, Tybalt murdered,
Doting like me, and like me banished,
Then mightst thou speak, then mightst thou tear
   thy hair,
And fall upon the ground, as I do now,
Taking the measure of an unmade grave. 70

[Knocking within.]

Friar Lawrence
Arise; one knocks. Good Romeo, hide thyself.
Romeo
Not I; unless the breath of heart-sick groans,
Mist-like, enfold me from the search of eyes.

[Knocking.]

Friar Lawrence
Hark how they knock! Who's there? Romeo, arise;
Thou wilt be taken. – Stay awhile. – Stand up; 75

[Knocking.]

Run to my study. – By and by. – God's will,
What simpleness is this! – I come, I come. *[Knocking.]*

85. *O woeful sympathy!* This refers to the similarity between Romeo and Juliet in their grief.

91. It seems that the Nurse, having spoken sharply to Romeo for his behaviour, is shocked into sympathy by his grief-stricken face when he looks up at her.

98. *My conceal'd lady* the fact that she is his lady (that is, his wife) has not yet been made known . . . it is still secret ('concealed').

Who knocks so hard? Whence come you? What's
    your will?
Nurse
    [Within] Let me come in and you shall know my
      errand;
    I come from Lady Juliet.
Friar Lawrence
                    Welcome, then.   80

            [Enter NURSE.]

Nurse
    O holy friar, O, tell me, holy friar,
    Where's my lady's lord, where's Romeo?
Friar Lawrence
    There on the ground, with his own tears made drunk.
Nurse
    O, he is even in my mistress' case,
    Just in her case!
Friar Lawrence
              O woeful sympathy!   85
    Piteous predicament!
Nurse
                Even so lies she,
    Blubbering and weeping, weeping and blubb'ring.
    Stand up, stand up; stand, an you be a man;
    For Juliet's sake, for her sake, rise and stand;
    Why should you fall into so deep an O?   90
Romeo
    Nurse!
Nurse
    Ah, sir! ah, sir! Well, death's the end of all.
Romeo
    Spak'st thou of Juliet? How is it with her?
    Doth not she think me an old murderer,
    Now I have stain'd the childhood of our joy   95
    With blood remov'd but little from her own?
    Where is she? and how doth she? and what says
    My conceal'd lady to our cancell'd love?

102–8. Romeo speaks of his body as though it were a house that could be destroyed. In that destruction he wishes that his name, which has caused Juliet so much grief, may be wiped out also.

106. *anatomy* body.

110. *denote* signify, show.

112–113. *seemly* could mean proper or fitting in terms of behaviour and appearance, so the Friar's words here suggest that Romeo's womanly behaviour (crying!) is *unseemly* in someone appearing (*seeming*) to be a man. The mix of woman and man in Romeo makes an *ill-beseeming beast* – an unnatural creature.
115. *better tempered* better balanced.

122. *thy shape* your manly form.
thy wit your intelligence and understanding.
123. *Which* who *a usurer* moneylender.
122–5. Romeo is compared to a rich money-lender *(he abound'st in all)*, who does not use his wealth, however, to do honour to *(bedeck)* what most deserves it, that is, his *shape*, his *love* and his *wit*.
126–7. His noble form is just a sham and a fake *(wax)*, which shows nothing of a proper courage.
128–9. The love he professes for Juliet is really just a lie, and this perjury is destroying the marriage vows that he has sworn.

Nurse
O, she says nothing, sir, but weeps and weeps;
And now falls on her bed, and then starts up,   100
And Tybalt calls; and then on Romeo cries,
And then down falls again.

Romeo
                          As if that name,
Shot from the deadly level of a gun,
Did murder her; as that name's cursed hand
Murder'd her kinsman. O, tell me, friar, tell me,   105
In what vile part of this anatomy
Doth my name lodge? Tell me that I may sack
The hateful mansion,

                    [Drawing his sword.]

Friar Lawrence
                          Hold thy desperate hand.
Art thou a man? Thy form cries out thou art:
Thy tears are womanish; thy wild acts denote   110
The unreasonable fury of a beast.
Unseemly woman in a seeming man!
And ill-beseeming beast in seeming both!
Thou hast amaz'd me. By my holy order,
I thought thy disposition better temper'd.   115
Hast thou slain Tybalt? Wilt thou slay thyself?
And slay thy lady that in thy life lives,
By doing damned hate upon thyself?
Why rail'st thou on thy birth, the heaven, and earth?
Since birth, and heaven, and earth, all three do meet 120
In thee at once; which thou at once wouldst lose.
Fie, fie! thou sham'st thy shape, thy love, thy wit;
Which, like a usurer, abound'st in all,
And usest none in that true use indeed
Which should bedeck thy shape, thy love, thy wit.   125
Thy noble shape is but a form of wax,
Digressing from the valour of a man;
Thy dear love sworn but hollow perjury,
Killing that love which thou hast vow'd to cherish;

130–4. 'Your intelligence is misguided in the direction both of your manly vigour and your love, and like an ignorant soldier who unwittingly sets his gunpowder alight and blows himself to pieces, you destroy yourself with that part of you which should be your safeguard.' It should be remembered that the whole of this speech, up to this point, is a rebuke to Romeo for trying to kill himself. In the remainder of it, the Friar turns from rebuke to encouragement and gives Romeo the reasons for faith and hope.

142. *array* dress and impressive appearance.

148–149. Romeo must leave Mantua before nightfall (i.e before the guards – the Watch – are posted on the gates or other exits).

151. *blaze* make known.

Thy wit, that ornament to shape and love,   130
Misshapen in the conduct of them both,
Like powder in a skilless soldier's flask,
Is set afire by thine own ignorance,
And thou dismember'd with thine own defence.
What, rouse thee, man! Thy Juliet is alive,   135
For whose dear sake thou wast but lately dead;
There art thou happy. Tybalt would kill thee,
But thou slowest Tybalt; there art thou happy too.
The law, that threaten'd death, becomes thy friend,
And turns it to exile; there art thou happy.   140
A pack of blessings lights upon thy back;
Happiness courts thee in her best array;
But, like a misbehav'd and sullen wench,
Thou pout'st upon thy fortune and thy love.
Take heed, take heed, for such die miserable.   145
Go, get thee to thy love, as was decreed,
Ascend her chamber, hence and comfort her.
But look thou stay not till the watch be set,
For then thou canst not pass to Mantua,
Where thou shalt live till we can find a time   150
To blaze your marriage, reconcile your friends,
Beg pardon of the Prince, and call thee back
With twenty hundred thousand times more joy
Than thou went'st forth in lamentation.
Go before, nurse; commend me to thy lady;   155
And bid her hasten all the house to bed,
Which heavy sorrow makes them apt unto;
Romeo is coming.

Nurse

O Lord, I could have stay'd here all the night
To hear good counsel; O, what learning is!   160
My lord, I'll tell my lady you will come.

Romeo

Do so, and bid my sweet prepare to chide.

Nurse

Here, sir, a ring she bid me give you, sir.
Hie you, make haste, for it grows very late.

166. *here stands all your state* 'this is what you must do.'

169. *Sojourn* stay.

171. *hap* happening, event.

[Exit.]

Romeo
    How well my comfort is reviv'd by this!   165
Friar Lawrence
    Go hence; good night; and here stands all your state:
    Either be gone before the watch be set,
    Or by the break of day disguis'd from hence.
    Sojourn in Mantua; I'll find out your man,
    And he shall signify from time to time   170
    Every good hap to you that chances here.
    Give me thy hand. 'tis late; farewell; good night.
Romeo
    But that a joy past joy calls out on me,
    It were a grief so brief to part with thee.
    Farewell.   175

[Exeunt.]

SCENE IV

1–2. Capulet is explaining that, because of Tybalt's death *(Things have fall'n out, sir, so unluckily),* he has had no opportunity to approach Juliet about the proposed marriage with Paris.

11. *mew'd up to her heaviness* she has shut herself away in her grief. Lady Capulet, of course, thinks that this grief has been caused by the death of Tybalt; the audience knows that it is for the banishment of her husband, Romeo.

12–13. *make a desperate tender Of my child's love* 'risk a bold offer to you of my daughter's love' – he is relying on the probability that Juliet will obey her father's wishes about whom she marries.

22. The questions are addressed to Paris.

23. *we'll keep no great ado* 'we won't have a showy wedding.'

Scene IV

Capulet's house

[Enter CAPULET, LADY CAPULET, and PARIS.]

Capulet
    Things have fall'n out, sir, so unluckily
    That we have had no time to move our daughter.
    Look you, she lov'd her kinsman Tybalt dearly,
    And so did I. Well, we were born to die.
    'Tis very late; she'll not come down to-night,   5
    I promise you, but for your company,
    I would have been abed an hour ago.

Paris
    These times of woe afford no time to woo.
    Madam, good night; commend me to your daughter.

Lady Capulet
    I will, and know her mind early to-morrow;   10
    To-night she's mew'd up to her heaviness.

Capulet
    Sir Paris, I will make a desperate tender
    Of my child's love. I think she will be rul'd
    In all respects by me; nay, more, I doubt it not.
    Wife, go you to her ere you go to bed;   15
    Acquaint her here of my son Paris' love
    And bid her, mark you me, on Wednesday next –
    But, soft! what day is this?

Paris
                    Monday, my lord.

Capulet
    Monday! ha, ha! Well, Wednesday is too soon.
    A Thursday let it be; a Thursday, tell her,   20
    She shall be married to this noble earl.
    Will you be ready? Do you like this haste?
    We'll keep no great ado – a friend or two;
    For, hark you, Tybalt being slain so late,
    It may be thought we held him carelessly,   25

30. *a Thursday* on Thursday.

Being our kinsman, if we revel much;
Therefore we'll have some half a dozen friends,
And there an end. But what say you to Thursday?

Paris

My lord, I would that Thursday were to-morrow.

Capulet

Well, get you gone; a Thursday be it then.   30
Go you to Juliet ere you go to bed;
Prepare her, wife, against this wedding-day.
Farewell, my lord. Light to my chamber, ho!
Afore me, it is so very very late
That we may call it early by and by.   35
Good night.

[Exeunt.]

SCENE V

In Shakespeare's theatre, this scene, taking place on the upper stage, would have started as soon as Capulet moved off the main platform – emphasizing that even at the moment that Capulet was arranging a marriage for her, Juliet, already married, was with her husband just above his head.

1–2. Evidently the song of the lark has aroused Romeo to the fact that he must be away from Verona before full daylight. Juliet touchingly tries to keep him a little longer by pretending it is a nightingale that he hears.

7. *envious streaks* the first light of dawn, called *envious* because it is summoning him to go, as though envious of his joy with Juliet.
9. *jocund* cheerful.

13. *meteor.* In Shakespeare's day, any luminous appearance in the sky was given the name; such things were thought to originate in the sun.

17–35. As soon as Romeo says he'll gladly stay and die for it, if Juliet wants him to, she in her turn becomes anxious for him, and urges him away.
20. 'the lingering light of the moon.' Cynthia (Diana) was the goddess of the moon *(reflex* = reflection).

23. *care* desire. *will* will-power.

Scene V

Capulet's orchard

[Enter ROMEO *and* JULIET, *aloft.]*

Juliet

    Wilt thou be gone? It is not yet near day;

    It was the nightingale, and not the lark,

    That pierc'd the fearful hollow of thine ear;

    Nightly she sings on yond pomegranate tree.

    Believe me, love, it was the nightingale.   5

Romeo

    It was the lark, the herald of the mom,

    No nightingale. Look, love, what envious streaks

    Do lace the severing clouds in yonder east;

    Night's candles are burnt out, and jocund day

    Stands tiptoe on the misty mountain tops.   10

    I must be gone and live, or stay and die.

Juliet

    Yond light is not daylight; I know it, I:

    It is some meteor that the sun exhales

    To be to thee this night a torch-bearer,

    And light thee on thy way to Mantua;   15

    Therefore stay yet; thou need'st not to be gone.

Romeo

    Let me be ta'en, let me be put to death;

    I am content, so thou wilt have it so.

    I'll say yon grey is not the morning's eye,

    'Tis but the pale reflex of Cynthia's brow;   20

    Nor that is not the lark whose notes do beat

    The vaulty heaven so high above our heads.

    I have more care to stay than will to go.

    Come death, and welcome! Juliet wills it so.

    How is't, my soul? Let's talk – it is not day.   25

Juliet

    It is, it is; hie hence, be gone, away!

    It is the lark that sings so out of tune,

28. *sharps* shrill notes.
29–30. *division ... divideth* another pun – *division* here means melody.

32. Juliet seems to be regretting the beauty of the lark's song, saying that, since it is what is driving Romeo away, it would be more agreeable if it sounded like the ugly croaking of a toad.
33. *affray* frighten.
34. *hunts-up* music played to rouse prospective hunters in the morning.

43. For Juliet, Romeo is everything – master, husband and lover.

Straining harsh discords and unpleasing sharps.
Some say the lark makes sweet division;
This doth not so, for she divideth us.   30
Some say the lark and loathed toad change eyes;
O, now I would they had chang'd voices too!
Since arm from arm that voice doth us affray,
Hunting thee hence with hunts-up to the day.
O, now be gone! More light and light it grows.   35

Romeo
More light and light – more dark and dark our woes!

[Enter NURSE.]

Nurse
Madam!

Juliet
Nurse?

Nurse
Your lady mother is coming to your chamber.
The day is broke; be wary, look about.   40

[Exit.]

Juliet
Then, window, let day in and let life out.

Romeo
Farewell, farewell! One kiss, and I'll descend.

[He goeth down.]

Juliet
Art thou gone so, love – lord, ay, husband, friend!
I must hear from thee every day in the hour,
For in a minute there are many days;   45
O, by this count I shall be much in years
Ere I again behold my Romeo!

Romeo
Farewell!
I will omit no opportunity
That may convey my greetings, love, to thee.   50

Juliet
O, think'st thou we shall ever meet again?

181

52–3. in answer to Juliet's ominous question, Romeo reassures her saying that he's sure they'll meet again, and that their current problems will simply be part of their happy conversations in the future.

54. *an ill-divining soul* 'to divine' means to see into the future – Juliet has a premonition of disaster – another of the many reminders that the young lovers are fated to a tragic end. This vision is a particularly accurate one.

59. Their misery at parting drains the blood from their faces.

60–4. 'Fortune is known to be changeable; why then does it have anything to do with Romeo, who is well-known for being firm and unchangeable? But let Fortune be changeable; for if Romeo's luck changes, he will be able to come back.'

73. *wit* good sense.

Romeo

    I doubt it not; and all these woes shall serve

    For sweet discourses in our times to come.

Juliet

    O God, I have an ill-divining soul!

    Methinks I see thee, now thou art below,   55

    As one dead in the bottom of a tomb;

    Either my eyesight fails or thou look'st pale.

Romeo

    And trust me, love, in my eye so do you;

    Dry sorrow drinks our blood. Adieu, adieu!

[Exit below.]

Juliet

    O Fortune, Fortune! all men call thee fickle.   60

    If thou art fickle, what dost thou with him

    That is renown'd for faith? Be fickle. Fortune;

    For then, I hope, thou wilt not keep him long,

    But send him back.

Lady Capulet

    [Within] Ho, daughter! are you up?

Juliet

    Who is't that calls? It is my lady mother.   65

    Is she not down so late, or up so early?

    What unaccustom'd cause procures her hither?

[Enter LADY CAPULET.]

Lady Capulet

    Why, how now, Juliet!

Juliet

              Madam, I am not well.

Lady Capulet

    Evermore weeping for your cousin's death?

    What, wilt thou wash him from his grave with tears?   70

    An if thou couldst, thou couldst not make him live;

    Therefore have done. Some grief shows much of love;

    But much of grief shows still some want of wit.

76. *feeling loss* a loss deeply felt.

81. 'Villain is a name that cannot possibly be given to Romeo.'

85–86. Juliet's words are full of irony – even in playing along with her mother, she says she wishes she were the only one who could avenge Tybalt's death (presumably to keep the killer – Romeo – to herself!)

89. *runagate* runaway.

97. *temper it* mix it. Juliet presumably takes her mother's promise to have Romeo poisoned *(give him such an unaccustomed dram)* seriously, and plans to have a hand in mixing the poison, so that she can make it harmless.

Juliet

    Yet let me weep for such a feeling loss.

Lady Capulet

    So shall you feel the loss, but not the friend   75
    Which you weep for.

Juliet

                 Feeling so the loss,
    I cannot choose but ever weep the friend.

Lady Capulet

    Well, girl, thou weep'st not so much for his death
    As that the villain lives which slaughtered him.

Juliet

    What villain, madam?

Lady Capulet

                 That same villain, Romeo.   80

Juliet

    [Aside] Villain and he be many miles asunder! –
    God pardon him! I do, with all my heart;
    And yet no man like he doth grieve my heart.

Lady Capulet

    That is because the traitor murderer lives.

Juliet

    Ay, madam, from the reach of these my hands.   85
    Would none but I might venge my cousin's death!

Lady Capulet

    We will have vengeance for it, fear thou not;
    Then weep no more. I'll send to one in Mantua –
    Where that same banish'd runagate doth live –
    Shall give him such an unaccustom'd dram   90
    That he shall soon keep Tybalt company;
    And then I hope thou wilt be satisfied.

Juliet

    Indeed I never shall be satisfied
    With Romeo till I behold him – dead –
    Is my poor heart so for a kinsman vex'd.   95
    Madam, if you could find out but a man
    To bear a poison, I would temper it,
    That Romeo should, upon receipt thereof,

101–2. In these lines and previously in the conversation, much of what Juliet says has quite a different meaning from that which Lady Capulet supposes it to have, and the audience, of course, realizes this. Consider, for example, what Juliet actually means in lines 99–100, and what her mother thinks she means.

107. *a careful father* a father who cares for you.

122. Again, Juliet's words, intended to be taken one way by her mother as an expression of how much she rejects marrying Paris (to the extent she'd rather marry a murderer) are understood quite differently by the audience.

Soon sleep in quiet. O, how my heart abhors
To hear him nam'd, and cannot come to him,   100
To wreak the love I bore my cousin Tybalt
Upon his body that hath slaughter'd him!

Lady Capulet

Find thou the means, and I'll find such a man.
But now I'll tell thee joyful tidings, girl.

Juliet

And joy comes well in such a needy time.   105
What are they, beseech your ladyship?

Lady Capulet

Well, well, thou hast a careful father, child;
One who, to put thee from thy heaviness,
Hath sorted out a sudden day of joy
That thou expects not, nor I look'd not for.   110

Juliet

Madam, in happy time, what day is that?

Lady Capulet

Marry, my child, early next Thursday morn
The gallant, young, and noble gentleman,
The County Paris, at Saint Peter's Church,
Shall happily make thee there a joyful bride.   115

Juliet

Now, by Saint Peter's Church, and Peter too,
He shall not make me there a joyful bride.
I wonder at this haste, that I must wed
Ere he that should be husband comes to woo.
I pray you tell my lord and father, madam,   120
I will not marry yet; and when I do, I swear
It shall be Romeo, whom you know I hate,
Rather than Paris. These are news indeed!

Lady Capulet

Here comes your father; tell him so yourself,
And see how he will take it at your hands.   125

[Enter CAPULET and NURSE.]

Capulet

When the sun sets, the air doth drizzle dew;

129. *a conduit* a water-pipe.
131. *counterfeit'st* play, take on the form/appearance of …
131. *a bark* a ship.

138. *our decree* that is, the decision that she is to marry Paris on the following Thursday.

146–8. Juliet tries to avoid making her father angry by saying that she is grateful for the trouble he has taken, though she cannot be proud of the man he has chosen.

149. *chopt logic* clever talk.
151. *minion* saucy creature.
153. *fettle your fine joints* get yourself ready. The words also convey the idea that Juliet thinks much too much of herself.
155. *hurdle* a wooden frame on which traitors were dragged through the streets.
156. *green-sickness carrion green-sickness* was the name given to an illness common to young women (anaemia) which made them look pale, and *carrion* is dead meat. Juliet is no doubt pale with anxiety – *tallow face* in line 157 refers to this also.
157. Lady Capulet is evidently shocked by the violence of Capulet's insulting language to their daughter.

But for the sunset of my brother's son
It rains downright.
How now! a conduit, girl? What, still in tears?
Evermore show'ring? In one little body   130
Thou counterfeit'st a bark, a sea, a wind;
For still thy eyes, which I may call the sea,
Do ebb and flow with tears. The bark thy body is,
Sailing in this salt flood; the winds thy sighs,
Who, raging with thy tears, and they with them,   135
Without a sudden calm will overset
Thy tempest-tossed body. How now, wife!
Have you delivered to her our decree?

Lady Capulet

Ay, sir; but she will none, she gives you thanks.
I would the fool were married to her grave!   140

Capulet

Soft I take me with you, take me with you, wife.
How will she none? Doth she not give us thanks?
Is she not proud? Doth she not count her blest,
Unworthy as she is, that we have wrought
So worthy a gentleman to be her bridegroom?   145

Juliet

Not proud you have, but thankful that you have.
Proud can I never be of what I hate,
But thankful even for hate that is meant love.

Capulet

How how, how how, chopt logic! What is this?
'Proud' – and 'I thank you' – and 'I thank you not' – 150
And yet 'not proud'? Mistress minion, you,
Thank me no thankings, nor proud me no prouds,
But fettle your fine joints 'gainst Thursday next,
To go with Paris to Saint Peter's Church,
Or I will drag thee on a hurdle thither.   155
Out, you green-sickness carrion! Out, you baggage!
You tallow-face!

Lady Capulet

            Fie, fie! what, are you mad?

164. *My fingers itch* presumably he means he is about to strike her.

168. *hilding* a worthless girl.
168–9. As on previous occasions, the Nurse strongly defends Juliet.

171. *smatter with your gossips, go* 'Oh! go away and chatter with the other old women.'

172. *O, God-i-goden!* literally 'Oh! Good evening to you'. Capulet is beside himself with anger and is trying to dismiss the Nurse.

181. *Of fair demesnes* owning a fine estate.

Juliet
    Good father, I beseech you on my knees,
    Hear me with patience but to speak a word.
Capulet
    Hang thee, young baggage! disobedient wretch!   160
    I tell thee what – get thee to church a Thursday,
    Or never after look me in the face.
    Speak not, reply not, do not answer me;
    My fingers itch. Wife, we scarce thought us blest
    That God had lent us but this only child;   165
    But now I see this one is one too much,
    And that we have a curse in having her.
    Out on her, hilding!
Nurse
               God in heaven bless her!
    You are to blame, my lord, to rate her so.
Capulet
    And why, my Lady Wisdom? Hold your tongue,   170
    Good Prudence; smatter with your gossips, go.
Nurse
    I speak no treason.
Capulet
               O, God-i-goden!
Nurse
    May not one speak?
Capulet
               Peace, you mumbling fool!
    Utter your gravity o'er a gossip's bowl,
    For here we need it not.
Lady Capulet
               You are too hot.   175
Capulet
    God's bread! it makes me mad:
    Day, night, hour, tide, time, work, play,
    Alone, in company, still my care hath been
    To have her match'd; and having now provided
    A gentleman of noble parentage,   180
    Of fair demesnes, youthful, and nobly train'd,

183. 'As suitable a man as one could possibly want.'
184. *puling* whimpering.
185. *mammet* doll.
185. *in her fortune's tender* in the face of what fortune offers her.

188. *I'll pardon you* meaning, of course, with threatening sarcasm, 'I'll show you the kind of pardon you'll get!'

196. *I'll not be forsworn* 'I won't be made to go back on my word' – that is, his promise to Paris that he could marry Juliet.

204. Lady Capulet's last word is exactly what one would expect from her: 'Do what you like; I wash my hands of you.'

206. *my faith in heaven* 'I have made a vow which is recorded in heaven' – that is, her marriage vow to Romeo.
207–9. Juliet says she could only be released from her marriage vow by the death of her husband.
210–11. She cries out in misery that heaven should play such tricks upon one as defenceless as herself.

Stuff'd, as they say, with honourable parts,
Proportion'd as one's thought would wish a man –
And then to have a wretched puling fool,
A whining mammet, in her fortune's tender,   185
To answer, 'I'll not wed, I cannot love,
I am too young, I pray you pardon me'!
But, an you will not wed, I'll pardon you.
Graze where you will, you shall not house with me.
Look to't, think on't; I do not use to jest.   190
Thursday is near; lay hand on heart, advise:
An you be mine, I'll give you to my friend;
An you be not, hang, beg, starve, die in the streets,
For, by my soul, I'll ne'er acknowledge thee,
Nor what is mine shall never do thee good.   195
Trust to't, bethink you, I'll not be forsworn.

[Exit.]

Juliet

Is there no pity sitting in the clouds
That sees into the bottom of my grief?
O, sweet my mother, cast me not away!
Delay this marriage for a month, a week;   200
Or, if you do not, make the bridal bed
In that dim monument where Tybalt lies.

Lady Capulet

Talk not to me, for I'll not speak a word;
Do as thou wilt, for I have done with thee.

[Exit.]

Juliet

O God! – O nurse! how shall this be prevented?   205
My husband is on earth, my faith in heaven;
How shall that faith return again to earth,
Unless that husband send it me from heaven
By leaving earth? Comfort me, counsel me.
Alack, alack, that heaven should practise stratagems   210
Upon so soft a subject as myself!

214. *and all the world to nothing* the odds of a bet; the Nurse is saying that it is as certain as anything can be that Romeo will not return.

215. *to challenge you* to lay claim to. The Nurse's worldly advice is typical of her rather basic outlook on life; she is quite incapable of appreciating the love of Romeo and Juliet, but she is well-meaning, despite her limitations.

228. *beshrew* curse. Juliet's muttered *Amen* in line 229 is an angry endorsement of the Nurse's suggested curse upon herself.

231–4. Juliet, aware now that even the Nurse is against her, quickly pretends to accept her advice.

236. *Ancient damnation* 'damnable old woman.' Once, the Nurse has left, Juliet is able to speak her mind and reflects angrily on how the Nurse, who had praised Romeo, quickly changed to endorsing Paris as a potential husband. She says she will no longer seek her advice, and intends to visit the Friar.

What say'st thou! Hast thou not a word of joy?
Some comfort, nurse.

Nurse

               Faith, here it is:
Romeo is banished; and all the world to nothing
That he dares ne'er come back to challenge you;   215
Or, if he do, it needs must be by stealth.
Then, since the case so stands as now it doth,
I think it best you married with the County.
O, he's a lovely gentleman!
Romeo's a dishclout to him; an eagle, madam,   220
Hath not so green, so quick, so fair an eye
As Paris hath. Beshrew my very heart,
I think you are happy in this second match,
For it excels your first; or, if it did not,
Your first is dead, or 'twere as good he were   225
As living here and you no use of him.

Juliet

Speak'st thou from thy heart?

Nurse

And from my soul too, else beshrew them both.

Juliet

Amen!

Nurse

What?   230

Juliet

Well, thou hast comforted me marvellous much.
Go in; and tell my lady I am gone,
Having displeas'd my father, to Lawrence' cell
To make confession, and to be absolved.

Nurse

Marry, I will; and this is wisely done.   235

[Exit.]

Juliet

Ancient damnation! O most wicked fiend!
Is it more sin to wish me thus forsworn,
Or to dispraise my lord with that same tongue

241. *twain* two (as in separated from each other).

Which she hath prais'd him with above compare
So many thousand times? Go, counsellor;   240
Thou and my bosom henceforth shall be twain.
I'll to the friar to know his remedy;
If all else fail, myself have power to die.

[Exit.]

ACT IV SCENE I

3. 'I certainly don't want to check his haste.'

5. The Friar says that a marriage in which the lady has had no opportunity to express an opinion is not normal, and that he disapproves.

9–14. Paris says that Capulet considers it dangerous for Juliet to spend so much time on her own brooding over her grief, but that it might be easily forgotten in his company. (Of course, Capulet has said nothing of the sort!)
12. *inundation* flood.

18–43. Throughout this conversation with Paris, Juliet's replies are cautious and ambiguous so that she neither commits herself to him, or reveals the reason why she cannot marry him.

ACT FOUR

Scene I

Friar Lawrence's cell

[*Enter* FRIAR LAWRENCE *and* COUNTY PARIS.]

Friar Lawrence
On Thursday, sir? The time is very short.
Paris
My father, Capulet will have it so,
And I am nothing slow to slack his haste.
Friar Lawrence
You say you do not know the lady's mind;
Uneven is the course; I like it not.   5
Paris
Immoderately she weeps for Tybalt's death,
And therefore have I little talk'd of love;
For Venus smiles not in a house of tears.
Now, sir, her father counts it dangerous
That she do give her sorrow so much sway,   10
And in his wisdom hastes our marriage,
To stop the inundation of her tears;
Which, too much minded by herself alone,
May be put from her by society.
Now do you know the reason of his haste.   15
Friar Lawrence
[*Aside*] I would I knew not why it should be slow'd. –
Look, sir, here comes the lady toward my cell.

[*Enter* JULIET.]

Paris
Happily met, my lady and my wife!
Juliet
That may be, sir, when I may be a wife.
Paris
That may be must be, love, on Thursday next.   20

27–8. Juliet means that compliments about someone who is not present are worth more than what may be just flattery.

22–35. What can we read into Paris's character from this exchange? Does an arrogance come across in his statement that he is 'sure' that Juliet will confess she loves him? Perhaps the reality is that he is delighted Juliet's father has set the wedding date so soon as it means Juliet has little chance to escape from it, or persuade her father to change his mind.

34. *to my face* Shakespeare is playing with words again – the meanings are (1) about my face, (2) openly.

39. *pensive* thoughtful.
40. *entreat* ask for, beg.
41. *God shield I should disturb devotion* 'God forbid that I should interfere with your devotions.'

Juliet
  What must be shall be.
Friar Lawrence
                    That's a certain text.
Paris
  Come you to make confession to this father?
Juliet
  To answer that, I should confess to you.
Paris
  Do not deny to him that you love me.
Juliet
  I will confess to you that I love him.   25
Paris
  So will ye, I am sure, that you love me.
Juliet
  If I do so, it will be of more price
  Being spoke behind your back than to your face,
Paris
  Poor soul, thy face is much abus'd with tears.
Juliet
  The tears have got small victory by that,   30
  For it was bad enough before their spite.
Paris
  Thou wrong's! it more than tears with that report.
Juliet
  That is no slander, sir, which is a truth;
  And what I spake, I spake it to my face.
Paris
  Thy face is mine, and thou hast slander'd it.   35
Juliet
  It may be so, for it is not mine own.
  Are you at leisure, holy father, now,
  Or shall I come to you at evening mass?
Friar Lawrence
  My leisure serves me, pensive daughter, now.
  My lord, we must entreat the time alone.   40
Paris
  God shield I should disturb devotion!

47. *compass* range.
48. *prorogue* delay.

54. *presently* immediately.
56–7. 'Before this hand will be ready to put the seal to another document.'
57. *deed* legal contract.

59. *both* that is, hand and heart.

64. *the commission of thy years and art* the authority you have as a result of your age and wisdom. We must imagine a long-pause between lines 65 and 66, during which Juliet stands, dagger in hand, whilst the Friar thinks what to do.
66–7. *I long to die ... remedy* 'I am more than willing to die, if you can suggest no way out of the difficulty.'

69–70. 'which requires a course of action as dangerous as the outcome we want to avoid.'

Juliet, on Thursday early will I rouse ye;
Till then, adieu, and keep this holy kiss.

[Exit.]

Juliet

O, shut the door, and when thou hast done so,
Come weep with me – past hope, past cure, past help. 45

Friar Lawrence

O, Juliet, I already know thy grief;
It strains me past the compass of my wits.
I hear thou must, and nothing may prorogue it,
On Thursday next be married to this County.

Juliet

Tell me not, friar, that thou hear'st of this, 50
Unless thou tell me how I may prevent it;
If, in thy wisdom, thou canst give no help,
Do thou but call my resolution wise,
And with this knife I'll help it presently.
God join'd my heart and Romeo's, thou our hands; 55
And ere this hand, by thee to Romeo's seal'd,
Shall be the label to another deed,
Or my true heart with treacherous revolt
Turn to another, this shall slay them both.
Therefore, out of thy long-experienc'd time, 60
Give me some present counsel; or, behold,
'Twixt my extremes and me this bloody knife
Shall play the umpire, arbitrating that
Which the commission of thy years and art
Could to no issue of true honour bring. 65
Be not so long to speak; I long to die,
If what thou speak'st speak not of remedy.

Friar Lawrence

Hold, daughter; I do spy a kind of hope,
Which craves as desperate an execution
As that is desperate which we would prevent. 70
If, rather than to marry County Paris,
Thou hast the strength of will to slay thyself,
Then is it likely thou wilt undertake

75. **That** (you) who.
76. **if thou dar'st** if you dare (to do this).

79. **thievish ways** streets full of thieves.

81. **charnel house** a store-house for human bones.

83. **reeky shanks** rotting legbones.
83. **chapless skulls** skulls from which the jawbones have fallen.

93. **vial** small bottle for liquids.

96. **humour** fluid.
97. **his native progress** its natural beat.
97. **surcease** stop.

100. **eyes' windows** eyelids.

102. **supple government** power of movement.

A thing like death to chide away this shame,
That cop'st with death himself to scape from it;   75
And, if thou dar'st, I'll give thee remedy.

Juliet

O, bid me leap, rather than marry Paris,
From off the battlements of any tower,
Or walk in thievish ways, or bid me lurk
Where serpents are; chain me with roaring bears,   80
Or hide me nightly in a charnel house,
O'er-cover'd quite with dead men's rattling bones,
With reeky shanks and yellow chapless skulls;
Or bid me go into a new-made grave,
And hide me with a dead man in his shroud –   85
Things that, to hear them told, have made me tremble
And I will do it without fear or doubt,
To live an unstain'd wife to my sweet love.

Friar Lawrence

Hold, then; go home, be merry, give consent
To marry Paris. Wednesday is to-morrow;   90
Tomorrow night look that thou lie alone,
Let not the nurse lie with thee in thy chamber.
Take thou this vial, being then in bed,
And this distilled liquor drink thou off;
When presently through all thy veins shall run   95
A cold and drowsy humour; for no pulse
Shall keep his native progress, but surcease;
No warmth, no breath, shall testify thou livest;
The roses in thy lips and cheeks shall fade
To paly ashes, thy eyes' windows fall,   100
Like death when he shuts up the day of life;
Each part, depriv'd of supple government,
Shall, stiff and stark and cold, appear like death;
And in this borrow'd likeness of shrunk death
Thou shalt continue two and forty hours,   105
And then awake as from a pleasant sleep.
Now, when the bridegroom in the morning comes
To rouse thee from thy bed, there art thou dead.
Then, as the manner of our country is,

110. *bier* the stand on which a coffin, or dead body, is carried or placed.
111. *ancient vault* old burial chamber.
113. *against thou shall awake* in preparation for the time when you will awake.
114. *drift* plan.

119. *inconstant toy* frivolous change of mind.
120. *abate thy valour* lessen your courage.

In thy best robes, uncovered on the bier,   110
Thou shalt be borne to that same ancient vault
Where all the kindred of the Capulets lie.
In the meantime, against thou shalt awake,
Shall Romeo by my letters know our drift,
And hither shall he come; and he and I   115
Will watch thy waking, and that very night
Shall Romeo bear thee hence to Mantua.
And this shall free thee from this present shame,
If no inconstant toy nor womanish fear
Abate thy valour in the acting it.   120

Juliet
Give me, give me! O, tell not me of fear!

Friar Lawrence
Hold; get you gone, be strong and prosperous
In this resolve. I'll send a friar with speed
To Mantua, with my letters to thy lord.

Juliet
Love give me strength! and strength shall help
    afford.   125
Farewell, dear father!

[Exeunt.]

SCENE II

2. *cunning* skilful.

3–9. The Servingman is making fun with the proverb that says that it is a poor cook that will not **lick his own fingers,** that is, taste his own food.

10. 'We haven't enough provisions in stock for an occasion like this.'

12. *Ay, forsooth* Yes, indeed she has.

14. *peevish* irritable *harlotry* an insulting term for a girl – 'silly creature.'

15. *shrift* confession.

Scene II

Capulet's house

*[Enter CAPULET, LADY CAPULET, nurse, and
two or three SERVINGMEN.]*

Capulet
So many guests invite as here are writ.

[Exit a SERVINGMAN.]

Sirrah, go hire me twenty cunning cooks.
Servingman
You shall have none ill, sir; for I'll try if they can lick
their fingers.
Capulet
How canst thou try them so?   5
Servingman
Marry, sir, 'tis an ill cook that cannot lick his own
fingers; therefore he that cannot lick his fingers goes
not with me.
Capulet
Go, be gone.

[Exit SECOND SERVINGMAN.]

We shall be much unfurnished for this time.   10
What, is my daughter gone to Friar Lawrence?
Nurse
Ay, forsooth.
Capulet
Well, he may chance to do some good on her:
A peevish self-will'd harlotry it is.

[Enter JULIET.]

Nurse
See where she comes from shrift with merry look.   15

16. *gadding* spending aimless time.

19. *behests* commands.
20. *fall prostrate* cast down in submission.

24. *knot knit up* marriage completed.

26. *becoined* suitable.

28. *stand up* Juliet has evidently knelt dutifully to her father.

31–2. Characteristically, as soon as the Friar has taken a course of action which Capulet supposes is convenient to him (Capulet), he is full of the old man's praises. The audience will recognise the irony in what he says.

36, 38–9. It should be noted that Capulet has brought the marriage forward a day and that Lady Capulet is protesting that this will not give them sufficient time for preparations.

Capulet

How now, my headstrong! Where have you been
  gadding?

Juliet

Where I have learnt me to repent the sin
Of disobedient opposition
To you and your behests; and am enjoin'd
By holy Lawrence to fall prostrate here,   20
To beg your pardon. Pardon, I beseech you.
Henceforward I am ever rul'd by you.

Capulet

Send for the County; go tell him of this.
I'll have this knot knit up to-morrow morning.

Juliet

I met the youthful lord at Lawrence' cell,   25
And gave him what becoined love I might,
Not stepping o'er the bounds of modesty.

Capulet

Why, I am glad on't; this is well – stand up –
This is as't should be. Let me see the County;
Ay, marry, go, I say, and fetch him hither.   30
Now, afore God, this reverend holy friar,
All our whole city is much bound to him.

Juliet

Nurse, will you go with me into my closet
To help me sort such needful ornaments
As you think fit to furnish me to-morrow?   35

Lady Capulet

No, not till Thursday; there is time enough.

Capulet

Go, nurse, go with her. We'll to church to-morrow.

[Exeunt JULIET and NURSE.]

Lady Capulet

We shall be short in our provision;
'tis now near night.

Capulet

                    Tush, I will stir about,

43. *I'll play the huswife for this once* Capulet declares that he will see to the business of getting in provisions himself; now that he has got his own way, he is all good humour.

44. *They are all forth* Capulet has called for servants, *(What ho!)*, but apparently they are all out on errands.

47. 'Since this disobedient girl has been saved.'

And all things shall be well, I warrant thee, wife.   40
Go thou to Juliet, help to deck up her;
I'll not to bed to-night; let me alone.
I'll play the huswife for this once. What, ho!
They are all forth; well, I will walk myself
To County Paris, to prepare up him   45
Against to-morrow. My heart is wondrous light
Since this same wayward girl is so reclaim'd.

[Exeunt.]

SCENE III

1. *attires* outfits.

3. *orisons* prayers.
4. *state* spiritual condition.
5. *cross* perverse. Juliet is pretending to confess that her obstinacy to her parents is sinful.

7. *cull'd* collected.
8. *As are behoveful* as are needed.
state ceremonies, i.e. the wedding.

14–23. Juliet is about to take the Friar's potion, which will send her into a deep sleep; she expects that she will then be taken from the tomb by Romeo and not see her parents again. Her speech is full of anxiety and uncertainty – at one point she almost calls the Nurse back, and then is concerned that the potion might not work. The first part of the speech contains three questions, all to herself, but by the time she lays down her dagger she seems resolved. However, new worries soon come into her head.
15. *faint cold fear* a terror that makes Juliet feel faint and uneasy.
23. *this* the dagger. What does Juliet mean by *'This shall forbid it'*?

Scene III

Juliet's chamber

[Enter JULIET and NURSE.]

Juliet

    Ay, those attires are best; but, gentle nurse,
    I pray thee, leave me to myself to-night,
    For I have need of many orisons
    To move the heavens to smile upon my state,
    Which well thou know'st is cross and full of sin.   5

[Enter LADY CAPULET.]

Lady Capulet

    What, are you busy, ho? Need you my help?

Juliet

    No, madam; we have cull'd such necessaries
    As are behoveful for our state to-morrow.
    So please you, let me now be left alone,
    And let the nurse this night sit up with you;   10
    For I am sure you have your hands full all
    In this so sudden business.

Lady Capulet

                Good night.
    Get thee to bed, and rest; for thou hast need.

[Exeunt LADY CAPULET and NURSE.]

Juliet

    Farewell! God knows when we shall meet again.
    I have a faint cold fear thrills through my veins,   15
    That almost freezes up the heat of life;
    I'll call them back again to comfort me.
    Nurse! – What should she do here?
    My dismal scene I needs must act alone.
    Come, vial.   20
    What if this mixture do not work at all?
    Shall I be married, then, to-morrow morning?
    No, no; this shall forbid it. Lie thou there.

24–58 The whole speech is a very convincing picture of Juliet's midnight terror. This main part of it, rather than calming Juliet, actually works her up into a state of near madness. In it, she wonders if the Friar has deliberately poisoned her to cover up his part in the marriage, and even when she has rejected that possibility in her mind, she then wonders if she'll be choked ('stifled') by the foul air of the burial tomb. This leads her to wondering whether, even if she should survive the vault's ghastly air, she'll be driven mad by being surrounded by dead bodies, including her own cousin, Tybalt. In this distracted, almost hysterical state, believing she can see Tybalt's ghost coming for Romeo, she swallows the liquid in order to escape the vision of her dead cousin.

29. *'He has always proved a holy man.'*

37. *conceit* thought.

38. Juliet's terror is reflected in the way the sentence breaks up.

42. *green in earth* only recently buried.

47. *mandrakes* the mandrake is a poisonous plant which, because it has a forked root, is thought to resemble the human body: it was fabled to shriek when pulled out of the earth. However, Juliet is presumably imagining these shrieks to be uttered by the spirits.

49. *distraught* driven mad.

50. *Environed* surrounded.

57. *Stay, Tybalt, stay* Juliet rises from her bed and holds out her hands to ward off this apparition.

[Laying down her dagger.]

What if it be a poison which the friar
Subtly hath minister'd to have me dead,   25
Lest in this marriage he should be dishonoured,
Because he married me before to Romeo?
I fear it is; and yet methinks it should not,
For he hath still been tried a holy man.
How, if, when I am laid into the tomb,   30
I wake before the time that Romeo
Come to redeem me? There's a fearful point.
Shall I not then be stifled in the vault,
To whose foul mouth no healthsome air breathes in
And there die strangled ere my Romeo comes?   35
Or, if I live, is it not very like
The horrible conceit of death and night,
Together with the terror of the place –
As in a vault, an ancient receptacle
Where for this many hundred years the bones   40
Of all my buried ancestors are pack'd;
Where bloody Tybalt, yet but green in earth,
Lies fest'ring in his shroud; where, as they say,
At some hours in the night spirits resort –
Alack, alack, is it not like that I,   45
So early waking – what with loathsome smells,
And shrieks like mandrakes' torn out of the earth,
That living mortals, hearing them, run mad –
O, if I wake, shall I not be distraught,
Environed with all these hideous fears,   50
And madly play with my forefathers' joints,
And pluck the mangled Tybalt from his shroud,
And, in this rage, with some great kinsman's bone,
As with a club, dash out my desp'rate brains?
O, look! methinks I see my cousin's ghost   55
Seeking out Romeo, that did spit his body
Upon a rapier's point. Stay, Tybalt, stay.
Romeo, I come. This do I drink to thee.

[She drinks and falls upon her bed within the curtains.]

SCENE IV

The action is continuous; no sooner has Juliet fallen on her bed within the curtains, than Lady Capulet reappears on the lower stage, bustling about the wedding preparations. Evidently, the household has been up all night.

2. *the pastry* the part of the kitchen where pastries were made.

4. *The curfew bell*. This can certainly not carry its normal meaning of an evening bell, in this context; perhaps it was a bell rung in the morning to show that the period of curfew (during which household fires had to be put out) was over.

5. *good Angelica* so that is what the Nurse is called!

6. *cot-quean* a man who does woman's work. This is a notable example of the Nurse's frankness, and it shows how much freedom she is given within the house.

8. *watching* staying up all night.

9. *not a whit* not at all.

11. *a mouse-hunt* one who chases after women, particularly at night.

12. 'I'll see you don't get up to any of those games now.'

13. 'You're jealous, that's what it is.' This cheerful exchange is in contrast to his behaviour to the women earlier on.

Scene IV

Capulet's house

[Enter LADY CAPULET and NURSE.]

Lady Capulet
    Hold, take these keys, and fetch more spices, nurse.
Nurse
    They call for dates and quinces in the pastry.

[Enter CAPULET.]

Capulet
    Come, stir, stir, stir! The second cock hath crow'd,
    The curfew bell hath rung, 'tis three o'clock.
    Look to the bak'd meats, good Angelica;   5
    Spare not for cost.
Nurse
                    Go, you cot-quean, go,
    Get you to bed; faith, you'll be sick to-morrow
    For this night's watching.
Capulet
    No, not a whit; what! I have watch'd ere now
    All night for lesser cause, and ne'er been sick.   10
Lady Capulet
    Ay, you have been a mouse-hunt in your time;
    But I will watch you from such watching now.

[Exeunt LADY CAPULET and NURSE.]

Capulet
    A jealous-hood, a jealous-hood!

*[Enter three or four SERVINGMEN with spits and logs
                    and baskets.]*

                            Now, fellow,
    What is there?
First Fellow
    Things for the cook, sir; but I know not what.   15

18–19. *I have a head, sir ... matter.* The servingman explains that he has enough commonsense to find logs without Peter's help.

20. *a merry whoreson, ha!* Capulet's modem counterpart might say, 'He's a cheerful bastard!'

21. *Thou shall be logger-head* Capulet puns on this remark, quipping that he has a wooden-head or blockhead.

Capulet

Make haste, make haste. *[Exit* FIRST FELLOW.*]*

              Sirrah, fetch drier logs;

Call Peter; he will show thee where they are.

Second Fellow

I have a head, sir, that will find out logs,

And never trouble Peter for the matter.

Capulet

Mass, and well said; a merry whoreson, ha!   20

Thou shall be logger-head. *[Exit* SECOND FELLOW.*]*

             Good faith, 'tis day;

The County will be here with music straight,

For so he said he would. *[Play music]* I hear him near.

Nurse! Wife! What, ho! What, nurse, I say!

[Re-enter NURSE.*]*

Go waken Juliet, go and trim her up;   25

I'll go and chat with Paris. Hie, make haste,

Make haste. The bridegroom he is come already

Make haste, I say.

[Exeunt.]

SCENE V

4–5. *You take your pennyworths now. Sleep for a week* 'You get some sound sleep now (because you'll get very little when Paris is with you).'
6. *hath set up his rest* an image from jousting; to have a lance at rest is to have it in readiness; of course, there are sexual overtones related to a man's 'lance'.

14–64. This very long-winded expression of grief in formal verse is perhaps the most unconvincing part of the play for a modern audience, but works better on the stage than on the page. The most moving words are those spoken by Capulet towards the end, when his metaphor about the 'untimely frost' cuts through his wife and the Nurse's hysterical cries.

Scene V

Juliet's chamber

[Enter NURSE.]

Nurse

Mistress! What, mistress! Juliet! Fast, I warrant her, she.
Why, lamb! Why, lady! Fie, you slug-a-bed!
Why, love, I say! madam! sweetheart! Why, bride!
What, not a word? You take your pennyworths now.
Sleep for a week; for the next night, I warrant,   5
The County Paris hath set up his rest
That you shall rest but little. God forgive me!
Marry, and amen. How sound is she asleep!
I needs must wake her. Madam, madam, madam!
Ay, let the County take you in your bed;   10
He'll night you up, i' faith. Will it not be?

[Draws the curtains.]

What, dress'd, and in your clothes, and down again!
I must needs wake you. Lady! lady! lady!
Alas, alas! Help, help! my lady's dead!
O well-a-day that ever I was born!   15
Some aqua-vita, ho! My lord! My lady!

[Enter LADY CAPULET.]

Lady Capulet

What noise is here?

Nurse

               O lamentable day!

Lady Capulet

What is the matter?

Nurse

             Look, look! O heavy day!

Lady Capulet

O me, O me! My child, my only life,
Revive, look up, or I will die with thee!   20

35–7. The idea of Death as a young girl's lover is a very widespread one in folk-tales and in art.

Help, help! Call help.

[Enter CAPULET.]

Capulet
  For shame, bring Juliet forth; her lord is come.
Nurse
  She's dead, deceas'd, she's dead; alack the day!
Lady Capulet
  Alack the day, she's dead, she's dead, she's dead!
Capulet
  Ha! let me see her. Out, alas! she's cold;   25
  Her blood is settled, and her joints are stiff.
  Life and these lips have long been separated.
  Death lies on her like an untimely frost
  Upon the sweetest flower of all the field.
Nurse
  O lamentable day!
Lady Capulet
                    O woeful time!   30
Capulet
  Death, that hath ta'en her hence to make me wail,
  Ties up my tongue and will not let me speak.

*[Enter FRIAR LAWRENCE and COUNTY PARIS, with
        MUSICIANS.]*

Friar Lawrence
  Come, is the bride ready to go to church?
Capulet
  Ready to go, but never to return.
  O son, the night before thy wedding day   35
  Hath Death lain with thy wife. There she lies,
  Flower as she was, deflowered by him.
  Death is my son-in-law. Death is my heir;
  My daughter he hath wedded; I will die,
  And leave him all; life, living, all is Death's.   40
Paris
  Have I thought long to see this morning's face,
  And doth it give me such a sight as this?

44–5. 'This is the most miserable hour that time, in its eternal progress onward, has ever revealed.'

47. *solace* take comfort.

55. *beguil'd* tricked, cheated.

70. Juliet's soul is in heaven (*his* = Death's).
71. *promotion* her social advancement (by a good marriage).

Lady Capulet
    Accurs'd, unhappy, wretched, hateful day!
    Most miserable hour that e'er time saw
    In lasting labour of his pilgrimage!   45
    But one, poor one, one poor and loving child,
    But one thing to rejoice and solace in,
    And cruel Death hath catch'd it from my sight!

Nurse
    O woe! O woeful, woeful, woeful day!
    Most lamentable day, most woeful day   50
    That ever, ever, I did yet behold!
    O day! O day! O day! O hateful day!
    Never was seen so black a day as this.
    O woeful day, O woeful day!

Paris
    Beguil'd, divorced, wronged, spited, slain!   55
    Most detestable Death, by thee beguil'd,
    By cruel cruel thee quite overthrown!
    O love! O life! – not life, but love in death!

Capulet
    Despis'd, distressed, hated, martyr'd, kill'd! –
    Uncomfortable time, why cam'st thou now   60
    To murder, murder our solemnity?
    O child! O child! my soul, and not my child!
    Dead art thou; alack, my child is dead,
    And with my child my joys are buried.

Friar Lawrence
    Peace, ho, for shame! Confusion's cure lives not   65
    In these confusions. Heaven and yourself
    Had part in this fair maid; now heaven hath all,
    And all the better is it for the maid.
    Your part in her you could not keep from death,
    But heaven keeps his part in eternal life.   70
    The most you sought was her promotion,
    For 'twas your heaven she should be advanc'd;
    And weep ye now, seeing she is advanc'd
    Above the clouds, as high as heaven itself?
    O, in this love, you love your child so ill   75

80–1. This, of course, is an essential part of the Friar's plan.

82–3. 'Our foolish human nature makes us grieve for her death, although reason laughs at our laments, knowing the absurdity of tears when she has gone to heaven.'

84–90. This speech, in contrast to the previous lamentations, is quite moving. There is here a control of expression and emotion and it is touching that the celebrations, which we have seen in preparation, must now be changed for the funeral.

88. *sullen dirges* gloomy funeral song.
89. *corse* corpse, body.

94. *lour upon you for some ill* 'frown upon you for some offence you have committed.'
95. What do you think of the Friar's deceit and his moralizing message here? Do you approve?

99. *the case may be amended* a pun. In the previous line the word means 'a state of affairs'; here the Musician presumably means a cover for his instrument.

That you run mad, seeing that she is well
She's not well married that lives married long,
But she's best married that dies married young.
Dry up your tears, and stick your rosemary
On this fair corse, and, as the custom is,   80
In all her best array bear her to church;
For though fond nature bids us all lament,
Yet nature's tears are reason's merriment.

Capulet

All things that we ordained festival
Turn from their office to black funeral: 85
Our instruments to melancholy bells,
Our wedding cheer to a sad burial feast,
Our solemn hymns to sullen dirges change;
Our bridal flowers serve for a buried corse;
And all things change them to the contrary.   90

Friar Lawrence

Sir, go you in; and, madam, go with him;
And go. Sir Paris. Every one prepare
To follow this fair corse unto her grave.
The heavens do lour upon you for some ill;
Move them no more by crossing their high will.   95

[Exeunt all but NURSE *and* MUSICIANS.*]*

First Musician

Faith, we may put up our pipes and be gone.

Nurse

Honest good fellows, ah, put up, put up;
For well you know this is a pitiful case.

[Exit.]

First Musician

Ay, by my troth, the case may be amended.

[Enter PETER.*]*

Peter

Musicians, O, musicians, 'Heart's ease,' 'Heart's ease'   100

104. *dump* mournful melody.

111. *gleek* a mocking comment.
111–12. *give you the minstrel* 'call you a minstrel.' Minstrel was a term of abuse: see Act III, Scene I, line 44.

115. *carry* put up with.
115. *crotchets* (1) in music the name of a note of a particular length, (2) insults.
117. *you note us* another pun. Peter used the word to mean 'understand' ; the Musician means 'set us to music'.
118. *put up* put away. *put out* display.
119. *dry-beat* beat soundly.

122–4. The words of a well-known song of the time.

O, an you will have me live, play 'Heart's ease'.

First Musician

Why 'Heart's ease'?

Peter

O, musicians, because my heart itself plays 'My heart is full of woe'. O, play me some merry dump to comfort me.   105

First Musician

Not a dump we! Tis no time to play now.

Peter

You will not, then?

First Musician

No.

Peter

I will then give it you soundly.

First Musician

What will you give us?   110

Peter

No money, on my faith, but the gleek. I will give you the minstrel.

First Musician

Then will I give you the serving-creature.

Peter

Then will I lay the serving-creature's dagger on your pate. I will carry no crotchets: I'll re you, I'll fa you; 115 do you note me?

First Musician

An you re us and fa us, you note us.

Second Musician

Pray you put up your dagger, and put out your wit.

Peter

Then have at you with my wit! I will dry-beat you with an iron wit, and put up my iron dagger. Answer me 120 like men.

> 'When griping grief the heart doth wound
> And doleful dumps the mind oppress,
> Then music with her silver sound' –

129. *sound for silver* i.e. play for money.

132. *I cry you mercy* I beg your pardon.

137. *pestilent* plague-ridden, diseased.

Why 'silver sound'? Why 'music with her silver sound'? 125
What say you, Simon Catling?

First Musician

Marry, sir, because silver hath a sweet sound.

Peter

Pretty! What say you, Hugh Rebeck?

Second Musician

I say 'silver sound' because musicians sound for silver.

Peter

Pretty too! What say you, James Soundpost? 130

Third Musician

Faith, I know not what to say.

Peter

O, I cry you mercy, you are the singer; I will say for
you. It is 'music with her silver sound' because musicians have no gold for sounding.

'Then music with her silver sound 135
With speedy help doth lend redress.'

[Exit.]

First Musician

What a pestilent knave is this same!

Second Musician

Hang him. Jack! Come, we'll in here; tarry for the
mourners, and stay dinner.

[Exeunt.]

ACT V SCENE I

1–2. Previously Romeo has had premonitions of doom, but now, as the lovers' deaths draw close, ironically he is having joyous dreams.
2. *presage* forecast.
3. *bosom's lord* i.e. his heart.

10–11. Romeo is saying that if his dreams of Juliet are so delightful, how much more wonderful it will be to be actually with her.

12–15. Romeo's stream of questions indicates his eagerness for news.

17. Balthasar's reply, echoing Romeo's words, is at first ambiguous; he considers that she is *well* because, although dead, her soul is in heaven. He puts it like this to break the shock of the news.

21. *took post* hired a horse.
24. There is a pause before Romeo speaks, as he gathers the full horror of Balthasar's message.
24. *Then I defy you, stars* Romeo, in an outburst of passion, violently defies fate and the influence of the stars, which are trying to separate him from Juliet.

ACT FIVE
Scene I

Mantua. A street

[Enter ROMEO.]

Romeo

    If I may trust the flattering truth of sleep,
    My dreams presage some joyful news at hand.
    My bosom's lord sits lightly in his throne,
    And all this day an unaccustom'd spirit
    Lifts me above the ground with cheerful thoughts.   5
    I dreamt my lady came and found me dead –
    Strange dream, that gives a dead man leave to think
    And breath'd such life with kisses in my lips
    That I reviv'd, and was an emperor.
    Ah me! how sweet is love itself possess'd,   10
    When but love's shadows are so rich in joy!

[Enter BALTHASAR, Romeo's man.]

    News from Verona! How now, Balthasar!
    Dost thou not bring me letters from the friar?
    How doth my lady? Is my father well?
    How fares my Juliet? That I ask again,   15
    For nothing can be ill if she be well.

Balthasar

    Then she is well, and nothing can be ill.
    Her body sleeps in Capels' monument,
    And her immortal part with angels lives.
    I saw her laid low in her kindred's vault,   20
    And presently took post to tell it you.
    O, pardon me for bringing these ill news,
    Since you did leave it for my office, sir.

Romeo

    Is it e'en so? Then I defy you, stars.
    Thou knowest my lodging: get me fade and paper,   25

27–9. The wildness of Romeo's manner makes Balthasar fear that he will do something foolish.

34. *I will lie with thee to-night*. He will at least lie with her in death, he says with bitter irony.

37. *an apothecary* someone who prepared medicines.
38. *which* whom.
38–52. Romeo's description of the apothecary and his shop sets a suitable nightmarish atmosphere for the final stages of the story.
39. *weeds* clothes.
39. *overwhelming* overhanging.
40. *Culling of simples* gathering herbs.
40. *Meagre* gaunt.

45. *account* collection.

47. *Pack-thread* twine or string used for tying up packages

47. old cakes of roses compressed rose petals which were used for perfume.

49. *penury* poverty
51. *present* immediate. The sale of poisons was a capital offence in Mantua.
52. *caitiff* miserable.

And hire post-horses; I will hence to-night,
Balthasar
    I do beseech you, sir, have patience;
    Your looks are pale and wild, and do import
    Some misadventure.
Romeo
               Tush, thou art deceiv'd;
    Leave me, and do the thing I bid thee do.   30
    Hast thou no letters to me from the friar?
Balthasar
    No, my good lord.
Romeo
            No matter; get thee gone,
    And hire those horses; I'll be with thee straight,

[Exit BALTHASAR.*]*

    Well, Juliet, I will lie with thee to-night.
    Let's see for means. O mischief, thou art swift   35
    To enter in the thoughts of desperate men!
    I do remember an apothecary,
    And hereabouts 'a dwells, which late I noted
    In tatter'd weeds, with overwhelming brows,
    Culling of simples. Meagre were his looks;   40
    Sharp misery had worn him to the bones;
    And in his needy shop a tortoise hung,
    An alligator stuff'd, and other skins
    Of ill-shap'd fishes; and about his shelves
    A beggarly account of empty boxes,   45
    Green earthen pots, bladders, and musty seeds,
    Remnants of packthread, and old cakes of roses,
    Were thinly scatter'd, to make up a show.
    Noting this penury, to myself I said
    'An if a man did need a poison now,   50
    Whose sale is present death in Mantua,
    Here lives a caitiff wretch would sell it him.'
    O, this same thought did but forerun my need;
    And this same needy man must sell it me.
    As I remember, this should be the house   55

63–5. This image is meant to suggest very sudden death: 'That life may leave my body as suddenly as the shot from a cannon.'

67. *utters* sells.

69–71. Romeo says that the apothecary's physical condition bears witness to his poverty and distress.

75. 'Because of my poverty, I am forced against my will to agree.' It is unlikely that the apothecary carries poison on him, so presumably he goes back into his shop to get it.

80–85. Romeo is saying that gold/money being the root of evil is poison that he gives to the apothecary, but that what he has received in return is not poison, but will bring comfort.

Being holiday, the beggar's shop is shut.
What, ho! Apothecary!

[Enter APOTHECARY.]

Apothecary
                    Who calls so loud?
Romeo
  Come hither, man. I see that thou art poor.
  Hold, there is forty ducats; let me have
  A dram of poison, such soon-speeding gear   60
  As will disperse itself through all the veins
  That the life-weary taker may fall dead,
  And that the trunk may be discharg'd of breath
  As violently as hasty powder fir'd
  Doth hurry from the fatal cannon's womb.   65
Apothecary
  Such mortal drugs I have; but Mantua's law
  Is death to any he that utters them.
Romeo
  Art thou so bare and full of wretchedness
  And fear'st to die? Famine is in thy cheeks,
  Need and oppression starveth in thy eyes,   70
  Contempt and beggary hangs upon thy back,
  The world is not thy friend, nor the world's law;
  The world affords no law to make thee rich;
  Then be not poor, but break it and take this.
Apothecary
  My poverty but not my will consents.   75
Romeo
  I pay thy poverty and not thy will.
Apothecary
  Put this in any liquid thing you will
  And drink it off; and if you had the strength
  Of twenty men, it would dispatch you straight.
Romeo
  There is thy gold – worse poison to men's souls,   80
  Doing more murder in this loathsome world
  Than these poor compounds that thou mayst not sell.

85. *cordial* a comforting drink. It is comforting to Romeo because it will bring him the death he longs for.

I sell thee poison: thou hast sold me none.
Farewell; buy food, and get thyself in flesh.
Come, cordial and not poison, go with me   85
To Juliet's grave; for there must I use thee.

[Exeunt.]

SCENE II

5–12. In his agitation. Friar John gives a very confusing account of what has happened. It appears that he had gone to look for another Franciscan friar to go with him on his visit to Mantua. He eventually found the man he was looking for visiting the sick in a house which was suspected of harbouring the plague; the health authorities, as the custom was at that time, would not allow them to leave the house for fear of their spreading the infection.

6. *to associate me* to accompany me.

18. *nice* trivial.

18–19. *full of charge Of dear import* full of important news. The letter is, of course, the one informing Romeo of Juliet's fake death and instructing him to come to Verona to collect her when she awakens.

21. *iron crow* crowbar.

Scene II

Friar Lawrence's cell

[Enter FRIAR JOHN.*]*

Friar John
Holy Franciscan friar! Brother, ho!

[Enter FRIAR LAWRENCE.*]*

Friar Lawrence
This same should be the voice of Friar John.
Welcome from Mantua! What says Romeo?
Or, if his mind be writ, give me his letter.

Friar John
Going to find a barefoot brother out,   5
One of our order, to associate me,
Here in this city visiting the sick,
And finding him, the searchers of the town,
Suspecting that we both were in a house
Where the Infectious pestilence did reign,   10
Seal'd up the doors, and would not let us forth,
So that my speed to Mantua there was stay'd.

Friar Lawrence
Who bare my letter, then, to Romeo?

Friar John
I could not send it – here it is again –
Nor get a messenger to bring it thee,   15
So fearful were they of infection.

Friar Lawrence
Unhappy fortune! By my brotherhood,
The letter was not nice, but full of charge
Of dear import; and the neglecting it
May do much danger. Friar John, go hence;   20
Get me an iron crow, and bring it straight
Unto my cell.

Friar John
Brother, I'll go and bring it thee.

26. *beshrew* greatly blame.
27. *accidents* occurrences, mischances.

[Exit.]

FRIAR LAWRENCE
    Now must I to the monument alone.
    Within this three hours will fair Juliet wake;   25
    She will beshrew me much that Romeo
    Hath had no notice of these accidents.
    But I will write again to Mantua,
    And keep her at my cell till Romeo come –
    Poor living corse, clos'd in a dead man's tomb!   30

[Exit.]

SCENE III

Paris has come to lay flowers at Juliet's tomb and to watch over it during the night.

1–9. It is not clear why Paris is so anxious not to be seen.

12. *thy bridal bed* this would have been the first night after their wedding.
12. *Strew* scatter.
13. *canopy* an Elizabethan bed had a covering high over it, supported by posts at the corners. Since Juliet's ***bridal bed*** is in fact a tomb, she is covered over by the stone roof of the tomb.
14. He intends to sprinkle water on the tomb.
16. *obsequies* the ceremony of mourning.

20. *To cross* to hinder, prevent.

Stage direction ***mattock*** a type of pick, used for loosening soil.

Scene III

_____

Verona. A churchyard; in it the tomb of the Capulets

[Enter PARIS, and his PAGE bearing flowers and a torch.]

Paris

    Give me thy torch, boy; hence, and stand aloof;
    Yet put it out, for I would not be seen.
    Under yond yew trees lay thee all along,
    Holding thy ear close to the hollow ground;
    So shall no foot upon the churchyard tread –   5
    Being loose, unfirm, with digging up of graves –
    But thou shalt hear it. Whistle then to me,
    As signal that thou hear'st something approach.
    Give me those flowers. Do as I bid thee, go.

Page *[Aside]*

    I am almost afraid to stand alone   10
    Here in the churchyard; yet I will adventure.

[Retires.]

Paris

    Sweet flower, with flowers thy bridal bed I strew –
    O woe, thy canopy is dust and stones! –
    Which with sweet water nightly I will dew;
    Or, wanting that, with tears distill'd by moans.   15
    The obsequies that I for thee will keep,
    Nightly shall be to strew thy grave and weep.

[The PAGE whistles.]

    The boy gives warning something doth approach.
    What cursed foot wanders this way to-night
    To cross my obsequies and true love's rite?   20
    What, with a torch! Muffle me, night, awhile.

[Retires.]

*[Enter ROMEO and BALTHASAR, with a torch,
a mattock, and a crow of iron.]*

32. *dear employment* important business.
33. *jealous* suspicious.

37. *intents* intentions.
38. *inexorable* relentless.

43–4. Balthasar is a loyal servant and, fearing Romeo's intentions, he resolves to stay hidden.
45. *maw* stomach.
46. *the dearest morsel of the earth* is, of course, Juliet.

48. *in despite* to spite you. The tomb, already gorged with Juliet's body, is to receive his corpse also, whether it wants it or not.

Romeo

Give me that mattock and the wrenching iron.
Hold, take this letter; early in the morning
See thou deliver it to my lord and father.
Give me the light; upon thy life I charge thee,   25
Whate'er thou hear'st or seest, stand all aloof
And do not interrupt me in my course.
Why I descend into this bed of death
Is partly to behold my lady's face,
But chiefly to take thence from her dead finger   30
A precious ring – a ring that I must use
In dear employment; therefore hence, be gone.
But if thou, jealous, dost return to pry
In what I farther shall intend to do,
By heaven, I will tear thee joint by joint,   35
And strew this hungry churchyard with thy limbs.
The time and my intents are savage-wild,
More fierce and more inexorable far
Than empty tigers or the roaring sea.

Balthasar

I will be gone, sir, and not trouble ye.   40

Romeo

So shalt thou show me friendship. Take thou that;
Live and be prosperous; and farewell, good fellow.

Balthasar [Aside]

For all this same, I'll hide me hereabout;
His looks I fear, and his intents I doubt. *[Retires]*

Romeo

Thou detestable maw, thou womb of death,   45
Gorg'd with the dearest morsel of the earth,
Thus I enforce thy rotten jaws to open,
Breaking open the tomb
And, in despite, I'll cram thee with more food.

Paris

This is that banish'd haughty Montague
That murder'd my love's cousin – with which grief   50
It is supposed the fair creature died –
And here is come to do some villainous shame

53. *apprehend* arrest.
54. *unhallow'd toil* unholy work.

58–67. Romeo speaks gently to Paris for, meaning to kill himself shortly, he has no wish to quarrel. He also speaks as though very much the senior man *(gentle youth ... youth)*.

68. *conjuration* There is some doubt as to what Shakespeare actually wrote here – the meaning presumably is that Paris is not going to be talked round. Perhaps he means he won't be 'conjured' by his words into doing what he's told.
69. *felon* criminal.

To the dead bodies. I will apprehend him.
Stop thy unhallow'd toil, vile Montague.
Can vengeance be pursued further than death?   55
Condemned villain, I do apprehend thee.
Obey, and go with me; for thou must die.

Romeo

I must indeed; and therefore came I hither.
Good gentle youth, tempt not a desp'rate man;
Fly hence, and leave me. Think upon these gone;   60
Let them affright thee. I beseech thee, youth,
Put not another sin upon my head
By urging me to fury; O, be gone!
By heaven, I love thee better than myself,
For I come hither arm'd against myself.   65
Stay not, be gone; live, and hereafter say
A madman's mercy bid thee run away.

Paris

I do defy thy conjuration,
And apprehend thee for a felon here.

Romeo

Wilt thou provoke me? Then have at thee, boy!   70

[They fight.]

Page

O lord, they fight! I will go call the watch.

[Exit. PARIS *falls.]*

Paris

O, I am slain! If thou be merciful,
Open the tomb, lay me with Juliet. *[Dies]*

Romeo

In faith, I will. Let me peruse this face.
Mercutio's kinsman, noble County Paris!   75
What said my man, when my betossed soul
Did not attend him as we rode? I think
He told me Paris should have married Juliet.
Said he not so, or did I dream it so?

82. There is no sense of rivalry here; Romeo feels that Paris and he have both been caught up in a web of fate, both part of 'sour misfortune's book'

84. *A lantern* a room with a dome or other construction at the top, through which light can pass. Romeo is saying that Juliet's body is a source of light which turns the grave into a *lantern,* in this sense.

86. *a feasting presence* a presence chamber prepared for a feast. A presence chamber is a palace-room in which a king or queen receives guests.

87. *Death* Paris.

87. *a dead man* Romeo – he is about to kill himself. *interr'd* buried

88–120. This is a wonderful speech which must be read aloud to catch the rhythms and cadences, which are so expressive in Romeo's lingering farewell to his apparently dead wife and his resignation to the fate that has shadowed him throughout the play.

90. *lightning* we should spell the word 'lightening' today. It means an interval of light-heartedness.

91. Romeo gazes at his wife who lies seemingly dead in her wedding dress.

94. *ensign* banner. Juliet's face still has the fresh colour of a living person, not the paleness of the dead. The image is of a battle between Beauty and Death.

100. *sunder* break.

102–5. Wondering at Juliet's beauty, Romeo plays with the idea that Death has fallen in love ('is amorous') with her body and is preserving it from decay, in order that he may remain her lover.

105. *paramour* mistress.

111. *the yoke of inauspicious stars* 'the controlling influence of an unhappy fate.'

115. *A dateless bargain* an eternal agreement. *engrossing* all-consuming.

Or am I mad, hearing him talk of Juliet, 80
To think it was so? O, give me thy hand,
One writ with me in sour misfortune's book!
I'll bury thee in a triumphant grave.
A grave? O no! A lantern, slaughter'd youth;
For here lies Juliet, and her beauty makes 85
This vault a feasting presence full of light.
Death, lie thou there, by a dead man interr'd.

[Laying PARIS *in the tomb.]*

How oft when men are at the point of death
Have they been merry! Which their keepers call
A lightning before death. O, how may I 90
Call this a lightning? O my love! my wife!
Death, that hath suck'd the honey of thy breath,
Hath had no power yet upon thy beauty.
Thou art not conquer'd; beauty's ensign yet
Is crimson in thy lips and in thy cheeks, 95
And death's pale flag is not advanced there.
Tybalt, liest thou there in thy bloody sheet?
O, what more favour can I do to thee
Than with that hand that cut thy youth in twain
To sunder his that was thine enemy? 100
Forgive me, cousin. Ah, dear Juliet,
Why art thou yet so fair? Shall I believe
That unsubstantial Death is amorous,
And that the lean abhorred monster keeps
Thee here in dark to be his paramour? 105
For fear of that I still will stay with thee,
And never from this palace of dim night
Depart again. Here, here will I remain
With worms that are thy chambermaids. O, here
Will I set up my everlasting rest, 110
And shake the yoke of inauspicious stars
From this world-wearied flesh. Eyes, look your last.
Arms, take your last embrace. And, lips, O you
The doors of breath, seal with a righteous kiss
A dateless bargain to engrossing death! 115

116. *Come, bitter conduct* he is now talking to the vial of poison which he is holding.

116. *conduct* conductor (the vessel that will conduct the poison into his body).

117–18. Compare Act II, Scene ii, lines 82–4.

118. *desperate pilot* himself.

118. *thy sea-sick weary bark* his body, tired of life, is compared to a ship after a long voyage.

122. *Who's there?* A lantern, which the Friar is carrying, lights up Balthasar.

126. *discern* make out from looking.

136. *unthrifty thing* unfortunate event or happening.

Come, bitter conduct, come, unsavoury guide.
Thou desperate pilot, now at once run on
The dashing rocks thy sea-sick weary bark.
Here's to my love! *[Drinks]* O true apothecary!
Thy drugs are quick. Thus with a kiss I die. *[Falls]*   120

[Enter FRIAR LAWRENCE, *with lantern, crow, and spade.]*

Friar Lawrence
Saint Francis be my speed! How oft to-night
Have my old feet stumbled at graves! Who's there?
Balthasar
Here's one, a friend, and one that knows you well?
Friar Lawrence
Bliss be upon you! Tell me, good my friend,
What torch is yond that vainly lends his light   125
To grubs and eyeless skulls? As I discern,
It burneth in the Capels' monument.
Balthasar
It doth so, holy sir; and there's my master,
One that you love.
Friar Lawrence
                    Who is it?
Balthasar
                              Romeo.
Friar Lawrence
How long hath he been there?
Balthasar
                              Full half an hour.   130
Friar Lawrence
Go with me to the vault.
Balthasar
                    I dare not, sir.
My master knows not but I am gone hence,
And fearfully did menace me with death,
If I did stay to look on his intents.
Friar Lawrence
Stay, then, I'll go alone; fear comes upon me;   135
O, much I fear some ill unthrifty thing.

141. *sepulchre* tomb or burial vault.

144–7. Friar Lawrence's speech is very broken up, because he is moving about the tomb, discovering who is there.

152. *contagion* disease.

156–7. 'I will secure your entry into a convent.'
158. *the watch* men who patrolled the streets at night.
159. The Friar is no doubt concerned his own part in the events will be revealed if he stays; how are we to view his desire to save his own skin? Of course, it helps Shakespeare's purposes to have him leave in order to allow Juliet the stage to herself for her final emotional lines.

Balshasar

    As I did sleep under this yew tree here,
    I dreamt my master and another fought,
    And that my master slew him.

Friar Lawrence

                  Romeo!
    Alack, alack, what blood is this which stains   140
    The stony entrance of this sepulchre?
    What mean these masterless and gory swords
    To lie discoloured by this place of peace?

            [Enters the tomb.]

    Romeo! O, pale! Who else? What, Paris too?
    And steep'd in blood? Ah, what an unkind hour   145
    Is guilty of this lamentable chance!
    The lady stirs.

            [JULIET wakes.]

Juliet

    O comfortable friar! Where is my lord?
    I do remember well where I should be,
    And there I am. Where is my Romeo?   150

            [Noise within.]

Friar Lawrence

    I hear some noise. Lady, come from that nest
    Of death, contagion, and unnatural sleep;
    A greater power than we can contradict
    Hath thwarted our intents. Come, come away;
    Thy husband in thy bosom there lies dead;   155
    And Paris too. Come, I'll dispose of thee
    Among a sisterhood of holy nuns.
    Stay not to question, for the watch is coming;
    Come, go, good Juliet. I dare no longer stay.

Juliet

    Go, get thee hence, for I will not away.   160

163. *O churl!* She criticises Romeo for being unkind in having drunk all the poison himself.

166. *a restorative* death will restore them to one another.

172. *attach* arrest.

[Exit FRIAR LAWRENCE.]

What's here? A cup, clos'd in my true love's hand?
Poison, I see, hath been his timeless end.
O churl! drunk all, and left no friendly drop
To help me after? I will kiss thy lips;
Haply some poison yet doth hang on them,   165
To make me die with a restorative.
Thy lips are warm.

[Kisses him.]

First Watch
  [Within]   Lead, boy. Which way?
Juliet
  Yea, noise? Then I'll be brief. O happy dagger!

[Snatching ROMEO's dagger.]

This is thy sheath; there rust, and let me die.

[She stabs herself and falls on ROMEO's body.]

[Enter WATCH, with PARIS'S page.]

This is the place; there, where the torch doth burn.   170

First Watch
  The ground is bloody; search about the churchyard.
  Go, some of you, whoe'er you find attach.

[Exeunt some of the WATCH.]

Pitiful sight! here lies the County slain;
And Juliet bleeding, warm, and newly dead,
Who here hath lain this two days buried.   175
Go, tell the Prince; run to the Capulets;
Raise up the Montagues; some others search.

[Exeunt others of the WATCH.]

We see the ground whereon these woes do lie;

179. *true ground* true cause – another pun with *ground* (earth) in line 178.
180. 'We cannot discover without further evidence.'

187. *misadventure* unfortunate event.

195. *Juliet, dead before* the Watchman is puzzled; he saw Juliet dead and buried but now her body is still warm and apparently just killed from stabbing.

But the true ground of all these piteous woes
We cannot without circumstance descry.   180

[Re-enter some of the WATCH *with* BALTHASAR.*]*

Second Watch
Here's Romeo's man; we found him in the
churchyard.
First Watch
Hold him in safety till the Prince come hither.

[Re-enter FRIAR LAWRENCE *and another* WATCHMAN.*]*

Third Watch
Here is a friar that trembles, sighs, and weeps;
We took this mattock and this spade from him,
As he was coming from this churchyard's side.   185
First Watch
A great suspicion; stay the friar too.

[Enter the PRINCE *and* ATTENDANTS.*]*

Prince
What misadventure is so early up,
That calls our person from our morning rest?

[Enter CAPULET, LADY CAPULET, *and others.]*

Capulet
What should it be that is so shriek'd abroad?
Lady Capulet
The people in the street cry 'Romeo',   190
Some 'Juliet' and some 'Paris'; and all run,
With open outcry, toward our monument.
Prince
What fear is this which startles in our ears?
First Watch
Sovereign, here lies the County Paris slain;
And Romeo dead; and Juliet, dead before,   195
Warm and new kill'd.
Prince
Search, seek, and know how this foul murder comes.

202–3. Capulet points to the empty sheath that Romeo is wearing.

206. 'That calls me to my grave.' Lady Capulet is, of course, not old (she is in fact twenty-eight).

216. *ambiguities* mysteries.

218. 'I will lead you in your mourning.'
220. 'Bear these misfortunes patiently.'

222–4. This passage is confused; the Friar says that he is under the greatest suspicion, implicated both by the time and the place at which he was caught, but he is actually the least likely to have committed the crime.

First Watch
    Here is a friar, and slaughtered Romeo's man,
    With instruments upon them fit to open
    These dead men's tombs.   200
Capulet
    O heavens! O wife, look how our daughter bleeds!
    This dagger hath mista'en, for, lo, his house
    Is empty on the back of Montague,
    And it mis-sheathed in my daughter's bosom.
Lady Capulet
    O me! this sight of death is as a bell   205
    That warns my old age to a sepulchre.

[Enter MONTAGUE and OTHERS.]

Prince
    Come, Montague, for thou art early up
    To see thy son and heir more early down.
Montague
    Alas, my liege, my wife is dead to-night;
    Grief of my son's exile hath stopp'd her breath.   210
    What further woe conspires against mine age?
Prince
    Look, and thou shalt see.
Montague
    O thou untaught! what manners is in this,
    To press before thy father to a grave?
Prince
    Seal up the mouth of outrage for a while,   215
    Till we can clear these ambiguities,
    And know their spring, their head, their true descent;
    And then will I be general of your woes,
    And lead you even to death. Meantime forbear,
    And let mischance be slave to patience.   220
    Bring forth the parties of suspicion.
Friar Lawrence
    I am the greatest, able to do least,
    Yet most suspected, as the time and place
    Doth make against me, of this direful murder;

225–6. 'Both to charge and condemn myself and at the same time to exonerate myself.'

228. *my short date of breath* 'the short time I have to live.'

236. *You* he turns to Capulet.

242. *tutor'd by my art* 'taught by my knowledge of medicines.'

246. *as* on.

252. *prefixed* prearranged.

259. *entreated* begged.

And here I stand, both to impeach and purge   225
Myself condemned and myself excus'd.

Prince

Then say at once what thou dost know in this.

Friar Lawrence

I will be brief, for my short date of breath
Is not so long as is a tedious tale.
Romeo, there dead, was husband to that Juliet;   230
And she, there dead, that Romeo's faithful wife.
I married them; and their stol'n marriage-day
Was Tybalt's doomsday, whose untimely death
Banish'd the new-made bridegroom from this city;
For whom, and not for Tybalt, Juliet pin'd.   235
You, to remove that siege of grief from her,
Betroth'd, and would have married her perforce,
To County Paris. Then comes she to me,
And with wild looks bid me devise some mean
To rid her from this second marriage,   240
Or in my cell there would she kill herself.
Then gave I her, so tutor'd by my art,
A sleeping potion; which so took effect
As I intended, for it wrought on her
The form of death. Meantime I writ to Romeo   245
That he should hither come as this dire night
To help to take her from her borrow'd grave,
Being the time the potion's force should cease.
But he which bore my letter, Friar John,
Was stay'd by accident, and yesternight   250
Return'd my letter back. Then all alone
At the prefixed hour of her waking
Came I to take her from her kindred's vault;
Meaning to keep her closely at my cell
Till I conveniently could send to Romeo.   255
But when I came, some minute ere the time
Of her awakening, here untimely lay
The noble Paris and true Romeo dead.
She wakes; and I entreated her come forth,
And bear this work of heaven with patience.   260

265

264–5. *and to the marriage Her nurse is privy.* 'Her Nurse knows all about the marriage.'

269. *still* always. The Friar's long speech, which may seem unnecessary to a modern audience, is, in fact, needed to prepare the way for the parents' reconciliation, which is the conclusion of the play and an essential part of Shakespeare's scheme. See Prologue to Act I, Scene i, line 11.

281. *stand aloof* stand away.

283. *drew on him* drew his sword on him.

292. 'That fate finds a way to kill your children through their love for each other.'
293. *winking at* 'shutting my eyes to.' ***discords*** conflicts, disagreements.

But then a noise did scare me from the tomb,
And she, too desperate, would not go with me,
But, as it seems, did violence on herself.
All this I know, and to the marriage
Her nurse is privy; and if ought in this   265
Miscarried by my fault, let my old life
Be sacrific'd, some hour before his time,
Unto the rigour of severest law.

Prince

We still have known thee for a holy man.
Where's Romeo's man? What can he say to this?   270

Balthasar

I brought my master news of Juliet's death;
And then in post he came from Mantua
To this same place, to this same monument.
This letter he early bid me give his father;
And threaten'd me with death, going in the vault,   275
If I departed not and left him there.

Prince

Give roe the letter, I will look on it.
Where is the County's page that rais'd the watch?
Sirrah, what made your master in this place?

Page

He came with flowers to strew his lady's grave;   280
And bid me stand aloof, and so I did.
Anon comes one with light to ope the tomb;
And by and by my master drew on him;
And then I ran away to call the watch.

Prince

This letter doth make good the friar's words,   285
Their course of love, the tidings of her death;
And here he writes that he did buy a poison
Of a poor pothecary, and therewithal
Came to this vault to die, and lie with Juliet.
Where be these enemies? Capulet, Montague,   290
See what a scourge is laid upon your hate,
That heaven finds means to kill your joys with love!
And I, for winking at your discords too,

294. *brace* two, i.e., Paris and Mercutio.

296–7. Montague's hand in reconciliation is all that Capulet, as Juliet's father, requires as a marriage gift *(jointure)* from the bridegroom's father.

Have lost a brace of kinsmen. All are punish'd.

Capulet
O brother Montague, give me thy hand.   295
This is my daughter's jointure, for no more
Can I demand.

Montague
But I can give thee more;
For I will raise her statue in pure gold,
That whiles Verona by that name is known,
There shall no figure at such rate be set   300
As that of true and faithful Juliet.

Capulet
As rich shall Romeo's by his lady's lie –
Poor sacrifices of our enmity!

Prince
A glooming peace this morning with it brings;
The sun for sorrow will not show his head.   305
Go hence, to have more talk of these sad things;
Some shall be pardon'd and some punished;
For never was a story of more woe
Than this of Juliet and her Romeo.

[Exeunt.]

SUMMING UP

It was mentioned in the Introduction that the action of the play is simple and compressed, although holding a great variety of material, and this observation is borne out by our knowledge of the time scheme, which is very tightly constructed. The entire movement is completed in six days. It may also be clear now that *Romeo and Juliet* is not primarily a tragedy which arises from the characteristics of the two lovers, but that it is rather the working out of the process of Fate.

It so happens that the Montagues and Capulets are quarrelling – we are not aware of the cause – and that Romeo and Juliet are born into this feud. It also so happens that Romeo falls in love with a Capulet, and then gets involved in the killing of Tybalt against his will, which brings about the Prince's sentence of banishment. Romeo's exile coincides with Capulet's decision to marry Juliet to Paris and this leads to Friar Lawrence's attempt to help, which fails when Friar John is unable to deliver the letter. When we see, in addition to the social environment of Verona, the nature of Romeo and Juliet's passion, we understand that the combination of those people and those circumstances could not result in a different ending.

It is often misleading to think about Shakespeare's plays simply in terms of characters. In *Romeo and Juliet* for example, the social conditions in Verona, the plot, and the language of the play are each just as important as characterization. Nevertheless the play obviously does include a number of characters so vividly put before us that we are bound to be interested in them as persons, as well as in their contribution to the working out of the plot of the play.

Capulet, Juliet's father, is wealthy and well into middle age; he likes to pose as an indulgent father – witness his conversation with Paris when the young man first asks about marrying Juliet – and as the benevolent head of an important family in Verona. He can be heartily good-humoured when everything is going his way but when he does not get his own way, he quickly appears as an overbearing brute. The language he uses to his young daughter is unforgivably insulting – even the Nurse and Lady Capulet protest – and shows the essential coarseness of a man who is insensitive to any feelings but his own. He contributes more than anyone else to the tragic story of his daughter, but is quite unaware of what he is doing.

His wife is by comparison only slightly drawn for us: much younger (she is, we gather, only twenty-eight), she seems to be a cold unsympathetic woman; her principal part in the play is to make more pitiful the isolation of Juliet, when even her mother refuses sympathy.

The Nurse, the other prominent figure of the household to which Juliet belongs, is, by common consent, one of the most real and living of all the characters Shakespeare created. She is talkative – nothing can stop her rattling on; she quickly loses the point of what she is saying in a flood of detail. She is full of vitality, has a simple sense of humour and, most evidently, she has a coarse mind. Her thoughts turn with the slightest provocation, or with none, to sex, and to sex in the most earthy way. It is in this that her part in the play is most evidently seen, providing a most effective contrast to the purity and idealism of Juliet.

Of all the characters in the play, it is Juliet who develops and matures most remarkably. We first see her as a child-like and obedient young girl, with little experience of personal relationships beyond her family attachments, and apparently submissive to her mother's arrangement of the marriage with Paris:

> I'll look to like, if looking liking move;
> But no more deep will I endart mine eye
> Than your consent gives strength to make it fly

However, her love for Romeo quite transforms her character; we see her awakened into womanhood, and learning a set of personal values which rise above Verona's accepted social conventions. Her new-found maturity is revealed in the scene at her bedroom window when she expresses her complete faith in and love for Romeo. This development in her character is again exhibited in her unembarrassed attitude to sexuality. We must appreciate that she is a young girl and that this is her first and only love-affair and yet despite her inexperience she quickly forms an adult attitude to sex. She recognizes but does not distort its great importance in their relationship. The growth in her character also reveals her great courage and determination. She does not yield to Capulet's disgracefully violent abuse and she completely ignores the Nurse's suggestion that she should marry Paris to get out of her difficulties. Alone in her bedroom, she dares to take the Friar's potion and when she awakens in the tomb to find her lover dead, there is no hesitation in her resolve,

> *Yea, noise ? Then I'll be brief. O happy dagger!*
> *This is thy sheath; there rust, and let me die*

The development of Romeo throughout the play complements that of Juliet; however, we may feel that he does not grow up as remarkably as she does. When we first see him, he is entangled in his affair with Rosaline; however, it must be made clear that this experience is very different from the passion he will later feel for Juliet. It was conventional in Elizabethan times for young men to sigh after, and write poetry to, hard-hearted ladies, and suffer when rejected. These were not so much authentic love-affairs as a sort of social affectation: the pretence of love and the posing as a desolate lover were all a kind of game. Romeo's relationship with Rosaline takes this form in the play. His advances are not returned by her and his infatuation seems to be a sickness, an affliction:

> *She hath forsworn to love, and in that vow*
> *Do I live dead that live to tell it now.*

We may initially feel with the Friar that Romeo's new love for Juliet is too impetuous to be really important, but are soon convinced of his seriousness, as Friar Lawrence is too. He is greatly involved with Juliet during the middle acts of the play, but we still see him jesting with his friends and getting caught up in a fatal sword-fight, which he has recognized as foolhardy. His futile revenge is to cost the lovers their lives. It is when we see his sheer hysteria after the news of his banishment that we realize that his involvement with Juliet has become total. Romeo does not achieve Juliet's stature until the final scenes of the play, when he cries.

> *Then I defy you, stars.*

and accepts death to be with his love. He shows in that last fine soliloquy that he will cling to what was best in his human experience; the lovers have found a sublime unity.

Friar Lawrence as a character in the play is more important for what he does than for what he is. He marries the young lovers in haste, so making it necessary for Juliet to defy her father when he arranges the wedding with Paris. The Friar then provides her with the means, the sleeping potion, by which she may hope to escape from her impossible situation, and it is his arrangements which break down when the letter fails to reach Romeo, an incident which leads directly to Romeo's suicide. He is old, gentle and sympathetic as is fitting to his vocation, but rather alarmed by the rashness and impetuosity of young lovers. He sees the harm done by the family quarrel between Capulets and Montagues, and hopes that the marriage might be a means of healing it. That is all we know about him: but it is sufficient for the purpose of the play.

Tybalt is the kind of man the Elizabethans would have recognized at once: proud and quick-tempered, and concerned to be up with the latest trends in manner and in speech. Although he is supposed to be an Italian, Shakespeare, his English creator, presents him in such a way as to show through the comments of Mercutio the prejudices of some Englishmen, then and now, against their compatriots who copy foreign continental habits. Tybalt's particular enthusiasm is fencing, which he practises after the manner of the French, his conversation larded with a full range of technical terms. He is an exhibitionist, a show-off, *'the courageous captain of compliments'*. As with his uncle Capulet, his character is aptly fitted to the contribution he makes to the plot: it is his showiness that goads Mercutio into the duel which leads to Romeo's banishment.

Mercutio, like the Nurse, is more interesting for what he is than for what he does. His single important contribution to the action of the play is his challenge to Tybalt, which leads to his death and so to Romeo's banishment. But during that part of the play in which he is on the stage there is vivacity, a gaiety and high-spiritedness, which disappears with him. He is the principal exponent of the kind of word-play which was discussed in the Introduction, and when this provokes Romeo into retorting in the same way as in Act II, Scene iv, the result is a dazzling display of verbal fireworks. It is he, too, who is the source of most of the outrageous sexual humour in *Romeo and Juliet*, particularly in baiting Romeo about his love-sickness for Rosaline. It is in this matter too that he has another dramatic function to perform: to Mercutio, who has never been touched by love, sex is a subject for humour, and Shakespeare makes very clear to us the contrast between him and Romeo by giving as a prologue to the love duet at Juliet's window a scene in which Mercutio's bawdy is at its broadest. Romeo, on Shakespeare's stage, listens to this unseen, and he dismisses it in a line –

He jests at scars that never felt a wound.

Shakespeare's judgement was wholly sound in removing him at a particular point: the tragic course of events in the second half of the play could have no place for the impudent gaiety of a Mercutio, and in the light of the elevated passion of the two lovers his attitude to sexuality would have seemed discordant, perhaps even silly. In this respect, his character is deficient, but on the other hand one loves him for all that he is, for being a man who even at death has a pun on his lips:

> *Ask for me tomorrow, and you shall find me a grave man.*

No consideration of *Romeo and Juliet* should neglect to give proper consideration to the fact that what made it possible for Shakespeare to raise a familiar and ordinary Italian short story to the level of a splendid play was his command of language.

An examination of two of Capulet's speeches will give some idea of how the man's character and moods are created for us through the phrases and rhythms that he uses (Act I, Scene v, lines 14–31). Here Capulet is jocular, being familiar with the young ladies and exchanging sentimental memories with his contemporaries. Notice how these first characteristics are given expression through the choice of words and the quick movement of the sounds in *'am I come near ye now?'* and *'give room; and foot it girls'*. For the expression of the other mood, Shakespeare employs a long, falling rhythm: *'For you and I are past our dancing days* and *'Tis gone, 'tis gone, 'tis gone!'*

In another scene (Act III, Scene v, lines 151–157), we see Capulet in an abusive and bullying mood; here, the repeated alliteration seems to make the words spit out and the brutality of the expression indicates the coarseness of the man. The phrase 'But fettle your fine joints 'gainst Thursday next', sounds as if he is treating his daughter as an animal. When he is even angrier, the rhythm is made to break down altogether, and only short wild words can explode from Capulet's mouth (line 193).

In complete contrast to this, we can see how Shakespeare organizes language to create the sententious, moralizing character of Friar Lawrence (Act II, Scene iii, lines 1–30; Act III Scene iii, lines 108–158). Here Shakespeare employs elaborate sentences, giving himself time for the full development of similes and metaphors, and in the second speech, carrying an involved but logical argument through to its conclusion.

When we turn from the Friar to the poetry of Juliet's speech, we see Shakespeare controlling the language to create an urgent yet gentle appeal in Act III, Scene ii, lines 17–25. The repeated words, 'come', 'night', 'Romeo' express Juliet's longing to be with her lover and yet the beauty of the picture of snow upon a raven's back, and the quality of freshness of the words new snow maintain the serenity of the mood. Notice how in both instances the three short phrases are followed by images with an extended slow, flowing rhythm. Both the strength of her desire and the tenderness of her feelings are captured in the varying sounds.

If we turn to one of the finest passages of poetry in the play, that is, Romeo's last soliloquy (Act V, Scene iii, lines 106–120), we see how Shakespeare uses images and rhythms to make us understand that to Romeo death is welcome and to appreciate that what is happening is inevitable. Juliet's tomb is for Romeo a 'palace' and within the terms of the image even the worms which will eat their bodies are made less repulsive by being visualized as their 'chambermaids'. What he is going to is 'everlasting rest' – the phrase itself is suggestive of complete and final release. The word 'yoke' sums up the way Fate (the 'inauspicious stars') has controlled his life. And the long rhythms of the whole sentence suggest a movement to a full close, like the recognizably final cadence of a piece of music.

THEME INDEX

The 'Generation Gap'

Romeo and Juliet are driven to behave as they do because they know that there is no possibility of their feelings being understood by their parents. *'O Romeo, Romeo!'* cries Juliet, when she discovers the identity of her lover, *'wherefore art thou Romeo? Deny thy father and refuse thy name'*; (II ii 33–36). Juliet in particular suffers under an insensitive mother and an abusive father (III v 139–204). The Nurse, too, another of the older generation, although apparently unusually sympathetic, abandons Juliet when she most needs help; *'O most wicked fiend!'* Juliet calls her (III v 205–end).

The Family Feud

Their parents' attitudes towards the love of Romeo and Juliet are partly conditioned by the Capulet-Montague feud. It is certainly destructive of the love of the two young people, who themselves have little feeling for it. The situation is made clear in the sonnet spoken before the start of the play proper: *'Two households, both alike in dignity'*, says Chorus, *'From ancient grudge break to new mutiny'*. He speaks of *'the continuance of their parents' rage'*. *Which, but their children's end, nought could remove.* The theme is continued as soon as Sampson and Gregory appear, and dominates the first scene. (See also: I v 58–62; II ii 60–65; III i; V iii 290–303.)

Fate

It is through the family feud that Fate principally operates in the play. *'A pair of star-cross'd lovers'* (Prologue, Act I, line 6): these are the words in which Shakespeare introduces Romeo and Juliet to us. We know from the first that there is to be no 'living happily ever after' for these two: they are destined to die. A boy and a girl are born into families which make it impossible that a marriage between them could be acceptable. They meet, very improbably, and fall in love at first sight (I v 42–51 and 130–139). Within hours of a secret marriage, Romeo reluctantly fights Tybalt after a chance meeting in the streets, kills him and is banished (III i). On the very same day Juliet learns that she is to be forced into marriage with another man (III v 107–196). The messenger taking news of Friar Lawrence's scheme never reaches Romeo (V ii 5–20), and the timing of the events which close the play is such that Romeo kills himself before Juliet awakes, and Juliet kills herself before the Watch arrives, though all these events take place within a few minutes of one another (V ii and iii). In addition we may feel that Fate is operating at deeper and less expressible levels: is it possible for us to conceive of a love so wholly absorbing, so passionate, so idealized, being able to survive in the world as it is? (See V iii 110–112).

Love

Three aspects of sexual love are illustrated in *Romeo and Juliet*. First, the 'calf-love' of Romeo for Rosaline, which is little more than affectation (I i 195–end; II ii 45–end; I iv 14–39). Second, Paris's love for Juliet. This is deeper, but wholly proper and conventional: Paris makes an approach to Juliet's father first, and refers to her always with great respect (III iv; IV i 1–43; V iii 1–73). Third, the overwhelming passion of Romeo and Juliet which is conveyed most vividly and movingly (II ii, III ii, III v 1–36 and V iii 22–169).

Bawdy

There is a very different aspect of sex in the play – the bawdiness freely expressed by Mercutio, the Nurse and other characters. There is probably more humorous talk about sex in *Romeo and Juliet* than in any other play of Shakespeare's. The bawdy is there for two main reasons:

because it amused the audience (I i 1–32; II i 17–end) and because it enables a most significant contrast to be made between the gay flippancy of Mercutio's attitude to sex (together with the comic vulgarity of the Nurse's remarks) and the seriousness and beauty of the love of Romeo and Juliet.

Imagery

In *Romeo and Juliet* Shakespeare's style varies between a rather self-conscious use of words and devices (characteristic of his early work) and a much more profound employment of all the resources of language. The imagery of the play reflects this dual effect. At I iii 82–93 Lady Capulet compares Paris's face with a book, and elaborates the idea lengthily in a purely descriptive way. There are other examples of the same kind of imagery at II iii 9–12 and III v 197–8 and particularly in the speeches of Romeo before his whole life is changed by meeting Juliet: I i 184–188, I iv 19–22, etc. Elaboration sometimes achieves a deeper meaning, in reflecting the character of the speaker: e.g. the pompous Capulet makes detailed comparisons with his weeping daughter (III v 129–137) in a manner that is typical of him. In the second half of the play the imagery has a much more pervasive effect. When Juliet is waiting for Romeo at the beginning of III ii, she speaks elaborately of the night, but the elaborateness now stresses that the lovers look on the night as the positive and benevolent background for their love: the imagery is both witty and passionate.

But the most striking use of imagery lies at the heart of the play's development. When the lovers meet for the first time, at Capulet's house, they address each other in a beautifully artificial way, with plenty of wit but little passion (I v 91–108). In the garden scene and the balcony scene, however, everything is changed and intensified, and the imagery reflects this: II ii 26–32, 107–124, 158–167; III v 1–11, 17–36.etc.

The dominant feature of the play's imagery is the contrast between light and darkness, and the most remarkable aspect of this is the way in which Romeo and Juliet appear to each other as luminous objects in surrounding darkness (II ii 15–22; III ii 17–19 and 21–25; Viii 85–86). The emotional and dramatic effects of this are obvious.

Shakespeare: Words and Phrases

adapted from the Collins English Dictionary

abate 1 VERB to abate here means to lessen or diminish ❑ *There lives within the very flame of love/A kind of wick or snuff that will abate it* (*Hamlet 4.7*) 2 VERB to abate here means to shorten ❑ *Abate thy hours* (*A Midsummer Night's Dream 3.2*) 3 VERB to abate here means to deprive ❑ *She hath abated me of half my train* (*King Lear 2.4*)

abjure VERB to abjure means to renounce or give up ❑ *this rough magic I here abjure* (*Tempest 5.1*)

abroad ADV abroad means elsewhere or everywhere ❑ *You have heard of the news abroad* (*King Lear 2.1*)

abrogate VERB to abrogate means to put an end to ❑ *so it shall praise you to abrogate scurrility* (*Love's Labours Lost 4.2*)

abuse 1 NOUN abuse in this context means deception or fraud ❑ *What should this mean? Are all the rest come back?/Or is it some abuse, and no such thing?* (*Hamlet 4.7*) 2 NOUN an abuse in this context means insult or offence ❑ *I will be deaf to pleading and excuses/Nor tears nor prayers shall purchase our abuses* (*Romeo and Juliet 3.1*) 3 NOUN an abuse in this context means using something improperly ❑ *we'll digest/Th'abuse*

of distance (*Henry II Chorus*) 4 NOUN an abuse in this context means doing something which is corrupt or dishonest ❑ *Come, bring them away: if these be good people in a commonweal that do nothing but their abuses in common houses, I know no law: bring them away.* (*Measure for Measure 2.1*)

abuser NOUN the abuser here is someone who betrays, a betrayer ❑ *I ... do attach thee/For an abuser of the world* (*Othello 1.2*)

accent NOUN accent here means language ❑ *In states unborn, and accents yet unknown* (*Julius Caesar 3.1*)

accident NOUN an accident in this context is an event or something that happened ❑ *think no more of this night's accidents* (*A Midsummer Night's Dream 4.1*)

accommodate VERB to accommodate in this context means to equip or to give someone the equipment to do something ❑ *The safer sense will ne'er accommodate/His master thus.* (*King Lear 4.6*)

according ADJ according means sympathetic or ready to agree ❑ *within the scope of choice/Lies* *my consent and fair according voice* (*Romeo and Juliet 1.2*)

account NOUN account often means judgement (by God) or reckoning ❑ *No reckoning made, but sent to my account/With all my imperfections on my head* (*Hamlet 1.5*)

accountant ADJ accountant here means answerable or accountable ❑ *his offence is… /Accountant to the law* (*Measure for Measure 2.4*)

ace NOUN ace here means one or first referring to the lowest score on a dice ❑ *No die, but an ace, for him; for he is but one./Less than an ace, man; for he is dead; he is nothing.* (*A Midsummer Night's Dream 5.1*)

acquit VERB here acquit means to be rid of or free of. It is related to the verb quit ❑ *I am glad I am so acquit of this tinderbox* (*The Merry Wives of Windsor 1.3*)

afeard ADJ afeard means afraid or frightened ❑ *Nothing afeard of what thyself didst make* (*Macbeth 1.3*)

affiance NOUN affiance means confidence or trust ❑ *O how hast thou with jealousy infected/The sweetness of affiance* (*Henry V 2.2*)

affinity NOUN in this context, affinity means important connections, or relationships with important people ❑ *The Moor replies/That he you hurt is of great fame in Cyprus,/And great affinity* (*Othello 3.1*)

agnize VERB to agnize is an old word that means that you recognize or acknowledge something ❑ *I do agnize/A natural and prompt alacrity I find in hardness* (*Othello 1.3*)

ague NOUN an ague is a fever in which the patient has hot and cold

shivers one after the other ❑ *This is some monster of the isle with four legs, who hath got … an ague* (*The Tempest 2.2*)

alarm, alarum NOUN an alarm or alarum is a call to arms or a signal for soldiers to prepare to fight ❑ *Whence cometh this alarum and the noise?* (*Henry VI part I 1.4*)

Albion NOUN Albion is another word for England ❑ *but I will sell my dukedom,/To buy a slobbery and a dirty farm In that nook-shotten isle of Albion* (*Henry V 3.5*)

all of all PHRASE all of all means everything, or the sum of all things ❑ *The very all of all* (*Love's Labours Lost 5.1*)

amend VERB amend in this context means to get better or to heal ❑ *at his touch… They presently amend* (*Macbeth 4.3*)

anchor VERB if you anchor on something you concentrate on it or fix on it ❑ *My invention … Anchors on Isabel* (*Measure for Measure 2.4*)

anon ADV anon was a common word for soon ❑ *You shall see anon how the murderer gets the love of Gonzago's wife* (*Hamlet 3.2*)

antic 1 ADJ antic here means weird or strange ❑ *I'll charm the air to give a sound/While you perform your antic round* (*Macbeth 4.1*) 2 NOUN in this context antic means a clown or a strange, unattractive creature ❑ *If black, why nature, drawing an antic,/Made a foul blot* (*Much Ado About Nothing 3.1*)

apace ADV apace was a common word for quickly ❑ *Come apace* (*As You Like It 3.3*)

apparel NOUN apparel means clothes or clothing ❑ *one suit of apparel* (*Hamlet 3.2*)

appliance NOUN appliance here means cure ❑ *Diseases desperate grown/ By desperate appliance are relieved* (*Hamlet 4.3*)

argument NOUN argument here means a topic of conversation or the subject ❑ *Why 'tis the rarest argument of wonder that hath shot out in our latter times* (*All's Well That Ends Well 2.3*)

arrant ADJ arrant means absolute, complete. It strengthens the meaning of a noun ❑ *Fortune, that arrant whore* (*King Lear 2.4*)

arras NOUN an arras is a tapestry, a large cloth with a picture sewn on it using coloured thread ❑ *Behind the arras I'll convey myself/ To hear the process* (*Hamlet 3.3*)

art 1 NOUN art in this context means knowledge ❑ *Their malady convinces/ The great essay of art* (*Macbeth 4.3*) 2 NOUN art can also mean skill as it does here ❑ *He ... gave you such a masterly report/ For art and exercise in your defence* (*Hamlet 4.7*) 3 NOUN art here means magic ❑ *Now I want/ Spirits to enforce, art to enchant* (*The Tempest 5 Epilogue*)

assay 1 NOUN an assay was an attempt, a try ❑ *Make assay./ Bow, stubborn knees* (*Hamlet 3.3*) 2 NOUN assay can also mean a test or a trial ❑ *he hath made assay of her virtue* (*Measure for Measure 3.1*)

attend (on/upon) VERB attend on means to wait for or to expect ❑ *Tarry I here, I but attend on death* (*Two Gentlemen of Verona 3.1*)

auditor NOUN an auditor was a member of an audience or someone who listens ❑ *I'll be an auditor* (*A Midsummer Night's Dream 3.1*)

aught NOUN aught was a common word which meant anything ❑ *if my love thou holdest at aught* (*Hamlet 4.3*)

aunt 1 NOUN an aunt was another word for an old woman and also means someone who talks a lot or a gossip ❑ *The wisest aunt telling the saddest tale* (*A Midsummer Night's Dream 2.1*) 2 NOUN aunt could also mean a mistress or a prostitute ❑ *the thrush and the jay/ Are summer songs for me and my aunts/ While we lie tumbling in the hay* (*The Winter's Tale 4.3*)

avaunt EXCLAM avaunt was a common word which meant go away ❑ *Avaunt, you curs!* (*King Lear 3.6*)

aye ADV here aye means always or ever ❑ *Whose state and honour I for aye allow* (*Richard II 5.2*)

baffle VERB baffle meant to be disgraced in public or humiliated ❑ *I am disgraced, impeached, and baffled here* (*Richard II 1.1*)

bald ADJ bald means trivial or silly ❑ *I knew 'twould be a bald conclusion* (*The Comedy of Errors 2.2*)

ban NOUN a ban was a curse or an evil spell ❑ *Sometimes with lunatic bans... Enforce their charity* (*King Lear 2.3*)

barren ADJ barren meant empty or hollow ❑ *now I let go your hand, I am barren.* (*Twelfth Night 1.3*)

base ADJ base is an adjective that means unworthy or dishonourable ❑ *civet is of a baser birth than tar* (*As You Like It 3.2*)

283

base 1 ADJ base can also mean of low social standing or someone who was not part of the ruling class ❑ *Why brand they us with 'base'?* (*King Lear* 1.2) 2 ADJ here base means poor quality ❑ *Base cousin,/ Darest thou break first?* (*Two Noble Kinsmen* 3.3)

bawdy NOUN bawdy means obscene or rude ❑ *Bloody, bawdy villain!* (*Hamlet* 2.2)

bear in hand PHRASE bear in hand means taken advantage of or fooled ❑ *This I made good to you In our last conference, passed in probation with you/ How you were borne in hand* (*Macbeth* 3.1)

beard VERB to beard someone was to oppose or confront them ❑ *Com'st thou to beard me in Denmark?* (*Hamlet* 2.2)

beard, in one's PHRASE if you say something in someone's beard you say it to their face ❑ *I will verify as much in his beard* (*Henry V* 3.2)

beaver NOUN a beaver was a visor on a battle helmet ❑ *O yes, my lord, he wore his beaver up* (*Hamlet* 1.2)

become VERB if something becomes you it suits you or is appropriate to you ❑ *Nothing in his life became him like the leaving it* (*Macbeth* 1.4)

bed, brought to PHRASE to be brought to bed means to give birth ❑ *His wife but yesternight was brought to bed* (*Titus Andronicus* 4.2)

bedabbled ADJ if something is bedabbled it is sprinkled ❑ *Bedabbled with the dew, and torn with briers* (*A Midsummer Night's Dream* 3.2)

Bedlam NOUN Bedlam was a word used for Bethlehem Hospital which was a place the insane were sent to ❑ *The country give me proof and precedent/ Of Bedlam beggars* (*King Lear* 2.3)

bed-swerver NOUN a bed-swerver was someone who was unfaithful in marriage, an adulterer ❑ *she's/ A bed-swerver* (*Winter's Tale* 2.1)

befall 1 VERB to befall is to happen, occur or take place ❑ *In this same interlude it doth befall/ That I present a wall* (*A Midsummer Night's Dream* 5.1) 2 VERB to befall can also mean to happen to someone or something ❑ *fair befall thee and thy noble house* (*Richard III* 1.3)

behoof NOUN behoof was an advantage or benefit ❑ *All our surgeons/ Convent in their behoof* (*Two Noble Kinsmen* 1.4)

beldam NOUN a beldam was a witch or old woman ❑ *Have I not reason, beldams as you are?* (*Macbeth* 3.5)

belike ADV belike meant probably, perhaps or presumably ❑ *belike he likes it not* (*Hamlet* 3.2)

bent 1 NOUN bent means a preference or a direction ❑ *Let me work,/ For I can give his humour true bent,/ And I will bring him to the Capitol* (*Julius Caesar* 2.1) 2 ADJ if you are bent on something you are determined to do it ❑ *for now I am bent to know/ By the worst means the worst.* (*Macbeth* 3.4)

beshrew VERB beshrew meant to curse or wish evil on someone ❑ *much beshrew my manners and my pride/ If Hermia meant to say Lysander lied* (*A Midsummer Night's Dream* 2.2)

betime (s) ADV betime means early ❑ *To business that we love we rise betime* (*Antony and Cleopatra 4.4*)

bevy NOUN bevy meant type or sort, it was also used to mean company ❑ *many more of the same bevy* (*Hamlet 5.2*)

blazon VERB to blazon something meant to display or show it ❑ *that thy skill be more to blazon it* (*Romeo and Juliet 2.6*)

blind ADJ if you are blind when you do something you are reckless or do not care about the consequences ❑ *are you yet to your own souls so blind/ That two you will war with God by murdering me* (*Richard III 1.4*)

bombast NOUN bombast was wool stuffing (used in a cushion for example) and so it came to mean padded out or long-winded. Here it means someone who talks a lot about nothing in particular ❑ *How now my sweet creature of bombast* (*Henry IV part I 2.4*)

bond 1 NOUN a bond is a contract or legal deed ❑ *Well, then, your bond, and let me see* (*Merchant of Venice 1.3*) 2 NOUN bond could also mean duty or commitment ❑ *I love your majesty/ According to my bond* (*King Lear 1.1*)

bottom NOUN here bottom means essence, main point or intent ❑ *Now I see/ The bottom of your purpose* (*All's Well That Ends Well 3.7*)

bounteously ADV bounteously means plentifully, abundantly ❑ *I prithee, and I'll pay thee bounteously* (*Twelfth Night 1.2*)

brace 1 NOUN a brace is a couple or two ❑ *Have lost a brace of kinsmen* (*Romeo and Juliet 5.3*) 2 NOUN if you are in a brace position it means you are ready ❑ *For that it stands not in such warlike brace* (*Othello 1.3*)

brand VERB to mark permanantly like the markings on cattle ❑ *the wheeled seat/ Of fortunate Caesar ... branded his baseness that ensued* (*Anthony and Cleopatra 4.14*)

brave ADJ brave meant fine, excellent or splendid ❑ *O brave new world/ That has such people in't* (*The Tempest 5.1*)

brine NOUN brine is sea-water ❑ *He shall drink nought brine, for I'll not show him/ Where the quick freshes are* (*The Tempest 3.2*)

brow NOUN brow in this context means appearance ❑ *doth hourly grow/ Out of his brows* (*Hamlet 3.3*)

burden 1 NOUN the burden here is a chorus ❑ *I would sing my song without a burden* (*As You Like It 3.2*) 2 NOUN burden means load or weight (this is the current meaning) ❑ *the scarfs and the bannerets about thee did manifoldly dissuade me from believing thee a vessel of too great a burden* (*All's Well that Ends Well 2.3*)

buttons, in one's PHRASE this is a phrase that means clear, easy to see ❑ *Tis in his buttons he will carry't* (*The Merry Wives of Windsor 3.2*)

cable NOUN cable here means scope or reach ❑ *The law ... Will give her cable* (*Othello 1.2*)

cadent ADJ if something is cadent it is falling or dropping ❑ *With cadent tears fret channels in her cheeks* (*King Lear 1.4*)

canker VERB to canker is to decay, become corrupt ❑ *And, as with age his body uglier grows,/So his mind cankers* (*The Tempest* 4.1)

canon, from the PHRASE from the canon is an expression meaning out of order, improper ❑ *Twas from the canon* (*Coriolanus* 3.1)

cap-a-pie ADV cap-a-pie means from head to foot, completely ❑ *I am courtier cap-a-pie* (*The Winter's Tale* 4.4)

carbonadoed ADJ if something is carbonadoed it is cut or scored (scratched) with a knife ❑ *it is your carbonadoed* (*All's Well That Ends Well* 4.5)

carouse VERB to carouse is to drink at length, party ❑ *They cast their caps up and carouse together* (*Anthony and Cleopatra* 4.12)

carrack NOUN a carrack was a large old ship, a galleon ❑ *Faith, he tonight hath boarded a land-carrack* (*Othello* 1.2)

cassock NOUN a cassock here means a military cloak, long coat ❑ *half of the which dare not shake the snow from off their cassocks lest they shake themselves to pieces* (*All's Well That Ends Well* 4.3)

catastrophe NOUN catastrophe here means conclusion or end ❑ *pat he comes, like the catastrophe of the old comedy* (*King Lear* 1.2)

cautel NOUN a cautel was a trick or a deceptive act ❑ *Perhaps he loves you now/And now no soil not cautel doth besmirch* (*Hamlet* 1.2)

celerity NOUN celerity was a common word for speed, swiftness ❑ *Hence hath offence his quick celerity/When it is borne in high authority* (*Measure for Measure* 4.2)

chafe NOUN chafe meant anger or temper ❑ *this Herculean Roman does become/The carriage of his chafe* (*Anthony and Cleopatra* 1.3)

chanson NOUN chanson was an old word for a song ❑ *The first row of the pious chanson will show you more* (*Hamlet* 2.2)

chapman NOUN a chapman was a trader or merchant ❑ *Not uttered by base sale of chapman's tongues* (*Love's Labours Lost* 2.1)

chaps, chops NOUN chaps (and chops) was a word for jaws ❑ *Which ne'er shook hands nor bade farewell to him/Till he unseamed him from the nave to th' chops* (*Macbeth* 1.2)

chattels NOUN chattels were your moveable possessions. The word is used in the traditional marriage ceremony ❑ *She is my goods, my chattels* (*The Taming of the Shrew* 3.3)

chide VERB if you are chided by someone you are told off or reprimanded ❑ *Now I but chide, but I should use thee worse* (*A Midsummer Night's Dream* 3.2)

chinks NOUN chinks was a word for cash or money ❑ *he that can lay hold of her/Shall have the chinks* (*Romeo and Juliet* 1.5)

choleric ADJ if something was called choleric it meant that they were quick to get angry ❑ *therewithal unruly waywardness that infirm and choleric years bring with them* (*King Lear* 1.1)

chuff NOUN a chuff was a miser,

someone who clings to his or her money ❏ *ye fat chuffs* (*Henry IV part I 2.2*)

cipher NOUN cipher here means nothing ❏ *Mine were the very cipher of a function* (*Measure for Measure 2.2*)

circummured ADJ circummured means that something is surrounded with a wall ❏ *He hath a garden circummured with brick* (*Measure for Measure 4.1*)

civet NOUN a civet is a type of scent or perfume ❏ *Give me an ounce of civet* (*King Lear 4.6*)

clamorous ADJ clamorous means noisy or boisterous ❏ *Be clamorous and leap all civil bounds* (*Twelfth Night 1.4*)

clangour, clangor NOUN clangour is a word that means ringing (the sound that bells make) ❏ *Like to a dismal clangour heard from far* (*Henry VI part III 2.3*)

cleave VERB if you cleave to something you stick to it or are faithful to it ❏ *Thy thoughts I cleave to* (*The Tempest 4.1*)

clock and clock, 'twixt PHRASE from hour to hour, without stopping or continuously ❏ *To weep 'twixt clock and clock* (*Cymbeline 3.4*)

close ADJ here close means hidden ❏ *Stand close; this is the same Athenian* (*A Midsummer Night's Dream 3.2*)

cloud NOUN a cloud on your face means that you have a troubled, unhappy expression ❏ *He has cloud in's face* (*Anthony and Cleopatra 3.2*)

cloy VERB if you cloy an appetite you satisfy it ❏ *Other women cloy/The appetites they feed* (*Anthony and Cleopatra 2.2*)

cock-a-hoop, set PHRASE if you set cock-a-hoop you become free of everything ❏ *You will set cock-a-hoop* (*Romeo and Juliet 1.5*)

colours NOUN colours is a word used to describe battle-flags or banners. Sometimes we still say that we nail our colours to the mast if we are stating which team or side of an argument we support ❏ *the approbation of those that weep this lamentable divorce under her colours* (*Cymbeline 1.5*)

combustion NOUN combustion was a word meaning disorder or chaos ❏ *prophesying ... Of dire combustion and confused events* (*Macbeth 2.3*)

comely ADJ if you are or something is comely you or it is lovely, beautiful, graceful ❏ *O, what a world is this, when what is comely/Envenoms him that bears it!* (*As You Like It 2.3*)

commend VERB if you commend yourself to someone you send greetings to them ❏ *Commend me to my brother* (*Measure for Measure 1.4*)

compact NOUN a compact is an agreement or a contract ❏ *what compact mean you to have with us?* (*Julius Caesar 3.1*)

compass 1 NOUN here compass means range or scope ❏ *you would sound me from my lowest note to the top of my compass* (*Hamlet 3.2*) 2 VERB to compass here means to achieve, bring about or make happen ❏ *How now shall this be compassed?/Canst thou bring me to the party?* (*Tempest 3.2*)

comptible ADJ comptible is an old word meaning sensitive ❏ *I am very comptible, even to the least sinister usage.* (*Twelfth Night 1.5*)

confederacy NOUN a confederacy is a group of people usually joined together to commit a crime. It is another word for a conspiracy ❏ *Lo, she is one of this confederacy!* (*A Midsummer Night's Dream 3.2*)

confound VERB if you confound something you confuse it or mix it up; it also means to stop or prevent ❏ *A million fail, confounding oath on oath.* (*A Midsummer Night's Dream 3.2*)

contagion NOUN contagion is an old word for disease or poison ❏ *hell itself breathes out/Contagion to this world* (*Hamlet 3.2*)

contumely NOUN contumely is an old word for an insult ❏ *the proud man's contumely* (*Hamlet 3.1*)

counterfeit 1 VERB if you counterfeit something you copy or imitate it ❏ *Meantime your cheeks do counterfeit our roses* (*Henry VI part I 2.4*) 2 VERB in this context counterfeit means to pretend or make believe ❏ *I will counterfeit the bewitchment of some popular man* (*Coriolanus*)

coz NOUN coz was a shortened form of the word cousin ❏ *sweet my coz, be merry* (*As You Like It 1.2*)

cozenage NOUN cozenage is an old word meaning cheating or a deception ❏ *Thrown out his angle for my proper life,/And with such coz'nage* (*Hamlet 5.2*)

crave VERB crave used to mean to beg or request ❏ *I crave your pardon* (*The Comedy of Errors 1.2*)

crotchet NOUN crotchets are strange ideas or whims ❏ *thou hast some strange crotchets in thy head now* (*The Merry Wives of Windsor 2.1*)

cuckold NOUN a cuckold is a man whose wife has been unfaithful to him ❏ *As there is no true cuckold but calamity* (*Twelfth Night 1.5*)

cuffs, go to PHRASE this phrase meant to fight ❏ *the player went to cuffs in the question* (*Hamlet 2.2*)

cup VERB in this context cup is a verb which means to pour drink or fill glasses with alcohol ❏ *cup us til the world go round* (*Anthony and Cleopatra 2.7*)

cur NOUN cur is an insult meaning dog and is also used to mean coward ❏ *Out, dog! out, cur! Thou drivest me past the bounds/Of maiden's patience* (*A Midsummer Night's Dream 3.2*)

curiously ADV in this context curiously means carefully or skilfully ❏ *The sleeves curiously cut* (*The Taming of the Shrew 4.3*)

curry VERB curry means to flatter or to praise someone more than they are worth ❏ *I would curry with Master Shallow that no man could better command his servants* (*Henry IV part II 5.1*)

custom NOUN custom is a habit or a usual practice ❏ *Hath not old custom made this life more sweet/Than that of painted pomp?* (*As You Like It 2.1*)

cutpurse NOUN a cutpurse is an old word for a thief. Men used to carry their money in small bags (purse) that hung from their belts; thieves would cut the purse from the belt and steal their money ❏ *A cutpurse of the empire and the rule* (*Hamlet 3.4*)

dainty ADJ dainty used to mean splendid, fine ❑ *Why, that's my dainty Ariel!* (*Tempest 5.1*)

dally VERB if you dally with something you play with it or tease it ❑ *They that dally nicely with words may quickly make them wanton* (*Twelfth Night 3.1*)

damask COLOUR damask is a light-red or pink colour ❑ *Twas just the difference/ Betwixt the constant red and mingled damask* (*As You Like It 3.5*)

dare 1 VERB dare means to challeng or, confront ❑ *He goes before me, and still dares me on* (*A Midsummer Night's Dream 3.3*) 2 VERB dare in this context means to present, deliver or inflict ❑ *all that fortune, death, and danger dare* (*Hamlet 4.4*)

darkly ADV darkly was used in this context to mean secretly or cunningly ❑ *I will go darkly to work with her* (*Measure for Measure 5.1*)

daw NOUN a daw was a slang term for idiot or fool (after the bird jackdaw which was famous for its stupidity) ❑ *Yea, just so much as you may take upon a knife's point and choke a daw withal* (*Much Ado About Nothing 3.1*)

debile ADJ debile meant weak or feeble ❑ *And debile minister great power* (*All's Well That Ends Well 2.3*)

deboshed ADJ deboshed was another way of saying corrupted or debauched ❑ *Men so disordered, deboshed and bold* (*King Lear 1.4*)

decoct VERB to decoct was to heat up, warm something ❑ *Can sodden water,/ A drench for sur-reained jades*

... Decoct their cold blood to such valiant heat? (*Henry V 3.5*)

deep-revolving ADJ deep-revolving here uses the idea that you turn something over in your mind when you are thinking hard about it and so means deep-thinking, meditating ❑ *The deep-revolving Buckingham/ No more shall be the neighbour to my counsels* (*Richard III 4.2*)

defect NOUN defect here means shortcoming or something that is not right ❑ *Being unprepared/ Our will became the servant to defect* (*Macbeth 2.1*)

degree 1 NOUN degree here means rank, standing or station ❑ *Should a like language use to all degrees,/ And mannerly distinguishment leave out/ Betwixt the prince and beggar* (*The Winter's Tale 2.1*) 2 NOUN in this context, degree means extent or measure ❑ *her offence/ Must be of such unnatural degree* (*King Lear 1.1*)

deify VERB if you deify something or someone you worship it or them as a God ❑ *all.. deifying the name of Rosalind* (*As You Like It 3.2*)

delated ADJ delated here means detailed ❑ *the scope/ Of these delated articles* (*Hamlet 1.2*)

delicate ADJ if something was described as delicate it meant it was of fine quality or valuable ❑ *thou wast a spirit too delicate* (*The Tempest 1.2*)

demise VERB in this context demise means to transmit, give or convey ❑ *what state ... Canst thou demise to any child of mine?* (*Richard III 4.4*)

deplore VERB to deplore means to express with grief or sorrow ❑ *Never more/ Will I my master's tears to you deplore* (*Twelfth Night 3.1*)

depose VERB if you depose someone you make them take an oath, or swear something to be true ❑ *Depose him in the justice of his cause* (*Richard II 1.3*)

depositary NOUN a depositary is a trustee ❑ *Made you ... my depositary* (*King Lear 2.4*)

derive 1 VERB to derive means to comes from or to descend (it usually applies to people) ❑ *No part of it is mine,/ This shame derives itself from unknown loins.* (*Much Ado About Nothing 4.1*) 2 VERB if you derive something from someone you inherit it ❑ *Treason is not inherited ...Or, if we derive it from our friends/ What's that to me?* (*As You Like It 1.3*)

descry VERB to see or catch sight of ❑ *The news is true, my lord. He is descried* (*Anthony and Cleopatra 3.7*)

desert 1 NOUN desert means worth or merit ❑ *That dost in vile misproson shackle up/ My love and her desert* (*All's Well That Ends Well 2.3*) 2 ADJ desert is used here to mean lonely or isolated ❑ *if that love or gold/ Can in this desert place buy entertainment* (*As You LIke It 2.4*)

design 1 VERB to design means to indicate or point out ❑ *we shall see/ Justice design the victor's chivalry* (*Richard II 1.1*) 2 NOUN a design is a plan, an intention or an undertaking ❑ *hinder not the honour of his design* (*All's Well That Ends Well 3.6*)

designment NOUN a designment was a plan or undertaking ❑ *The desperate tempest hath so bang'd the Turks,/ That their designment halts* (*Othello 2.1*)

despite VERB despite here means to spite or attempt to thwart a plan ❑ *Only to despite them I will endeavour anything* (*Much Ado About Nothing 2.2*)

device NOUN a device is a plan, plot or trick ❑ *Excellent, I smell a device* (*Twelfth Night 2.3*)

disable VERB to disable here means to devalue or make little of ❑ *he disabled my judgement* (*As You Like It 5.4*)

discandy VERB here discandy means to melt away or dissolve ❑ *The hearts ... do discandy , melt their sweets* (*Anthony and Cleopatra 4.12*)

disciple VERB to disciple is to teach or train ❑ *He ...was/ Discipled of the bravest* (*All's Well That Ends Well 1.2*)

discommend VERB if you discommend something you criticize it ❑ *my dialect which you discommend so much* (*King Lear 2.2*)

discourse NOUN discourse means conversation, talk or chat ❑ *which part of it I'll waste/ With such discourse as I not doubt shall make it/ Go quick away* (*The Tempest 5.1*)

discover VERB discover used to mean to reveal or show ❑ *the Prince discovered to Claudio that he loved my niece* (*Much Ado About Nothing 1.2*)

disliken VERB disguise, make unlike ❑ *disliken/ The truth of your own seeming* (*The Winter's Tale 4.4*)

dismantle VERB to dismantle is to remove or take away ❑ *Commit a thing so monstrous to dismantle/*

So many folds of favour (*King Lear 1.1*)

disponge VERB disponge means to pour out or rain down ❑ *The poisonous damp of night disponge upon me* (*Anthony and Cleopatra 4.9*)

distrain VERB to distrain something is to confiscate it ❑ *My father's goods are all distrained and sold* (*Richard II 2.3*)

divers ADJ divers is an old word for various ❑ *I will give out divers schedules of my beauty* (*Twelfth Night 1.5*)

doff VERB to doff is to get rid of or dispose ❑ *make our women fight/ To doff their dire distresses* (*Macbeth 4.3*)

dog VERB if you dog someone or something you follow them or it closely ❑ *I will rather leave to see Hector than not to dog him* (*Troilus and Cressida 5.1*)

dotage NOUN dotage here means infatuation ❑ *Her dotage now I do begin to pity* (*A Midsummer NIght's Dream 4.1*)

dotard NOUN a dotard was an old fool ❑ *I speak not like a dotard nor a fool* (*Much Ado About Nothing 5.1*)

dote VERB to dote is to love, cherish, care without seeing any fault ❑ *And won her soul; and she, sweet lady, dotes,/ Devoutly dotes, dotes in idolatry* (*A Midsummer Night's Dream 1.1*)

doublet NOUN a doublet was a man's close-fitting jacket with short skirt ❑ *Lord Hamlet, with his doublet all unbraced* (*Hamlet 2.1*)

dowager NOUN a dowager is a widow ❑ *Like to a step-dame or a dowage* (*A Midsummer Night's Dream 1.1*)

dowdy NOUN a dowdy was an ugly woman ❑ *Dido was a dowdy* (*Romeo and Juliet 2.4*)

dower NOUN a dower (or dowery) is the riches or property given by the father of a bride to her husband-to-be ❑ *Thy truth then by they dower* (*King Lear 1.1*)

dram NOUN a dram is a tiny amount ❑ *Why, everything adheres together that no dram of a scruple* (*Twelfth Night 3.4*)

drift NOUN drift is a plan, scheme or intention ❑ *Shall Romeo by my letters know our drift* (*Romeo and Juliet 4.1*)

dropsied ADJ dropsied means pretentious ❑ *Where great additions swell's and virtues none/ It is a dropsied honour* (*All's Well That Ends Well 2.3*)

drudge NOUN a drudge was a slave, servant ❑ *If I be his cuckold, he's my drudge* (*All's Well That Ends Well 1.3*)

dwell VERB to dwell sometimes meant to exist, to be ❑ *I'd rather dwell in my necessity* (*Merchant of Venice 1.3*)

earnest ADJ an earnest was a pledge to pay or a payment in advance ❑ *for an earnest of a greater honour/ He bade me from him call thee Thane of Cawdor* (*Macbeth 1.3*)

ecstasy NOUN madness ❑ *This is the very ecstasy of love* (*Hamlet 2.1*)

edict NOUN law or declaration ❑ *It stands as an edict in destiny.* (*A Midsummer Night's Dream 1.1*)

egall ADJ egall is an old word meaning equal ❏ *companions/Whose souls do bear an egall yoke of love* (*Merchant of Venice 2.4*)

eisel NOUN eisel meant vinegar ❏ *Woo't drink up eisel?* (*Hamlet 5.1*)

eke, eke out VERB eke meant to add to, to increase. Eke out nowadays means to make something last as long as possible – particularly in the sense of making money last a long time ❏ *Still be kind/And eke out our performance with your mind* (*Henry V Chorus*)

elbow, out at PHRASE out at elbow is an old phrase meaning in poor condition – as when your jacket sleeves are worn at the elbow which shows that it is an old jacket ❏ *He cannot, sir. He's out at elbow* (*Measure for Measure 2.1*)

element NOUN elements were thought to be the things from which all things were made. They were: air, earth, water and fire ❏ *Does not our lives consist of the four elements?* (*Twelfth Night 2.3*)

elf VERB to elf was to tangle ❏ *I'll ... elf all my hairs in knots* (*King Lear 2.3*)

embassy NOUN an embassy was a message ❏ *We'll once more hear Orsino's embassy.* (*Twelfth Night 1.5*)

emphasis NOUN emphasis here means a forceful expression or strong statement ❏ *What is he whose grief/ Bears such an emphasis* (*Hamlet 5.1*)

empiric NOUN an empiric was an untrained doctor sometimes called a quack ❏ *we must not ... prostitute our past-cure malady/To empirics* (*All's Well That Ends Well 2.1*)

emulate ADJ emulate here means envious ❏ *pricked on by a most emulate pride* (*Hamlet 1.1*)

enchant VERB to enchant meant to put a magic spell on ❏ *Damn'd as thou art, thou hast enchanted her,/ For I'll refer me to all things of sense* (*Othello 1.2*)

enclog VERB to enclog was to hinder something or to provide an obstacle to it ❏ *Traitors enscarped to enclog the guitless keel* (*Othello 1.2*)

endure VERB to endure was to allow or to permit ❏ *and will endure/Our setting down before't.* (*Macbeth 5.4*)

enfranchise VERB if you enfranchised something you set it free ❏ *Do this or this;/Take in that kingdom and enfranchise that;/ Perform't, or else we damn thee.'* (*Anthony and Cleopatra 1.1*)

engage VERB to engage here means to pledge or to promise ❏ *This to be true I do engage my life* (*As You Like It 5.4*)

engaol VERB to lock up or put in prison ❏ *Within my mouth you have engaoled my tongue* (*Richard II 1.3*)

engine NOUN an engine was a plot, device or a machine ❏ *their promises, enticements, oaths, tokens, and all these engines, of lust, are not the things they go under* (*All's Well That Ends Well 3.5*)

englut VERB if you were engulfed you were swallowed up or eaten whole ❏ *For certainly thou art so near the gulf,/Thou needs must be englutted.* (*Henry V 4.3*)

enjoined ADJ enjoined describes people joined together for the same reason ❏ *Of enjoined penitents/*

There's four or five (*All's Well That Ends Well 3.5*)

entertain 1 VERB to entertain here means to welcome or receive ❏ *Approach, rich Ceres, her to entertain.* (*The Tempest 4.1*) 2 VERB to entertain in this context means to cherish, hold in high regard or to respect ❏ *and I quake,/ Lest thou a feverous life shouldst entertain/ And six or seven winters more respect/ Than a perpetual honour.* (*Measure for Measure 3.1*) 3 VERB to entertain means here to give something consideration ❏ *But entertain it,/ And though you think me poor, I am the man/ Will give thee all the world.* (*Anthony and Cleopatra 2.7*) 4 VERB to entertain here means to treat or handle ❏ *your highness is not entertained with that ceremonious affection as you were wont* (*King Lear 1.4*)

envious ADJ envious meant spiteful or vindictive ❏ *he shall appear to the envious a scholar* (*Measure for Measure 3.2*)

ere PREP ere was a common word for before ❏ *ere this I should ha' fatted all the region kites* (*Hamlet 2.2*)

err VERB to err means to go astray, to make a mistake ❏ *And as he errs, doting on Hermia's eyes* (*A Midsummer Night's Dream 1.1*)

erst ADV erst was a common word for once or before ❏ *that erst brought sweetly forth/ The freckled cowslip* (*Henry V 5.2*)

eschew VERB if you eschew something you deliberately avoid doing it ❏ *What cannot be eschewed must be embraced* (*The Merry Wives of Windsor 5.5*)

escote VERB to escote meant to pay for, support ❏ *How are they escoted?* (*Hamlet 2.2*)

estimable ADJ estimable meant appreciative ❏ *I could not with such estimable wonder over-far believe that* (*Twelfth Night 2.1*)

extenuate VERB extenuate means to lessen ❏ *Which by no means we may extenuate* (*A Midsummer Night's Dream 1.1*)

fain ADV fain was a common word meaning gladly or willingly ❏ *I would fain prove so* (*Hamlet 2.2*)

fall NOUN in a voice or music fall meant going higher and lower ❏ *and so die/ That strain again! it had a dying fall* (*Twelfth Night 1.1*)

false ADJ false was a common word for treacherous ❏ *this is counter, you false Danish dogs!* (*Hamlet 4.5*)

fare VERB fare means to get on or manage ❏ *I fare well* (*The Taming of the Shrew Introduction 2*)

feign VERB to feign was to make up, pretend or fake ❏ *It is the more like to be feigned* (*Twelfth Night 1.5*)

fie EXCLAM fie was an exclamation of disgust ❏ *Fie, that you'll say so!* (*Twelfth Night 1.3*)

figure VERB to figure was to symbolize or look like ❏ *Wings and no eyes, figure unheedy haste* (*A Midsummer Night's Dream 1.1*)

filch VERB if you filch something you steal it ❏ *With cunning hast thou filch'd my daughter's heart* (*A Midsummer Night's Dream 1.1*)

flout VERB to flout something meant to scorn it ❏ *Why will you suffer her to flout me thus?* (*A Midsummer Night's Dream 3.2*)

fond ADJ fond was a common word meaning foolish ❑ *Shall we their fond pageant see?* (*A Midsummer Night's Dream 3.2*)

footing 1 NOUN footing meant landing on shore, arrival, disembarkation ❑ *Whose footing here anticipates our thoughts/ A se'nnight's speed.* (*Othello 2.1*) 2 NOUN footing also means support ❑ *there your charity would have lacked footing* (*Winter's Tale 3.3*)

forsooth ADV in truth, certainly, truly
❑ *I had rather, forsooth, go before you like a man* (*The Merry Wives of Windsor 3.2*)

forswear VERB if you forswear you lie, swear falsely or break your word ❑ *he swore a thing to me on Monday night, which he forswore on Tuesday morning* (*Much Ado About Nothing 5.1*)

freshes NOUN a fresh is a fresh water stream ❑ *He shall drink nought brine, for I'll not show him/ Where the quick freshes are.* (*Tempest 3.2*)

furlong NOUN a furlong is a measure of distance. It is the equivalent to one eight of a mile ❑ *Now would I give a thousand furlongs of sea for an acre of barren ground* (*Tempest 1.1*)

gaberdine NOUN a gaberdine is a cloak ❑ *My best way is to creep under his gaberdine* (*Tempest 2.2*)

gage NOUN a gage was a challenge to duel or fight ❑ *There is my gage, Aumerle, in gage to thine* (*Richard II 4.1*)

gait NOUN your gait is your way of walking or step ❑ *I know her by her gait* (*Tempest 4.1*)

gall VERB to gall is to annoy or irritate ❑ *Let it not gall your patience, good Iago,/ That I extend my manners* (*Othello 2.1*)

gambol NOUN frolic or play ❑ *Hop in his walks, and gambol in his eyes* (*A Midsummer Night's Dream 3.1*)

gaskins NOUN gaskins is an old word for trousers ❑ *or, if both break, your gaskins fall.* (*Twelfth Night 1.5*)

gentle ADJ gentle means noble or well-born ❑ *thrice-gentle Cassio!* (*Othello 3.4*)

glass NOUN a glass was another word for a mirror ❑ *no woman's face remember/ Save from my glass, mine own* (*Tempest 3.1*)

gleek VERB to gleek means to make a joke or jibe ❑ *Nay, I can gleek upon occasion* (*A Midsummer Night's Dream 3.1*)

gust NOUN gust meant taste, desire or enjoyment. We still say that if you do something with gusto you do it with enjoyment or enthusiasm ❑ *the gust he hath in quarrelling* (*Twelfth Night 1.3*)

habit NOUN habit means clothes ❑ *You know me by my habit* (*Henry V 3.6*)

heaviness NOUN heaviness means sadness or grief ❑ *So sorrow's heaviness doth heavier grow/ For debt that bankrupt sleep doth sorrow owe* (*A Midsummer Night's Dream 3.2*)

heavy ADJ if you are heavy you are said to be sad or sorrowful ❑ *Away from light steals home my heavy son* (*Romeo and Juliet 1.1*)

hie VERB to hie meant to hurry ❑ *My husband hies him home* (*All Well That Ends Well 4.4*)

hollowly ADV if you did something hollowly you did it insincerely ❑ *If hollowly invert/ What best is boded me to mischief!* (*Tempest 3.1*)

holy-water, court PHRASE if you court holy water you make empty promises, or make statements which sound good but have no real meaning ❑ *court holy-water in a dry house is better than this rain-water out o' door* (*King Lear 3.2*)

howsoever ADV howsoever was often used instead of however ❑ *But howsoever strange and admirable* (*A Midsummer Night's Dream 5.1*)

humour NOUN your humour was your mood, frame of mind or temperament ❑ *it fits my humour well* (*As You Like It 3.2*)

ill ADJ ill means bad ❑ *I must thank him only,/ Let my remembrance suffer ill report* (*Antony and Cleopatra 2.2*)

indistinct ADJ inseparable or unable to see a difference ❑ *Even till we make the main and the aerial blue/ An indistinct regard.* (*Othello 2.1*)

indulgence NOUN indulgence meant approval ❑ *As you from crimes would pardoned be,/ Let your indulgence set me free* (*The Tempest Epilogue*)

infirmity NOUN infirmity was weakness or fraility ❑ *Be not disturbed with my infirmity* (*The Tempest 4.1*)

intelligence NOUN here intelligence means information ❑ *Pursue her; and for this intelligence/ If I have thanks* (*A Midsummer Night's Dream 1.1*)

inwards NOUN inwards meant someone's internal organs ❑ *the thought whereof/ Doth like a poisonous mineral gnaw my inwards* (*Othello 2.1*)

issue 1 NOUN the issue of a marriage are the children ❑ *To thine and Albany's issues,/ Be this perpetual* (*King Lear 1.1*) 2 NOUN in this context issue means outcome or result ❑ *I am to pray you, not to strain my speech,/ To grosser issues* (*Othello*)

kind NOUN kind here means situation or case ❑ *But in this kind, wanting your father's voice,/ The other must be held the worthier.* (*A Midsummer Night's Dream 1.1*)

knave NOUN a knave was a common word for scoundrel ❑ *How absolute the knave is!* (*Hamlet 5.1*)

league NOUN A distance. A league was the distance a person could walk in one hour ❑ *From Athens is her house remote seven leagues* (*A Midsummer Night's Dream 1.1*)

lief, had as ADJ I had as lief means I should like just as much ❑ *I had as lief the town crier spoke my lines* (*Hamlet 1.2*)

livery NOUN livery was a costume, outfit, uniform usually worn by a servant ❑ *You can endure the livery of a nun* (*A Midsummer Night's Dream 1.1*)

loam NOUN loam is soil containing decayed vegetable matter and therefore good for growing crops and plants ❑ *and let him have some plaster, or some loam, or some rough-cast about him, to signify wall* (*A Midsummer Night's Dream 3.1*)

lusty ADJ lusty meant strong ❑ *and oared/ Himself with his good arms in lusty stroke/ To th' shore* (*The Tempest 2.1*)

maidenhead NOUN maidenhead means chastity or virginity ❏ *What I am, and what I would, are as secret as maidenhead* (*Twelfth Night 1.5*)

mark VERB mark means to note or pay attention to ❏ *Where sighs and groans,/ Are made not marked* (*Macbeth 4.3*)

marvellous ADJ very or extremely ❏ *here's a marvellous convenient place for our rehearsal* (*A Midsummer Night's Dream 3.1*)

meet ADJ right or proper ❏ *tis most meet you should* (*Macbeth 5.1*)

merely ADV completely or entirely ❏ *Love is merely a madness* (*As You Like It 3.2*)

misgraffed ADJ misgraffed is an old word for mismatched or unequal ❏ *Or else misgraffed in respect of years* (*A Midsummer Night's Dream 1.1*)

misprision NOUN a misprision meant an error or mistake ❏ *Misprision in the highest degree!* (*Twelfth Night 1.5*)

mollification NOUN mollification is appeasement or a way of preventing someone getting angry ❏ *I am to hull here a little longer. Some mollification for your giant* (*Twelfth Night 1.5*)

mouth, cold in the PHRASE a well-known saying of the time which meant to be dead ❏ *What, must our mouths be cold?* (*The Tempest 1.1*)

murmur NOUN murmur was another word for rumour or hearsay ❏ *and then 'twas fresh in murmur* (*Twelfth Night 1.2*)

murrain NOUN murrain was another word for plague, pestilence ❏ *A murrain on your monster, and*

the devil take your fingers! (*The Tempest 3.2*)

neaf NOUN neaf meant fist ❏ *Give me your neaf, Monsieur Mustardseed* (*A Midsummer Night's Dream 4.1*)

nice 1 ADJ nice had a number of meanings here it means fussy or particular ❏ *An therefore, goaded with most sharp occasions,/ Which lay nice manners by, I put you to/ The use of your own virtues* (*All's Well That Ends Well 5.1*) 2 ADJ nice here means critical or delicate ❏ *We're good… To set so rich a man/ On the nice hazard of one doubtful hour?* (*Henry IV part 1*) 3 ADJ nice in this context means carefully accurate, fastidious ❏ *O relation/ Too nice and yet too true!* (*Macbeth 4.3*) 4 ADJ trivial, unimportant ❏ *Romeo .. Bid him bethink/ How nice the quarrel was* (*Romeo and Juliet 3.1*)

nonpareil NOUN if you are nonpareil you are without equal, peerless ❏ *though you were crown'd/ The nonpareil of beauty!* (*Twelfth Night 1.5*)

office NOUN office here means business or work ❏ *Speak your office* (*Twelfth Night 1.5*)

outsport VERB outsport meant to overdo ❏ *Let's teach ourselves that honorable stop,/ Not to outsport discretion.* (*Othello 2.2*)

owe VERB owe meant own, possess ❏ *Lend less than thou owest* (*King Lear 1.4*)

paragon 1 VERB to paragon was to surpass or excede ❏ *he hath achieved a maid/ That paragons description and wild fame* (*Othello 2.1*) 2 VERB to paragon could also mean to compare with ❏ *I will give thee*

pate NOUN pate is another word for head ❑ *Back, slave, or I will break thy pate across* (*The Comedy of Errors 2.1*)

paunch VERB to paunch someone is to stab (usually in the stomach). Paunch is still a common word for a stomach ❑ *Batter his skull, or paunch him with a stake* (*The Tempest 3.2*)

peevish ADJ if you are peevish you are irritable or easily angered ❑ *Run after that same peevish messenger* (*Twelfth Night 1.5*)

peradventure ADV perhaps or maybe ❑ *Peradventure this is not Fortune's work* (*As You Like It 1.2*)

perforce 1 ADV by force or violently ❑ *my rights and royalties,/Plucked from my arms perforce* (*Richard II 2.3*) 2 ADV necessarily ❑ *The hearts of men, they must perforce have melted* (*Richard II 5.2*)

personage NOUN personage meant your appearance ❑ *Of what personage and years is he?* (*Twelfth Night 1.5*)

pestilence NOUN pestilence was a common word for plague or disease ❑ *Methought she purg'd the air of pestilence!* (*Twelfth Night 1.1*)

physic NOUN physic was medicine or a treatment ❑ *tis a physic/That's bitter to sweet end* (*Measure for Measure 4.6*)

place NOUN place means a person's position or rank ❑ *Sons, kinsmen, thanes,/And you whose places are the nearest* (*Macbeth 1.4*)

post NOUN here a post means a messenger ❑ *there are twenty weak and wearied posts/Come from the north* (*Henry IV part II 2.4*)

pox NOUN pox was a word for any disease during which the victim had blisters on the skin. It was also a curse, a swear word ❑ *The pox of such antic, lisping, affecting phantasims* (*Romeo and Juliet 2.4*)

prate VERB to prate means to chatter ❑ *if thou prate of mountains* (*Hamlet 5.1*)

prattle VERB to prattle is to chatter or talk without purpose ❑ *I prattle out of fashion, and I dote In mine own comforts* (*Othello 2.1*)

precept NOUN a precept was an order or command ❑ *and my father's precepts I therein do forget.* (*The Tempest 3.1*)

present ADJ present here means immediate ❑ *We'll put the matter to the present push* (*Hamlet 5.1*)

prithee EXCLAM prithee is the equivalent of please or may I ask – a polite request ❑ *I prithee, and I'll pay thee bounteously* (*Twelfth Night 1.2*)

prodigal NOUN a prodigal is someone who wastes or squanders money ❑ *he's a very fool, and a prodigal* (*Twelfth Night 1.3*)

purpose NOUN purpose is used here to mean intention ❑ *understand my purposes aright* (*King Lear 1.4*)

quaff VERB quaff was a common word which meant to drink heavily or take a big drink ❑ *That quaffing and drinking will undo you* (*Twelfth Night 1.3*)

quaint 1 ADJ clever, ingenious ❑ *with a quaint device* (*The Tempest 3.3*) 2 ADJ cunning ❑ *I'll... tell quaint lies* (*Merchant of Venice 3.4*) 3 ADJ pretty, attractive ❑ *The clamorous owl, that nightly hoots and wonders/At our quaint spirit* (*A Midsummer Night's Dream 2.2*)

quoth VERB an old word which means say ❑ *'Tis dinner time.' quoth I* (*The Comedy of Errors 2.1*)

rack NOUN a rack described clouds or a cloud formation ❑ *And, like this insubstantial pageant faded,/ Leave not a rack behind* (*The Tempest 4.1*)

rail VERB to rant or swear at. It is still used occasionally today ❑ *Why do I rail on thee* (*Richard II 5.5*)

rate NOUN rate meant estimate, opinion ❑ *My son is lost, and, in my rate, she too* (*The Tempest 2.1*)

recreant NOUN recreant is an old word which means coward ❑ *Come, recreant, come, thou child* (*A Midsummer Night's Dream 3.2*)

remembrance NOUN remembrance is used here to mean memory or recollection ❑ *our remembrances of days foregone* (*All's Well That Ends Well 1.3*)

resolute ADJ firm or not going to change your mind ❑ *You are resolute, then?* (*Twelfth Night 1.5*)

revels NOUN revels means celebrations or a party ❑ *Our revels now are ended* (*The Tempest 4.1*)

rough-cast NOUN a mixture of lime and gravel (sometimes shells too) for use on an outer wall ❑ *and let him have some plaster, or some loam, or some rough-cast about him, to signify wall* (*A Midsummer Night's Dream 3.1*)

sack NOUN sack was another word for wine ❑ *My man-monster hath drowned his tongue in sack.* (*The Tempest 3.2*)

sad ADJ in this context sad means serious, grave ❑ *comes me the Prince and Claudio... in sad conference* (*Much Ado About Nothing 1.3*)

sampler NOUN a piece of embroidery, which often showed the family tree ❑ *Both on one sampler, sitting on one cushion* (*A Midsummer Night's Dream 3.2*)

saucy ADJ saucy means rude ❑ *I heard you were saucy at my gates* (*Twelfth Night 1.5*)

schooling NOUN schooling means advice ❑ *I have some private schooling for you both.* (*A Midsummer Night's Dream 1.1*)

seething ADJ seething in this case means boiling – we now use seething when we are very angry ❑ *Lovers and madmen have such seething brains* (*A Midsummer Night's Dream 5.1*)

semblative ADJ semblative means resembling or looking like ❑ *And all is semblative a woman's part.* (*Twelfth Night 1.4*)

several ADJ several here means separate or different ❑ *twenty several messengers* (*Anthony and Cleopatra 1.5*)

shrew NOUN An annoying person or someone who makes you cross ❑ *Bless you, fair shrew.* (*Twelfth Night 1.3*)

shroud VERB to shroud is to hide or shelter ❏ *I will here, shroud till the dregs of the storm be past* (The Tempest 2.2)

sickleman NOUN a sickleman was someone who used a sickle to harvest crops ❏ *You sunburnt sicklemen, of August weary* (The Tempest 4.1)

soft ADV soft here means wait a moment or stop ❏ *But, soft, what nymphs are these* (A Midsummer Night's Dream 4.1)

something ADV something here means somewhat or rather ❏ *Be something scanter of your maiden presence* (Hamlet 1.3)

sooth NOUN truly ❏ *Yes, sooth; and so do you* (A Midsummer Night's Dream 3.2)

spleen NOUN spleen means fury or anger ❏ *That, in a spleen, unfolds both heaven and earth* (A Midsummer Night's Dream 1.1)

sport NOUN sport means recreation or entertainment ❏ *I see our wars/ Will turn unto a peaceful comic sport* (Henry VI part I 2.2)

strain NOUN a strain is a tune or a musical phrase ❏ *and so die/ That strain again! it had a dying fall* (Twelfth Night 1.1)

suffer VERB in this context suffer means perish or die ❏ *but an islander that hath lately suffered by a thunderbolt.* (The Tempest 2.2)

suit NOUN a suit is a petition, request or proposal (marriage) ❏ *Because she will admit no kind of suit* (Twelfth Night 1.2)

sup VERB to sup is to have supper ❏ *Go know of Cassio where he supped tonight* (Othello 5.1)

surfeit NOUN a surfeit is an amount which is too large ❏ *If music be the food of love, play on;/ Give me excess of it, that, surfeiting,/ The appetite may sicken* (Twelfth Night 1.1)

swain NOUN a swain is a suitor or person who wants to marry ❏ *take this transformed scalp/ From off the head of this Athenian swain* (A Midsummer Night's Dream 4.1)

thereto ADV thereto meant also ❏ *If she be black, and thereto have a wit* (Othello 2.1)

throstle NOUN a throstle was a name for a song-bird ❏ *The throstle with his note so true* (A Midsummer Night's Dream 3.1)

tidings NOUN tidings meant news ❏ *that upon certain tidings now arrived, importing the mere perdition of the Turkish fleet* (Othello 2.2)

transgress VERB if you transgress you break a moral law or rule of behaviour ❏ *Virtue that transgresses is but patched with sin* (Twelfth Night 1.5)

troth, by my PHRASE this phrase means I swear or in truth or on my word ❏ *By my troth, Sir Toby, you must come in earlier o' nights* (Twelfth Night 1.3)

trumpery NOUN trumpery means things that look expensive but are worth nothing (often clothing) ❏ *The trumpery in my house, go bring it hither/ For stale catch these thieves* (The Tempest 4.1)

twink NOUN In the wink of an eye or no time at all ❏ *Ay, with a twink* (The Tempest 4.1)

undone ADJ if something or someone is undone they are ruined, destroyed, brought down ❏ *You have undone a man of fourscore three* (*The Winter's Tale 4.4*)

varlets NOUN varlets were villains or ruffians ❏ *Say again: where didst thou leave these varlets?* (*The Tempest 4.1*)

vaward NOUN the vaward is an old word for the vanguard, front part or earliest ❏ *And since we have the vaward of the day* (*A Midsummer Night's Dream 4.1*)

visage NOUN face ❏ *when Phoebe doth behold/Her silver visage in the watery glass* (*A Midsummer Night's Dream 1.1*)

voice NOUN voice means vote ❏ *He has our voices* (*Coriolanus 2.3*)

waggish ADJ waggish means playful ❏ *As waggish boys in game themselves forswear* (*A Midsummer Night's Dream 1.1*)

wane VERB to wane is to vanish, go down or get slighter. It is most often used to describe a phase of the moon ❏ *but, O, methinks, how slow/This old moon wanes* (*A Midsummer Night's Dream 1.1*)

want VERB to want means to lack or to be without ❏ *a beast that wants discourse of reason/Would have mourned longer* (*Hamlet 1.2*)

warrant VERB to assure, promise, guarantee ❏ *I warrant your grace* (*As You Like It 1.2*)

welkin NOUN welkin is an old word for the sky or the heavens ❏ *The starry welkin cover thou anon/With drooping fog as black as Acheron* (*A Midsummer Night's Dream 3.2*)

wench NOUN wench is an old word for a girl ❏ *Well demanded, wench* (*The Tempest 1.2*)

whence ADV from where ❏ *Whence came you, sir?* (*Twelfth Night 1.5*)

wherefore ADV why ❏ *Wherefore, sweetheart? what's your metaphor?* (*Twelfth Night 1.3*)

wide-chopped ADJ if you were wide-chopped you were big-mouthed ❏ *This wide-chopped rascal* (*The Tempest 1.1*)

wight NOUN wight is an old word for person or human being ❏ *She was a wight, if ever such wight were* (*Othello 2.1*)

wit NOUN wit means intelligence or wisdom ❏ *thou didst conclude hairy men plain dealers, without wit* (*The Comedy of Errors 2.2*)

wits NOUN wits mean mental sharpness ❏ *we that have good wits have much to answer for* (*As You Like It 4.1*)

wont ADJ to wont is to be in the habit of doing something regularly ❏ *When were you wont to use my sister thus?* (*The Comedy of Errors 2.2*)

wooer NOUN a wooer is a suitor, someone who is hoping to marry ❏ *and of a foolish knight that you brought in one night here to be her wooer* (*Twelfth Night 1.3*)

wot VERB wot is an old word which means know or learn ❏ *for well I wot/Thou runnest before me* (*A Midsummer Night's Dream 3.2*)